"I'm surprised ⟨ get me out of jail."

"Why?" Shannon asked, glancing at Rick curiously.

He thought about that for a moment. "Because I don't deserve it, I suppose. I wasn't being truthful with you. In some ways I'm still not," he admitted.

Shannon smiled slightly. "Don't you think I know that?"

Rick studied her face. That enigmatic smile bothered him. She was one of the most intuitive women he had ever met. But more to the point, she was starting to get under his skin. By the end of this evening he could very well find himself telling her more than he should.

He wanted—even needed—to trust her. But there was only so much of himself that he could reveal—just yet.

Dear Reader,

At Harlequin Intrigue, we all agree—nothing is better on a cold winter night than cozying up with a good romantic mystery. So we've asked some of our favorite authors—and yours—to entertain us with some special stories this month, which are set around the holidays.

We hope you'll grab some cider and cuddle up with *The Kid Who Stole Christmas* by Linda Stevens—a Christmas mystery that we know will warm your heart!

Sincerely,

Debra Matteucci
Senior Editor & Editorial Coordinator
Harlequin Books
300 East 42nd Street
New York, NY 10017

Linda Stevens
The Kid Who Stole Christmas

Harlequin Books

TORONTO • NEW YORK • LONDON
AMSTERDAM • PARIS • SYDNEY • HAMBURG
STOCKHOLM • ATHENS • TOKYO • MILAN
MADRID • WARSAW • BUDAPEST • AUCKLAND

ISBN 0-373-22303-X

THE KID WHO STOLE CHRISTMAS

Copyright © 1994 by Steven and Melinda Hamilton

This edition published by arrangement with Harlequin Enterprises B.V.

® and TM are trademarks of the publisher. Trademarks indicated with ® are registered in the United States Patent and Trademark Office, the Canadian Trade Marks Office and in other countries.

Printed in U.S.A.

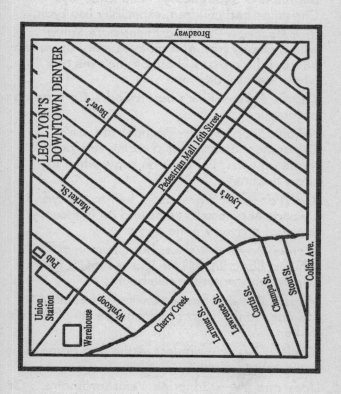

LEO LYON'S
DOWNTOWN DENVER

Broadway

Bayer's

Pedestrian Mall 16th Street

Lyon's

Market St.

Colfax Ave.

Pub

Union Station

Wynkoop

Warehouse

Cherry Creek

Larimer St.

Lawrence St.

Curtis St.

Champa St.

Stout St.

CAST OF CHARACTERS

Shannon O'Shaugnessy—She loves toys, Christmas and children, especially Leo Lyon.

Rick Hastings—A department-store Santa with a cloudy past and an even more uncertain future. If he crosses Shannon, he's the one who'd better watch out!

Charlie Prine—Rick's best friend... Or is he an accomplice?

Johann "Pop" Lyon—Founder of Lyon's Department Store, he is a cagey veteran of the retail wars. But does he know when to draw the line?

Leo Lyon—Pop's grandson, heir to the Lyon's Department Store fortune, and an innocent pawn of a rivalry gone awry.

Nathan Bayer—Ruthless businessman or white-collar criminal? He knows that it's the winner who writes the rule book.

Angela Bayer—Nathan's wife. A beautiful woman with a heart of ice and plenty of secrets of her own.

Chelsea Bayer—Hapless victim in a game of parental tug-o'-war.

Joey and Irv—Kidnappers extraordinaire... Or are they?

Prologue

An icy December wind swept down Denver's Sixteenth Street Mall, bringing with it a few crystals of white snow. It was a cold but fragrant wind, ripe with the strange mix of country-fresh mountain air laced with city exhaust fumes. The wind came from the west, confirming that there was a storm brewing in the high country, sharpening winter's already bitter edge.

Evidence of the last snowfall still coated the downtown streets with slush and lined pedestrian walkways with crusty, disagreeable soot-covered mounds. Undaunted, throngs of holiday shoppers jostled for position along the crowded sidewalks, swaddled in their cold-weather gear, looking like a colony of anxious penguins beneath the gray, threatening skies. But it wasn't the storm that had them worried. A far more important event was imminent. There were only seven more shopping days until Christmas, and panic was setting in.

At the northwest end of the mile-long mall, near Market Street, where the free shuttle buses that plied the busy open-air shopping center made their turnaround, a man stood in the lengthening afternoon shadows, watching passengers disembark. From his vantage point in the entry arch of an aged, brick office building, he could observe several different parking lots with just a slight turn of his head.

Most people getting off the shuttles at this end were leaving the downtown area. After stuffing their purchases into already full trunks, they got into their shiny, expensive cars and sped off, trying to beat Monday rush-hour traffic. Now and then, a young businessman or a group of boisterous college students would continue toward the trendy taverns across from Union Station. From that direction, the faint voices of an impromptu choir could be heard rendering a slightly tipsy version of "Jingle Bells."

The watcher did not share their merriment. He did envy them their warmer attire and cozy destinations, for his navy blue pea coat and faded jeans were scarcely adequate for the weather. But it was good camouflage and he was resigned to his fate. Hunching his broad shoulders against the cold, he moved from foot to foot in an attempt to keep his blood circulating.

Finally, he had watched long enough to satisfy himself that no one was watching him in return. He left the relative shelter of the doorway and shuffled down icy sidewalks toward the railroad tracks and their accompanying warehouse district, gritting his teeth against the frigid wind. When he found the building he sought, he forced himself to pause for a few moments and check out the area, though by now he barely had any feeling in his fingers or toes.

There was an unlocked entrance around back and he went inside. The place was still in use, as were most of Denver's downtown commercial properties, even such disreputable specimens as this. But they certainly weren't wasting money on electricity. As he made his way across the bare concrete floor, he could just make out the various shapes of storage boxes and crates that loomed ahead of him in the dim late-afternoon light.

It was quiet. That was why he'd picked this location. Occasionally, a clerk or loading-dock worker would show up to drop something off or cart something away, but not often, even at this time of year. At the moment, he was the only one moving around, and the only sound was the *clomp, clomp* of his heavy hiking boots echoing in the dusty silence.

When he reached the cubicle that served as the warehouse office, he stopped, alert to anything that might be unusual. Through the single, grimy window in the plywood wall, he could see a light on inside, a single overhead bulb. Beneath that bulb was a lone, cluttered desk. At the desk sat another man, clad in a gray business suit and black overcoat. He looked out of place and ill at ease with his surroundings. In his lap he held a leather briefcase.

He nearly dropped the case on the floor when the office door swung open. But then he saw that it was only the person he'd been waiting for, and he breathed a sigh of relief.

"You took your sweet time, Rick!" he admonished. "I'm about to freeze to death in this icebox!"

"Feels nice and toasty in here to me, Charlie," Rick said. "I guess it all depends on what you're used to. Want some coffee?"

"Sure. Decaf, please."

"This look like the Oxford Hotel to you?"

Charlie made a face. "Perhaps I'll just pass."

"Like I said, it's all in what you're used to."

Rick moved around the office, making himself at home. He brewed a cup of coffee in a cracked mug, using an old packet of instant and some rusty hot water from the rest room faucet. It was, he decided, some of the best he'd ever tasted, perhaps because he'd been standing in near-freezing temperatures for the better part of an hour. He took it over to the desk and took a seat across from the other man, grinning at his disdain.

"How the mighty have fallen," Charlie said.

Rick chuckled ruefully. "I was never all that mighty in the first place. Besides, I didn't fall. I was pushed."

"But you don't have to live like this."

"Actually, I do," Rick returned. "You're as acquainted with my finances as I am, perhaps more so."

"I mean, I could give you a loan. We can just call it an advance. That way, you could at least hole up in a motel for the duration. No one should be this alone during the holidays."

The instant coffee left a bitter taste in Rick's mouth, as did the feeling of resentment rising within him. Charlie was as much of a friend as a man like Rick could have. But Charlie simply didn't understand. Rick was alone no matter how many people were around him. The only companionship he allowed himself was that of his own anger.

"I appreciate the offer, Charlie," he said at last. "I really do. But I happen to enjoy the way I live. There's a certain purity to it."

"Purity, huh?" Charlie looked into Rick's eyes. There was a coldness in them that had grown stronger in recent weeks. "You're starting to scare me, my friend."

Rick shrugged. "Sorry. Just my street attitude coming out, I guess." He managed a sincere smile. "Now. You didn't fly to Denver just to freeze your buns off in here and shoot the breeze, did you?"

"Too true," Charlie agreed, popping open his briefcase. "I have some papers I need you to sign." He held them out to Rick, along with a pen.

Rick took them and scanned them quickly, then signed on the dotted line, nodding his approval. "How about the other arrangements?"

"On schedule and as planned. They'll handle the whole thing, start to finish. We'll be completely in the background." Charlie took the papers back and returned them to his briefcase, grinning broadly. "Until the payoff. Then you and Mr. Bonner will have no choice but to stop playing the vagabond."

"I suppose." He couldn't afford to think that far ahead right now. One day at a time was hard enough. The stakes were just too high. "I'm applying at Lyon's tomorrow afternoon."

Charlie shook his head, and again studied his friend's haggard face with a concerned, almost paternal air. "I'm not wild about that idea."

"I'm not overly thrilled with it myself, but I simply have to be there in person. Besides, I really could use the extra cash right now. Be it ever so humble, this place is still expensive." He smiled again. That made it two times in as many minutes. If he wasn't careful, he might become downright jovial. "I've taken all possible precautions. And there's no crime in hiring on for a part-time job, after all."

"I suppose not." Charlie stood up to go. "Still, watch your back, okay?"

"Sure." Rick got to his feet and shook Charlie's hand. "But don't worry about me, Charlie. When you've had everything in the world that ever meant anything to you taken away, there isn't much that scares you. Now, they can't hurt me, but I can most certainly hurt them."

Chapter One

"Leo! I'm warning you!" Shannon O'Shaughnessy glared at the heavily armed gunman confronting her, her emerald green eyes flashing defiantly. "Don't you dare!"

"Hah! Save your pitiful threats, Amazon." Leo raised his pistol and took aim. "Prepare to meet your doom."

With a maniacal laugh, he fired, not once, but twice, hitting Shannon directly between the eyes. Then he spun on the heel of one neon green sneaker and sprinted out of her grasp. He was down the aisle and gone in an instant.

"You can run but you can't hide!" Shannon yelled after him. He just laughed again. "I'll tell Pop!"

She took a tissue out of her pocket and wiped the water off her face, counting slowly to ten as she did so. It could have been worse. In addition to the squirt gun, her eight-year-old attacker was also toting the latest gross-out toy, a slime shooter. Besides, Shannon supposed she almost deserved to be squirted for making such lame threats.

Leo Lyon could not only run like the wind, he could also hide like a fox. That was especially true in Lyon's Department Store, a place that had been home to the boy for his whole young life. And telling eighty-year-old Johann Lyon about his grandson's unruly behavior never did much good; though bordering on the infirm, on his good days the old man could be quite a scalawag himself. Just last week, he'd almost nailed a startled customer with his wheelchair while racing Leo through Housewares. Even his junior employees called him Pop.

So, as usual, Shannon supposed she would have to deal with Leo in her own way. There was a boxful of hand-held water cannons in the storeroom, waiting for warmer weather.

"I wonder if I could rig one to fire chocolate syrup?" she mused aloud, then shook her head. "No, he'd probably enjoy that. Maybe carrot juice."

The entire staff was guilty of indulging Leo and his active imagination, but Shannon was especially indulgent. Though she had no children of her own, she loved them. She also loved her job. Managing a toy department was a little like having Christmas every day. And Christmas just happened to be Shannon's favorite time of year.

It was Leo's favorite, too, naturally. Since he was out of school for the holidays, that meant the pair of them had been having a jolly time—even if he did get out of hand now and again. Shannon was used to it. She had been something of a stand-in mother for him since he was three, when his parents had been killed in an auto accident. It was a role she enjoyed. In fact, she considered it a duty, because he was otherwise being raised by nannies, something she had endured herself as a child and knew to be a poor substitute.

Leo really was a good little boy, most of the time. He practically ran the whole store, of course, charmer that he was, with his head of very blond hair, cute button nose and impish blue eyes. And Shannon genuinely respected his opinion when choosing which toys to buy for her department.

But all children went a bit crazy at Christmas. Leo just happened to have an entire department store to do it in—which could be a dangerous combination. With only half an hour until opening time, it was imperative that Shannon find Leo and disarm him, lest he stir up an insurrection among the hundreds of other boys and girls that would be pouring into this department.

Shannon shivered at the thought, then took off down the stuffed-toy aisle, heading for the life-size dollhouse display at the far end. Leo often hid there.

The whole store was done up for Christmas, with tinsel and pine boughs and glittering colored lights. But Shannon's department was particularly nice, decorated in her preference for the old-fashioned. At the end of each aisle were huge reproductions of childhood favorites, teddy bears and baby dolls, spinning tops and brightly-patterned balls. A big fir tree took center stage, covered with shiny gold ornaments, silver garlands and candy canes. At the top sat a gleaming crystal star. As if guarding the presents beneath the tree, a unit of giant wooden soldiers was stationed nearby.

The enormous dollhouse, which was a year-round fixture in Lyon's, took on a magical glow at Christmas, thanks to the hundreds of candle-shaped lights that outlined every window and door. Shannon thought it looked like a fairyland castle.

To an eight-year-old boy, it became whatever he needed it to be most. At the moment, it was a hideout for his alter ego, Lionman, complete with glowing force-field windows to protect him from the redheaded Amazon on his trail.

Huddled just inside the front door, watching Shannon's cautious approach, Leo kept up a running commentary on the action, a sort of superhero's play-by-play announcer.

"Lionman checked the ammunition in his ion blaster and steeled his nerve," he said to himself in a soft, dramatically deep voice. "The Amazon was tricky. She would try to bewitch him before moving in for the kill."

Shannon stopped in front of the dollhouse. "Leo? Are you in there?" she asked, wary of an ambush.

"Lionman's hopes soared!" Leo exclaimed quietly. "His presence had not yet been detected."

"Come on, honey. We'll play later. I promised your grandfather I'd get some breakfast into you this morning."

"Cruel temptress! She knew Lionman had been without food or water for days. But she would pay. He raised his blaster. Soon he would have his revenge. . . ."

"Who are you talking to, Leo?" Shannon called, frowning. "It's not Bob, is it? Don't you dare encourage him, Bob!"

Leo feigned anguish and slumped against the dollhouse wall. "The mention of his trusted companion's name cut Lionman like a knife," he said, continuing his monologue. "Sir Bob had been defeated in battle just the day before. The Amazon was playing dirty."

Shannon looked around. The store was starting to come to life now. Christmas carols were playing softly over the public address system. A couple of other department heads were huddled near the perfume counter, conferring with one of the sales reps, who was touting this season's must-wear scent. She was relieved to see that Bob Jenkins, maintenance man and occasional accomplice to Leo's schemes, was up on a ladder preparing to change a bad fluorescent tube. He looked down at Shannon and waved. She waved back, distracted for a moment.

Once Bob was done with the light, he would go unlock the doors. There was already a line of shoppers outside, waiting impatiently in the cold morning air.

"Leo!" she exclaimed, taking a few hesitant steps toward the dollhouse. "Come on now. I'm not kidding."

"Lionman steadied his blaster. The Amazon was in range."

Shannon sighed. Luckily, there was still a threat that worked for each and every Christmas-crazed child—up to a certain age, anyway.

"All right for you, young man," she called out. "Don't blame me if all you get for Christmas is a lump of coal!"

Leo's eyes widened, and he clasped his chest, dropping his squirt gun. It clattered out the dollhouse door, and then he staggered out, as well, reeling as if struck by a fatal blow.

"Lionman is hit!" he cried. "The Amazon has unleashed the terrible power of her secret weapon. All is lost."

He fell to the floor, tongue lolling. Shannon bent over him, laughing. "All that's lost is most of your marbles, kiddo. Now, get up and dust yourself off. I have things to do."

"Can I help?" Leo asked, opening one eye.

"That would depend on your knowledge of magic words."

Leo got to his feet, looking contrite. "I'm sorry," he told Shannon, using his best hangdog expression.

"As well you should be. Haven't I told you not to shoot those things in the store, let alone at me?"

He colored slightly, but that was an easy feat for a boy with such a pale complexion. "Yes, ma'am. I was just playing."

She sighed. "I know."

"You won't tell Santa?"

"I don't have to tattle on you, Leo," she explained, trying to keep a straight face. "He knows when you've been bad or good."

Leo was getting over his initial regret, as evidenced by the mischievous gleam in his blue eyes. "Yeah, right. Do you have any idea how big a data base he'd need?"

Shannon looked skyward. "Why me?"

"Hey," Leo objected mildly as he came to stand beside her. "Don't blame me for being a computer-literate kid."

She took his hand. "Come on, Lionman. Let's hit the cafeteria. I need a cup of coffee."

Leo holstered his weapon and nodded. "I know what you mean," he agreed sagely. "Some chocolate milk would go down pretty good right now. It's going to be a long day."

"How so?"

"They're *all* long days before Christmas."

"You've got a point there."

Although Shannon loved the season, it did increase her work load. In addition to doing the decorations, and making sure they had enough stock on all the right toys, she was also in charge of hiring and watching over the department store Santas.

There was one main jolly old elf who had worked for the Lyon family for years, so that was never a bother—or hadn't been until recently. He was getting on in years and needed a lot more breaks, a tall order since it was a Lyon's tradition to have a Santa on duty from open to close the entire month of December. There was a time when Shannon had had to turn away Santa applicants. But they had thinned out over the past few years, and this year she had been having trouble finding anyone at all.

Or at least anyone she felt was worthy of representing such a venerable old department store as Lyon's.

For over fifty years, there had been a Lyon's in downtown Denver. Opened in the late forties by Johann "Pop" Lyon, a German craftsman, Lyon's began as a toy emporium. All the toys were made by Pop's own hand, the mainstay being his whimsical stuffed animals. His bestseller was a scraggly king of the jungle he dubbed Leopold, or Leo the Lion, a name he liked so much, he gave it to his firstborn son, who later passed it on to his own son.

Over the years, Lyon's gradually expanded, first adding a line of fine chocolates, then children's fancy-dress clothing and eventually other related sundries, until it became a full-fledged department store. There had been many changes and problems, but Lyon's held its own by maintaining a dedication to value and service. Today, it was a fixture in the downtown area, taking up one whole corner of a city block in a building four stories high. There was still a fine toy department, and even a lion or two, although they were now made by others.

In this, the age of the megamall and computer shopping, Lyon's had of course been forced to evolve. Pop no longer did much hands-on management, preferring to delegate authority to the heads of each individual department. Eventually, if he were so inclined, Leo might take the helm. Until then, the store would operate like the family unit it nearly was. Pop made the major decisions, those with seniority made the lesser ones as a group and everyone else simply did their own jobs.

Shannon was proud to be a part of it all, and proud of her department. To make her Santa Claus team, a man had to be kind, jovial, warmhearted and genuinely fond of children. Unfortunately, he had to be all that for a bargain-basement wage, since her budget was minimal after paying the main Santa's salary.

Each year, the pickings had gotten slimmer. Santa school graduates asked for too much money, as did employment agency clients. While city labor pools were fine for part-time help in the shipping department, the average day laborer didn't quite have what it took to hold a steady stream of fidgety children in his lap one after the other, seven days a week.

For the last couple of years, Shannon had been forced to rely on the friends, relatives and acquaintances of employees, and on occasion the employees themselves, scouting their ranks for any able-bodied male who happened to have some free time, a kind heart and the need of a little extra cash.

But this year, just this past week, in fact, even a couple of those last resorts had canceled out. So Shannon was now quite desperate. And everyone knew it. When she came into the cafeteria with Leo in tow, any man with even the hint of a twinkle in his eye finished his cornflakes and was off like a startled reindeer. The more portly among them were already long gone, having formed an early-warning network.

Which was why she nearly fell on her knees and kissed Madge Hensen's suede boots when the accountant came up to her and said she'd found a candidate. Or as she put it, a lamb to the slaughter.

"He's a bit eccentric, though," Madge added.

Shannon's eyes narrowed. "*How* eccentric?"

"Oh, you know," the other woman said vaguely. "The usual. He's an artist or a musician or something bohemian like that."

"Just how well do you know this person?"

"He's my sister's cousin's nephew. I think."

"Oh, jeez." Shannon groaned. "In other words, it could be Jack the Ripper, for all you know."

Madge started to walk away. "Fine. I did try..."

"Wait!" Shannon motioned the woman back. "Okay. I'll give the guy an interview at least. What's his name?"

"Um, I'm not sure. Roy or Roger, something like that. He's taking me to lunch. I'll send him down to see you after."

Leo, who thought this entire conversation was much more fascinating than his nearly empty bowl of sugar-frosted cereal, decided it was time he joined in.

"Is he bringing Trigger?" he asked.

"Who?"

"Roy Rogers," Leo returned.

Madge smiled at him. "Isn't that a little before your time, sweetie?"

"I'm into the classics," the boy informed her sagely.

Madge walked away, shaking her head. Shannon was doing her best to keep a straight face. "Good one, Leo," she said.

He grinned. "Thanks." After a long pull on his box of chocolate milk, he asked, "Can I help you interview Santas?"

Each year, Shannon had feared Leo would figure the whole thing out. Undoubtedly, it wouldn't be much longer. But so far, his innocence was intact. He had come to grips with the duplicate department store versions of Santa a few seasons ago by considering them to be emissaries of a sort, servants to the big man himself. To his mind, they were men who received the calling, like priests. This helped explain why some of them were better than others and why still others didn't make the grade at all. Many were chosen, few could answer.

But all of them had an inside track to the big guy himself, and were to be treated with deference until proven incompetent, at which time they were fair game.

"Actually, Leo, I don't think there'll be much of an interview. It's only six more days to Christmas, so he'll probably do just fine."

"Unless he's a raving maniac," Leo interjected.

"Right. Or really does ride in on a horse. Too messy."

Leo giggled. "Gross!"

When Leo was in the store, it wasn't unusual for him to follow Shannon around as she went about the daily business of running her department. And if he wasn't with her, he could usually be found "helping" someone else. All the employees were accustomed to having him around. He rarely got underfoot. In some cases, he actually was of help. Though the boy didn't press the issue, most of them got the feeling he considered himself an executive-in-training. Pop said he had retail in his blood.

Whatever his function, he was most certainly the center of attention wherever he went. And Leo thrived on it. It was small compensation for the loss of both his mother and father, but it must have helped, because he did seem to be a fairly normal boy in most respects. A bit advanced for his age, perhaps, especially his speech, but that was the result of his spending so much of his free time around adults.

In fact, the only aspect of his personality that caused anyone much concern was his habit of concocting wild, highly detailed fantasies. His alter ego, Lionman, was only one of several multilayered melodramas he'd developed to give vent to his imagination. But even these were harmless. Usually.

"HE'S AT IT AGAIN," Paul Sanchez said.

Shannon looked up from the inventory printout she was studying. Paul was one of the store security guards. She liked the burly, dedicated older man.

"Leo, you mean?" she asked.

"Who else?"

After breakfast, she and Leo had returned to the toy department, where Shannon went about her business while Leo compared Christmas lists with some of the children there to see Santa Claus. His extensive knowledge of Lyon's stock on hand was of great interest to them, if a source of consternation to their parents. Shannon had assumed he was still at it.

She looked around the busy department, not seeing the boy. "Where is he?"

"Sneaking around on the second floor somewhere," Paul returned with a vague gesture of one big hand. "But it's not what he's doing. It's what he's saying." He shook his head. "Kid'll drive me loony, I swear."

"He's Lionman today, I believe," Shannon said. She saw no problem with Leo's inventiveness. Her own childhood had been full of vivid fantasy games. "That one can get a bit strange."

"It's not that, either." Paul waved her comment aside impatiently, then leaned on the counter between them, speaking quietly. "It's the spies. They're back."

Shannon arched her eyebrows. "Oh."

"He says they're watching him. I wish you'd talk to him."

"I see." She leaned on the counter now, as well, and used the same conspiratorial tone. "I already talked to Leo, Paul. He explained the whole thing. They're after the plans."

"Plans?" Paul was confused. "What plans?"

"To the secret underground bunkers." Shannon looked around, making sure there was no one near. "That's where we're keeping the Arnie the Arachnid shipment."

"Arnie the Arachnid!" the guard exclaimed.

"Shh!" Shannon looked around again, this time in genuine alarm. "What are you trying to do? Start a riot? I was just pulling your leg, for heaven's sake!"

Arnie the Arachnid was the newest, hottest toy on the market—or more correctly, on television. To the best of anyone's knowledge, none had been shipped yet. But the black, six-inch-long squiggly plastic spiders had most certainly been advertised, relentlessly, since the first of December.

Supposedly made of a new heat-sensitive, nontoxic material that reacted safely with human skin, Arnie the Arachnid would temporarily bond himself to any body part warm enough to cause the reaction—a temperature easily attained by the squealing, hyperactive children shown dashing around in the ads. Evidently, adults terrified of spiders would generate the same amount of heat, because they were shown in the ads, as well, at the mercy of those same hyperactive children. Once a person calmed down, causing his or her skin temperature to drop a degree or two, then Arnie would drop off, as well.

Every child in the nation wanted one. Almost every adult did, too. However, the toy developer would only provide them on its own terms; a limited number of select outlets would be supplied on a percentage-paid basis, with delivery just before Christmas. Even a small cut of Arnie would be a fortune, and Lyon's was to be the only supplier in the Denver Metro area.

But so far, no store, anywhere, had received even one. The media was in a frenzy. Children were fixated. Parents were hounding merchandisers. There were outrageous offers being made in private newspaper ads, with nary an Arnie to be found—though police had arrested some counterfeiters.

It was a stroke of marketing genius. Such toys were typically flash-in-the-pan fads that disappeared as soon as the novelty wore off. A week after Christmas, remainder bins were full of them, with few takers. But this way, every Arnie was virtually sold already. Demand would stay high.

Provided that any were delivered. Which was why Shannon was so concerned that Paul Sanchez keep his voice down. "We're waiting for Arnie just like everybody else. That's probably why Leo concocted this story about spies," she said quietly.

The guard straightened and cleared his throat. "Yeah, well, I wish you'd tell him to stop. It makes me edgy."

She smiled. "Why do you think he does it, Paul?"

Finally, Paul smiled, as well, and then chuckled. "Can I help it if the kid's clever?"

"He is that. But it's just another of his tall tales," Shannon assured him. "There's no one after him. Really."

Chapter Two

A lot of things had troubled Rick when he had been forced to adopt what he euphemistically termed a low-profile lifestyle. Relying mainly on public transportation was one. Drifting from job to job was another. But the part that had taken him the longest to get used to was the way most people treated him. As if they were scared. Or annoyed.

It just didn't make any sense. He was clean, as were his clothes, though admittedly a bit shabby. His thick, brown hair was long around the edges, but that was mere carelessness, not a statement of any kind.

Granted, he was a big man, six foot, with a strong build, and had done a lot of physical work in the last few years, but there was little else about him that he considered threatening. Maybe he scowled a lot. But then, so did a good portion of the human race these days, especially members of the working class.

Perhaps that was the answer. A bumpy economy made people aware of how illusory their own security was. Anyone could fall from grace. Or perhaps there was something about an obviously well-bred, highly educated man living the life of a nomad that insulted their sense of order. At thirty-nine, he was supposed to look settled and steady, not like a rough-hewn rebel-without-a-cause. Little did they know.

Whatever it was, Charlie said it showed in his eyes. He was probably right, considering the way some people looked into them and then immediately looked away. Rick had to take his friend's word for it; these days, he barely recognized the man he saw in the mirror each morning.

The security guard standing just inside the entrance to Lyon's Department Store certainly gave him the once-over as Rick came through the door. He must have not liked what he saw, either, because he kept an eye on him all the way to the toy department. Rick was aware of this scrutiny. In a way, he supposed he couldn't really blame the guy. He had his job to do, and so did Rick.

Though the Lyon's building was old, architecturally the design had returned to favor so that it seemed quite modern. There was a large central area, open all the way to the fourth-floor ceiling with its ornate iron-braced skylight. More gold-and-green-colored ornate ironwork decorated the balustrades running around each descending level, over which customers could peer down onto the first floor. In the middle of this central space was the toy department, with its picturesque dollhouse and giant old-fashioned toys. And there, the centerpiece of the season, was the twinkling Christmas tree.

Looking down on all this from the second level, another man was watching Rick's progress across the sales floor. He was pudgy and quite nearly bald. His companion, thinner, with a head of wild, curly blond hair, stood only a few feet away, covertly studying some lacy red lingerie displayed on a curvaceous mannequin.

"Hey, Irv," the bald one called softly. "Come here."

Irv sighed and stepped over to the railing. "What's up, Joey? You spot him?"

"No, something else." Joey indicated the direction with a motion of his head. "See that guy down there in jeans, just passing the perfume counter?"

"Yeah," Irv said, barely sparing a glance. "So what?"

"Quit ogling the plaster ladies and take a good look."

Irv glared first at his partner, then toward the man in question, who had been forced to take a detour around the line of children waiting to see Santa Claus.

He frowned. "I know that guy. Who is that?"

"That's what I'm trying to figure out, mop-head," Joey said disparagingly. He thought for a moment. "Got it! Put a few pounds on, roll back the mileage... It's Rick Hastings!"

"Who?" Irv asked.

"Rick Hastings, Her Ladyship's ex-husband."

"Nah!" Irv dismissed that suggestion with a wave of his hand. "He's dead. Drank himself to death back in Phoenix."

Joey was shaking his head uncertainly. "No, he's not the type to hit the skids. And if so, he's risen from the ashes."

"Huh?"

"Never mind," Joey told him. "But if it is Rick Hastings, I don't like it. Let's get this done. Get on up to the third floor, I'll finish down here."

AROUND ONE in the afternoon, Shannon realized she wasn't going to make it to lunch again today, or at least not until it was closer to the dinner hour. Luckily, she kept a stash of candy bars in the storeroom for just such occasions. She'd just stuffed about three quarters of one into her mouth, when someone tapped her on the shoulder.

"I understand you're looking for a Santa?"

"Mmmph!" Startled, Shannon spun around, eyes wide. She swallowed thickly. "What are you doing back here?"

she demanded. They were in the corridor leading to the storeroom, a spot that was narrow, ill-lighted and not at all conducive to such chance encounters. "This is off limits!"

"Sorry." Rick held up his hands and backed out the way he had come, through a curtain that covered the opening to the corridor. "But one of the clerks said it would be okay."

Shannon followed him through the curtain, glaring at him. Now that they were back in the light and he could see her face more clearly, Rick smiled, then chuckled.

"What's so funny?" Shannon demanded.

He pointed to her mouth. "Domestic or imported?"

She looked at him as if he'd taken leave of his senses. But then she touched her cheek and felt something sticky. A glance in a nearby mirror confirmed it. When he'd startled her, she had smeared chocolate from her mouth up toward one ear. She looked ridiculous.

"Oh, for the love of..." Shannon let her words trail off and pulled a tissue from the pocket of her slacks. As she cleaned up in front of the mirror, she glanced at the man who had caused all this. "What did you say your name was?"

"Rick. Rick Hastings. I'm here about the Santa job."

"Oh." Satisfied with her appearance, Shannon turned to face him. "Roy Rogers."

"Pardon?"

Shannon chuckled. "Sorry, Rick." She held out her hand. "Shannon O'Shaughnessy, toy department manager."

They shook hands briefly. "Pleased to meet you," he said.

"Madge told me your name was Roy or Roger. But she always was lousy with names. Good thing she gets them right on the paychecks."

Rick didn't have the slightest idea what this woman was going on about, but he needed this job badly, so he just smiled and nodded. Shannon smiled back.

Females had caused Rick a lot of pain in his life. In fact, it had been quite some time since he'd been even remotely interested in any woman. There had been purely physical urges, naturally, but no real feelings except negative ones.

His feelings at the moment were difficult to define, and had a healthy dose of the physical involved in them. They were, however, anything but negative.

Shannon O'Shaughnessy was quite a woman. Her hair, cut in a flattering, shoulder-length style, looked like finely spun copper wire. She had eyes the color of emeralds, and they flashed with intelligence and good humor—even though the joke had been on her. Rick judged her to be nearly as tall as he was, making it easy for her to meet his gaze, which she did with calm self-assurance. Age was always a deceiving factor for him. He was almost forty and he knew he looked older; to be a manager, Shannon would probably have to be in her mid-thirties but looked younger.

Whatever, she was old enough to know when she was being studied. "Didn't I get it all?" she asked.

"Hmm?" Rick realized he'd been staring. "Oh. Yes. Sorry to interrupt your coffee break."

"Actually, it was lunch," Shannon admitted.

"It does look like they keep you hopping."

"That's in the morning. At this time of day, we're doing good just to walk," she said. "By closing, we crawl."

"I can imagine."

Rick looked around the bustling toy department. A little girl went running past, dragging a stuffed lion by the tail. He felt a pang of regret and looked away.

Shannon couldn't help noticing. "Is something wrong?"

"No," he replied, a bit too quickly. He managed a smile and added, "I rushed over my lunch, too. Heartburn."

Paul Sanchez strolled up nonchalantly. "Everything okay here, Shannon?" he asked politely.

Shannon wasn't fooled. She could see from the way Paul was checking out the other man that he was suspicious of Rick. Rick was aware of it, too, she noticed, and yet seemed oddly accepting of it, as if it happened all the time.

"We're fine, Paul. Rick is here to apply for the Santa job."

"Oh." This made all the difference in the world to Paul, who had been forced to fill in at that position a few times himself earlier this month and had no desire to repeat the performance. "Well, I'll let you get on with it, then," he said, hurrying off. "Good luck!"

"I take it the job is still open?" Rick asked, amused.

"Very open." Shannon laughed, too. "It's hard work and there are no benefits, but at least the pay is lousy. Still interested?"

He nodded. "Lousy pay is better than none."

Shannon needed someone for this position so badly that she hadn't even bothered to take a really good look at Rick Hastings until now. He was, as Madge had warned, an eccentric. Or at least dressed like one, considering he was here about a job.

But Shannon had never really been all that concerned with appearances. She had known, and even dated, a few of the snappy dressers who frequented Lyon's. Most were more interested in themselves than in her. Others had been interested in her, all right, but what they had in mind was a clothes-optional activity.

Rick had given her a solid masculine appraisal, as well, she knew. What with the black woolen slacks, cream-colored blouse and black-and-red-check blazer she had on today, though, whatever conclusions he'd come to must have been based largely on his imagination. Still, some men were good at that

There was something about him that Shannon couldn't put her finger on. He was handsome, in a rugged sort of way. But it was another quality that had her wondering about him. Rick Hastings looked a bit lost. Strong, self-assured and maybe just a little dangerous, too, judging by the oddly cold undercurrents in his eyes. Perhaps therein lay his appeal. A lot of men were lost; this one seemed intent on staying that way, and that had aroused Shannon's curiosity.

"You really don't seem the Santa type, Rick," she said.

Rick shrugged. "Like I said, I need the job."

A straightforward answer. Shannon liked that. She was inclined to like the man, too. But would the kids?

"How are you with children?" she asked.

This was the part that worried him, and had caused a good part of Charlie's concern for him, as well. "I used to be very good with kids. But it's been some time since I was around any." He looked at her, wondering if she would understand what he was about to say. "That's one of the reasons I want this job."

Shannon arched her eyebrows. "I see."

"Do you?" Rick asked, suddenly sure she was going to turn him down. "Do you really?"

"How long have you been divorced?"

The question hit Rick as if it had been a physical blow. He actually pulled back from Shannon a few inches. "You're very astute."

"Rude, too, I suppose," Shannon said by way of apology. "It comes from spending so much of my time around children. They're very direct, most of them. I enjoy that about them."

One of the clerks approached them. "Sorry to interrupt, Shannon," the woman said, "but there's a lady over there who wants to talk to you." She indicated a frazzled-looking older woman standing by the overflowing checkout counter. "It's about you-know-who."

"Not another one." Shannon groaned. "Excuse me a moment, Rick. This shouldn't take long."

She went to deal with the problem. The clerk smiled uncertainly at Rick, then returned to her register. Left to his own devices, Rick decided to take a look around. He was standing in front of a display of pistol-like gadgets, when Leo discovered him.

"Hi," Leo said.

Rick stopped his puzzled examination of the gadget in his hand to look down at the boy. "Hi."

"Slime," Leo said.

"No, thanks," Rick returned. "I just ate."

Leo grinned crookedly, not quite sure how to take that response. "I mean that's what that gun shoots," he explained. "Slime. I'd show you, but Shannon took away the demonstrator."

"Did she?" Rick studied the gun some more. "I don't suppose that was an arbitrary decision on her part?"

"What's arbitrary mean?"

"For no particular reason."

"Oh." Leo colored slightly. "I suppose she had a reason."

Rick smiled. "Is it fun to shoot?"

"Sort of," Leo replied with a shrug. "It'd be a lot better if the slime wasn't so thick. That way, it would go farther."

"And give a guy a head start running away."

"Right." Leo nodded his approval, both of the idea and of Rick. "Sometimes, arbitrary targets get mad for no reason when you slime 'em."

"I just bet they do." Chuckling appreciatively, Rick returned to his inspection of the device in question. "So you just fill it with water, add some of that powder to this other reservoir and it's ready to go?"

"Uh-huh."

"Seems to me if you added some kind of control onto it, you could change how much water got mixed with the powder," Rick said thoughtfully. "Make the slime thicker or thinner, depending on your range."

Leo thought that was a wonderful idea. "Neat! Hey, are you an engineer, or something?"

"Or something," Rick agreed.

"Well, I bet they'd pay you for that idea."

"I doubt it. Big companies aren't very good listeners."

"Why not?"

Rick shrugged. "Too busy making money, I guess."

"That's what Shannon says about the Arnie people. She says they don't care that some kids won't get one. I'll be right here in the store when they come, so I know I will," he added with obvious relief.

Frowning, Rick started to say something, but Shannon returned from talking to the distraught customer and had her own opinion on the subject.

"They don't care what their stupid marketing scheme is doing to the parents of those kids, either," Shannon said. "That's the third one in an hour. In person, that is. I lost count of the phone calls from parents who have to work the rest of the week, or can't make it into the city again for a while. For whatever reason, they're worried sick they won't get an Arnie and their boy or girl will be devastated."

"It's just a toy spider," Rick said quietly.

Both Leo and Shannon stared at him. "Just a toy spider?" Shannon asked incredulously. "It is *the* toy of the season. We don't know how many we'll get or when we'll get them. The company won't even let us take advance orders, so it's first come, first served. All we know for sure is that there won't be enough to go around."

"Maybe that's not such a bad thing," Rick maintained. "It might force some kids, and their parents, to be more thankful for what they do get. Like I said, it's just a toy spider. There are plenty of kids in this city and others I've lived in who would rather have a new coat for Christmas."

"Really?" Leo asked, surprised by this information.

Rick nodded solemnly. "And their parents are worried there may not be enough of those to go around, either."

Shannon closed her eyes and sighed. When she opened them, she was seeing her Santa applicant in a different light. His clothes. That defiant look in his eyes. The lost air about him. He probably wasn't homeless, but she could just bet he really did need the job.

There was more to it than that, though, she was certain. This wasn't much of a job, and he looked capable of doing ones that paid a lot more. Of course, those were usually hard, physical labor, of which he had undoubtedly done a fair share. Maybe he just wanted to be in where it was warm. He obviously wanted to be near children.

Shannon had a sudden, powerful urge to help this man, to find out how he had come to be in his present situation. She also felt an undeniable attraction to him. But she was head of Lyon's toy department and had a duty to hire people on the basis of their character, not her hormones.

Still, Madge had recommended him, after all. And his view of the Arnie affair would certainly be a welcome voice of reason at a time when almost everyone she came in contact with seemed to be losing their minds.

There was, of course, one final test. She had little doubt he'd pass with flying colors. "Mr. Hastings wants to be a Santa, Leo. What do you think?"

"I figured that's what he was here for," Leo replied with a knowing air. "I was checking him out."

Rick was somewhat taken aback by this information. "Oh, really? And here I thought you were just being friendly."

"I was. But a good executive can't let friendship stand in the way of making the right decisions." He walked around Rick once, looking him up and down. "A little skinny. And he doesn't seem very jolly. But we'll give him a try."

"I agree," Shannon said. She smiled at Rick, who was clearly befuddled by this cooperative effort. "Rick, meet Leo Lyon. He'll show you where to change. Then he'll show you where to sit. And then he'll sit on your lap."

"Don't worry," Leo assured him. "I'll take it easy on you, this being your first time and all. Come on." He grabbed Rick's hand and started pulling him toward the elevator. "How are you on the reindeer?"

"Reindeer?"

"The names. If you don't know all the names, you're in trouble. Especially with the five-year-olds. They look for the slightest weakness, and then *wham!* They murder ya."

Chapter Three

Over fifty years ago, on the day the first customer walked out of Pop Lyon's toy shop, Joe Bayer was standing across the street in front of his own dry goods emporium, holding up a sign proclaiming his competitor to be a liar and a cheat. From that high point, relations between the two men went steadily downhill. By comparison, Macy got along quite well with Gimbels.

When Pop expanded into the storefront next door, Joe added a second level to his establishment. Pop bought out the entire block, Joe went down the street and did the same. A building spree followed. At four stories, Lyon's was bigger. But Bayer's had an indoor fountain. Lyon's gave out trading stamps. Bayer's held one-cent sales.

In spite of this competition, or maybe because of it, both stores were hugely profitable. However, for some reason, there was always a tendency on the part of the public to think of Bayer's as the less pleasant alternative. They would shop there, especially for bargains, but if an item was similarly priced at the two stores, people preferred to buy from Lyon's.

This naturally drove Joe Bayer up the wall. He even went so far as to scatter pictures of his smiling face around the store to promote goodwill. In fact, he wasn't nearly as nice a man as Pop Lyon. His employees did not love him the way Pop's did, and weren't as happy in their work as Lyon's employees. Customer relations suffered.

The situation didn't improve upon Joe's death when his son Nathan took over operation of Bayer's. While Pop Lyon continued to refine his homespun method of internal management, Nathan dragged Bayer's into the world of incorporation and expansion, stock offerings and board meetings. He demanded obedient efficiency from his employees. And, like his father before him, Nathan was not a very nice man.

Such a man deserved a wife like Angela. Shrill, shrewish and unabashedly materialistic, Angela had the body of a goddess and the morals of an alley cat. She would use any and all of those attributes to get what she wanted. And what Angela Bayer wanted, every minute of every hour, was nothing less than her own way. She usually got it, because if she didn't, everyone knew there would be hell to pay.

At the moment, Nathan was making an installment.

"Can't?" Angela glowered at her husband of three years and repeated the word, emphasizing it as if she didn't know its meaning. "*Can't?* I don't want to hear that, Nathan!"

Nathan hadn't wanted to say it, either. He tried not to wince at her tone of voice. Like a wild animal, she would take any sign of weakness and turn it to her own advantage.

"There's nothing I can do, my love," he said calmly. "I don't have a magic lamp."

She narrowed her pale gray eyes to thin slits. "Is that supposed to be funny, Nathan?"

"No." He sighed. "I simply meant that what you're asking me to do is impossible. There are no Arnies to be had, at any price."

As slick as an eel, Angela changed tactics. She sat on the edge of his desk and leaned over, her oval, expertly made-up face in a pretty pout, her ample bosom displayed at the V of her yellow mohair sweater.

"But what shall I tell Chelsea and Todd?" she asked.

Nathan stared at her breasts; she was perched so close to him that he hardly had any choice. But it wasn't a hardship. The view was marvelous. Angela was a very beautiful woman.

From her rich mane of natural, honey-blond hair to her delicately painted toenails, she was one ripe, luscious curve after another. Sensuality smoldered in her eyes, was painted on her full mouth and tempted any man that watched the gentle sway of her hips as she walked. After three years, Nathan still couldn't quite believe his eyes when he woke up beside her every morning.

But such a luxury came with a steep price. Besides her demanding, self-indulgent ways and expensive tastes, there was her temper, which could be quick and unbelievably vile. She was also a flirt and a tease, leading on any man who looked at her, and the way she flaunted herself, there were many of those.

On the other hand, she could also be charming, a treat to have on his arm at a social gathering and a valuable asset to his career. It was a trade-off.

Nathan had no illusions. That she had married him for his money and position was obvious. That he had allowed her into his world—and his will—in return for the pleasures of her young body was just as obvious. She had given him a son, too, an heir to the Bayer empire—though she left that heir with a nanny most of the time, especially the nearer he got to the terrible twos. Everything else was as negotiable as next year's labor contracts.

"At his age, Angela," he said at last, "I don't think Todd is going to much care if he gets an Arnie for Christmas, or not. And all Chelsea wants is the same thing she asks for every year. A horse. Since she's getting the stupid thing this year—thanks to you—I'm sure she'll be thrilled."

"An Argentine polo pony is hardly just a stupid horse," Angela corrected. "I told you. It's an investment."

Nathan laughed curtly. "Sure it is. An investment in bankruptcy. Heaven forbid she might actually want to compete with the thing someday. There's a reason they call it the sport of kings, you know."

"I believe that's horse racing, dear," Angela corrected again, her white, perfect teeth clenched.

"Whatever." Nathan could sense her mood swinging again. He had to nip it in the bud by going on the attack. "Neither of the children needs or even wants an Arnie. *You're* the one who does, just so you can say you have it."

Little spots of color appeared on Angela's cheekbones. "So? You bought a Porsche for the same reason."

"I drive the car. You wouldn't even look at the stupid spider, now, would you? With its hairy legs and little beady eyes? They stick to your skin, you know, and won't come off."

"Stop it!" As quickly as she had colored with anger, Angela now went pale. She stood up, hugging herself.

"See? Now what would you do with an Arnie?"

Angela glared at him. "I don't want one, you stupid fool!" she returned sharply. "I want the shipment that Lyon's is getting. And so should you. You call yourself a Bayer? Hah! Your father is spinning in his grave."

The light was dawning in Nathan's mind. "I see. And you thought that by nagging me to find one, I might stumble onto a source? A black market source, maybe?"

"No, idiot! I thought you'd have the guts to make your own breaks this time. Those damn spiders are somewhere."

His eyes went wide. "You mean, you hoped I'd find them, and then *steal* them?"

"Don't look at me like that," Angela said. "You're not above it. You take so many nips and tucks in the deals you put together, you should have been a plastic surgeon. I have access to the books, remember? I know what goes on."

True. Angela was not just a pretty face. She had a mind for business, Nathan had seen it in action before. What he had not been aware of was that beneath those breasts beat the heart of a thief. He rather liked the idea.

"But you're not on top of everything, obviously," he told her with a self-satisfied smile. "For your information, I have done some digging. But this is the cagiest marketing gambit I've ever seen. I doubt we could trace this company down even if we did have the time, and we don't. Even the manufacturer is keeping a very, very low profile."

"Why, Nathan!" Angela exclaimed, pleasantly surprised. "You mean you've been holding out on me?"

He nodded. "I've even developed a plan, something of a Christmas present for the both of us. You see, dearest, we don't need to find the shipment."

"We don't?"

"No. We can make the shipment come to us."

Chapter Four

By seven-thirty in the evening, Rick had filled in for Hans, the main Santa, a total of six times—three bathroom breaks, one dinner break and two rest periods the normally self-composed elderly gentleman referred to as sanity breaks. Even so, the man was wearing down, and Rick had the feeling that he would soon find himself in charge until closing time.

Though Rick was bearing up stoically, he didn't know how the old guy did it. To think, he had envisioned this job as a pleasant change from physical labor.

The small of his back ached from helping the kids onto his lap. His left knee was killing him, since this was the one on which most children preferred to sit. That meant that even with the traditional heavy black boots on, his right shin was bruised and battered from the kicks—some accidental, some intentional—he had received from approximately seventy pairs of little feet. And if one more kid pulled his beard, which Leo had insisted he must glue to his face with spirit gum, Rick was quite certain he would scream.

Not that anyone would notice. For a supposedly happy occasion, there was certainly a lot of yelling going on. It was stressful for the children, standing in a long line with a hundred or so of their peers, waiting for a chance to make their fondest desires known. It was tiring, too. Some of them cracked under the pressure and started bawling. This had much the same effect as one barking dog in a quiet neighborhood; pretty soon, they were all doing it.

But for all the hollering and crying, the being thrown up on and some other even less pleasant accidents he had endured thus far, Rick had to admit he was enjoying himself. Because every now and then, in between the whiners and the grabbers, he would discover a gem.

At the moment, he had one on his lap, in the form of a six-year-old girl with the biggest brown eyes Rick had ever seen. She was looking at him. Just him. For the time being, even the candy cane each child received had been placed in the pocket of her cute paisley overalls and forgotten.

"And what's your name, little one?" Rick asked her.

"Susan," she replied softly.

"Susan." He smiled. "Susie?"

She shook her head solemnly, never once taking her eyes from his face. "No. Not Susie." Each word was spoken slowly and clearly, so there would be no mistake. "I like Susan."

"Then Susan it shall be," Rick said, treating her with the dignity she so obviously desired. "Have you been a good girl this year, Susan?"

"Not 'specially."

Rick arched his bushy white false eyebrows. "No?"

"My daddy doesn't think so."

Puzzled by this unprompted display of honesty, Rick looked to the girl's mother for confirmation. She was young, perhaps twenty, with the same big brown eyes as her daughter. Blushing furiously, the young woman gave a shrug and patted the little girl's sleek black hair.

"She's actually been pretty good. For Susan."

"I see," Rick said with a knowing smile, then returned his attention to Susan. "Maybe you'd better tell Santa what you did that made your father mad."

"I washed Peaches," the girl replied, at last lowering her gaze. Her jet black lashes were incredibly long and fluffy against her cheeks. "Daddy didn't like that."

"Peaches?" Rick asked.

"My kitty."

"Oh." Fearing some sort of horror story, Rick again looked at the child's mother. But she was just grinning ruefully and shaking her head, so he pressed onward. "Well, kitties don't much like anyone washing them. They'd usually rather do it themselves."

Susan was gazing at him again. But this time there was the strangest look in her eyes. "Peaches can't wash herself, Mr. Claus! She's stuffed!"

Realizing that it wouldn't do for Santa to admit such a faux pas, Rick decided to blunder on and hope for the best. "But your daddy didn't like it when you washed her?"

"Nope."

"Why not?" Rick asked. He wasn't about to stop now.

"I couldn't reach the sink. So I put her in the bathtub."

"And left her there," her mother continued. "For an hour. With the water running. Peaches is *very* clean now. So is everything else. The bathroom was on the second floor."

"Daddy went ballistic," Susan said. She had trouble with the word but obviously knew what it meant, because she pointed toward the ceiling. "Boom!"

Rick was having trouble keeping a straight face. Then he just gave up. It was his job to laugh. "Ho, ho, ho!"

Shannon could hear him laughing all the way over in the cosmetics department, where she was watching the register for a moment while the usual clerk took a quick break.

"My, that certainly is a jolly Santa!" the woman she was helping observed.

"He does seem to be getting into the spirit, doesn't he?" Shannon agreed.

The woman smiled. "Well, he's certainly raising my spirits!"

When the cosmetics clerk returned, Shannon went back to her own department, whistling along with the piped-in Christmas music. She had to admit Rick was raising her spirits, as well. She hadn't been sure he would work out. But after a hesitant start, during which just being around them seemed to make him sad, Rick proved to have a genuine affinity for children, and they for him. Even Leo approved of his performance, and he was a harsh judge.

But there was more to Shannon's improved mood than the fact that Rick was working out at the job. She could tell that she was actually doing him a service, and not only economically speaking. There was a spring in his step that hadn't been there when he'd come in that afternoon to apply for the job.

She wanted to get to know him better. Since he was due for a break and she was about to faint with hunger, she decided a good start would be to have a chat with him while grabbing a quick bite in the cafeteria. The pickings would be slim by now, but at least it would be quiet. Not that it really mattered. She just wanted him to fill out a couple of forms and maybe have a little employer-to-employee talk.

Sure she did. That's why she had put on a spritz of the most expensive French perfume Lyon's carried. And touched up her lipstick. She was already in cosmetics, so why not? Just because a woman tried to look her best, that didn't mean it was to impress a man.

"Shannon," she muttered to herself. "You're such a liar."

It wasn't that she was hard up for companionship. She had two cats, Buttons and Phil. And handsome customers were always asking her out. Of course, most of them were shopping for their kids and had wives at home, but it was the thought that counted, right?

There were also phone calls every now and then from her ex-husband who called to remind her that he still held her responsible for their lack of children and, ultimately, their lack of marriage.

Yes, Shannon had her pick of interesting diversions. But whether Rick had lost a child, too, or had endured a bitter divorce, Shannon knew that lost look. She had worn one of her own for a long time. Maybe she could help him. Maybe they could help each other. Stranger things had happened.

At last, Rick approached her. He was hobbling slightly, she noticed. "Knee or shin?" Shannon asked.

"Shin. The knee went numb an hour ago."

"That'll get stronger," she informed him. "And here's a trick for the shin." Shannon dug around beneath the sales counter to find him a magazine. "Stick that in your boot. I'm told it works wonders."

He grinned. "Thanks."

"Hey, I've got some forms Accounting needs you to fill out. Care to join me for a bite to eat while we take care of them?" she asked, as if the thought had suddenly occurred to her. "It's still a couple of hours till closing time."

Rick looked over toward Santa's workshop, actually just a little tableau set up where the kids could get their pictures taken with Santa—and a hidden area where the Santas could switch places without anyone's feeling they were being slighted. The crowds were thinning out a bit.

"I can't be long," he said. "Hans probably doesn't have much more than another thirty minutes in him."

"No problem," Shannon assured him. "I should have told you earlier. There's a cafeteria on the fourth floor. Not too fancy, but it's clean and cheap."

"That's the magic word."

They rode the elevator up. It was something of an ordeal. Rick didn't want to take the trouble of changing, so he went in costume. And of course, his fluffy white beard was glued on. He and Shannon were the object of some interested stares.

They went over the forms Rick needed to fill out, but it was just the basics, to keep the government happy, and didn't take them long. There were only sandwiches left, but they each bought one, ate, then lingered over coffee.

"Tough work, isn't it?" Shannon said.

Rick nodded. "I had no idea. But I'm having a blast."

"It shows." She laughed. "Sorry. But I feel a bit absurd. Like I'm having a private audience with Saint Nicholas, or something."

"Ho ho ho! And have *you* been a good little girl?"

Shannon winked coquettishly. "I always am, Santa."

"Hmm. That's not what Santa wanted to hear."

She noticed that Santa had a very wicked twinkle in his eyes as he looked at her. "Rick!"

He immediately sobered and looked away.

Shannon wasn't sure what to do. Obviously, Rick felt he'd taken their banter a step too far. She didn't feel that way. There was a definite attraction between them, and it wasn't going to just disappear. Shannon didn't want it to.

She didn't want to come on too strong, either. It had been nearly five years since her divorce from Greg, but she was still in a cautious mode, and perhaps always would be.

"It's difficult, isn't it?" Shannon began. "You get into such a pattern when you're married. And afterward, it just doesn't fit with anyone else. You have to start fresh."

Rick nodded. "As I said earlier, you're very astute."

"Well, I've just been there, that's all."

"Divorced?" he asked.

"Going on five years this March," Shannon replied. "Not that I keep track, necessarily. Heaven knows it was time for that particular union to end."

"Mine, too," he agreed, laughing. That surprised him. Rick hadn't thought he would ever be able to laugh about it. Perhaps it was because he would soon have the last laugh. "We just didn't have the same life in mind. Now I can't see how we ever thought we would make it."

"Ditto. Strange, isn't it?"

He shrugged. "In our case, it was lust, I suppose."

They both smiled. Shannon liked him, and could tell by the way Rick was looking at her that he liked her, too. It was a start. Where it would lead was anyone's guess, but it couldn't happen at a better time.

"Would you mind?" Shannon said, pointing to his beard. "I'll help you put it back on later."

"Gladly. It's getting itchy, anyway." Rick pulled on the fake beard gently to loosen it. He slowly peeled it off. "That's better," he said with a sigh of relief.

"Much," Shannon agreed. She stroked the downy soft whiskers that now lay on the table between them. "Christmas is my favorite time of year. But it can be…" She trailed off uncertainly.

"Lonely?" Rick offered.

She smiled. They were on the same wavelength. "That, too. But I was thinking of how it can be a rather melancholy reminder of the way things used to be. Not just of married days, either. Childhood days."

"Or days with your child," Rick said, his mood taking a sudden downswing. "Do you have any children?"

Shannon studied a tiny chip in her coffee mug. "No," she said quietly. "I don't."

"I have one. A girl. She's with her mother."

"That must be hard." Shannon reached out to touch his hand. In fact, she needed the contact right now, herself. "But at least you know that she's . . . that she's safe."

Rick wasn't the least bit comforted. "For all the good it does me," he said, a bitter edge to his voice. "I can't see her. Her mother forbids it."

"She can't do that!" Shannon exclaimed incredulously.

"Oh, but she did. All it took was money. She had lots of it, while I used up what little I had trying to stop her. I lost everything, including my little girl."

"Well, she can't take that from you," Shannon objected. "Not really. You'll always be her father."

Rick looked at her, his face bleak. "No, I'm not. Not anymore. I gave that up, too. I didn't have any choice."

"I don't understand."

"Neither do I," Rick muttered. He stood up, grabbing his beard from the table. "I'd better get back."

Shannon left a tip for the busboy, and then hurried to catch up with Rick. She barely managed to slip into the elevator with him. It was crowded.

"I'm sorry," she said quietly.

"For what? It's not your fault."

"I was prying," Shannon maintained. "It's a problem of mine. I just thought maybe I could help."

Rick took a deep breath, then blew it out slowly. He looked at her, and the concern he saw in those lovely green eyes touched his heart, a part of him that hadn't been treated very well.

"It's being handled, okay?" he told her. "Now, if you don't mind, I'd really rather not talk about it anymore."

When the elevator stopped at the main level, everyone got out, including some bemused shoppers who must have wondered what was going on between Santa and his red-headed companion. They made their way to the toy department, where she helped him glue on his beard, then got back to work herself.

It was about nine when Paul came to see her. He looked worried. "Have you seen Leo, Shannon? I can't find him anywhere."

"Now that you mention it, I haven't seen him for quite some time," Shannon returned. "Maybe Pop called for the car to come get him early."

Paul shook his head. "Pop just called for it now and told me to go round him up."

"Did you check electronics? He's absolutely addicted to that new video game with the wolves in it."

"I know. I checked there first thing."

"Hmm." Shannon thought for a moment. Then she shrugged. "Well, it's no use driving ourselves crazy looking for him all over the store. He could probably hide so well in here that we'd never find him. I'll just page him. That'll bring him running."

But it didn't. Shannon tried again, thinking he might not have heard the first time, with the same result. No Leo.

"Could he have fallen asleep somewhere?" Paul wondered.

"Maybe," Shannon said. "But he's been so wound up lately. He wouldn't have left the building, would he?"

"Never has," Paul said. "Not without asking, I mean. Besides, it's snowing like mad out there "

Thinking that could be the answer, Shannon went to the locker where the boy kept his coat. It wasn't there. Encouraged, she took a quick tour around the building, looking out every window. At any moment she expected to spot him out there building a snowman. But all she saw was falling snow and irritated shoppers.

Concerned now, they started a department-by-department search, asking every clerk. But since Leo had been around off and on all day, no one could pinpoint a time when they had noticed he *hadn't* been around for a while. The last time Shannon had seen him was when he'd been coaching Rick.

"Nope," Rick said when they asked him. "Once he finally got it through my head that Dopey wasn't one of the reindeer, he left me on my own. I don't remember his saying he was headed anyplace particular."

By this time, the store was getting ready to close, and Shannon's normally buoyant attitude was starting to crumble. She paged the boy again, the worry in her voice plain.

"Leo! Leo Lyon! You report to me this instant, young man! Or you'll get enough coal for Christmas to open your own power plant!"

When that failed, too, she started to cry. Even the fact that it was Rick who held her didn't fully register.

"Hey," he cajoled softly, "don't worry. We'll find him."

"I'm not so sure about that," Paul announced, returning to the toy department after making his final check of the store. "I've looked high and low and yelled until I'm blue in the face. He's not here." Then he held up a piece of paper. "And I found this in the dollhouse."

Shannon snatched it from him, impatiently brushing away her tears so she could read it. Even then it was a struggle, since Leo had written it himself.

Shannon read the note aloud so the employees gathered around could hear. " 'I can't say much about my mission. Spies are everywhere, and the government agents have sworn me to secrecy. We're off to fight evil, and deliver Arnie to all the boys and girls of the world.' " Tears sprang again to Shannon's eyes. "And he signed it Agent X."

"That's a new one," someone said.

"What government agents?" someone else wanted to know.

Paul's face was pale. "He kept talking about spies watching him. I told you there was something weird going on," he exclaimed, looking accusingly at Shannon.

"Oh, Lord!" she wailed. "Leo's been kidnapped!"

Chapter Five

"Are we there yet?"

"No, kid," the one called Irv replied. "Soon. Right, Agent Joey? We'll be there soon, huh?" He sounded worried.

The bald one muttered something under his breath. He was driving, and wasn't at all happy about it. According to him, the roads were slicker than snot.

Leo thought that sounded pretty slick. He was sitting in the back seat of their nifty, fully equipped luxury four-wheel drive, a can of soda in one hand and a double-fudge brownie in the other. From his position, he couldn't even see the road, but that was okay, because there wasn't much to see, anyway. It was pitch black outside, and snowing heavily.

They were on their way to what Joey called a safe house, from which they could direct their campaign against the forces of evil who threatened the Arnie shipment. At first, Leo hadn't been so sure about coming with them. But then, after swearing him to secrecy, Agent Joey and his brother Agent Irv had shown him their official badges and explained why it was necessary.

Since Lyon's was the rightful owner of the shipment, it was necessary for a member of the Lyon family to be with them, in case some important decision had to be made on the spot. But they thought the excitement would be too much for Pop, so Leo would have to come in his place.

Leo was proud to be of help. Besides, they designated him Agent X, and gave him an official badge, too. They had also given him his favorite supper at the Taco Shack, the one Pop never let him order because it gave Leo gas. And there was a sackful of brownies for dessert. Not to mention the cooler at his side filled with his pick of sodas.

If this was government work, Leo might have to change his mind about becoming an executive at Lyon's. After they gave him a medal for saving the Arnie shipment, he could probably have his pick of jobs. Maybe even president of the United States.

"Have you ever met the president, Agent Joey?"

"Huh?" Joey took his eyes off the road momentarily, and saw to his horror that Leo was out of his safety belt. "Jeez! Put that belt back on, kid!"

"It's Agent X," Irv reminded him solemnly, "you gotta use the code names, Agent Joey."

"I'll give *you* a code name, you putz! Get that kid back into that belt!"

Irv turned around in his seat and made sure Leo was buckled in. "There. Snug as a bug."

"Shannon always says that," Leo remarked. "When she helps me with my coat, or something." He looked at his cartoon-character watch and frowned. "I hope she found that note. She doesn't like it when I worry her. Can I call her later?"

"Everything's fine, kid," Joey said reassuringly. "It's all been handled. No reason to get upset." But he reached over and thumped Irv on the arm with the back of his hand. "Give Agent X a cookie."

Irv passed back what was left of the package to Leo. Most of the rest were presently stuffed in his mouth. He made a face, and Leo laughed so hard, soda came out his nose, which set Irv off, as well. Soon, they were both howling with laughter, much to Joey's dismay.

"Oh, man," he muttered. "This is going to be some couple of days. Like baby-sitting *two* eight-year-olds."

He was so perturbed, he almost missed his exit, and then nearly slid into a ditch making too fast a turn. This chain of events sobered up his passengers some, but Irv still had the giggles. Joey whacked him on the arm again.

"Just help me look for the driveway, will you?"

"Sure thing, Agent Joey."

"That's it!" Joey exclaimed. "I'm making a new rule. From now on, I'm just Joey, okay? Just Joey. And you're Irv, and he's Leo. Got that?"

"Got it," Irv said. "Just Joey."

"Roger," Leo agreed. "Want a cookie, Just Joey?"

That started Irv off all over again. Joey groaned and looked skyward. "Why me?" he asked.

"Shannon says that a lot, too," Leo observed.

They found the driveway Joey was looking for without further incident. He pulled down it, the headlights of the four-wheel drive sweeping across the thick pine trees lining each side. When he reached the house, he pushed a remote control attached to the visor and the garage door slid up. A light went on inside the garage at the same time, like a warm yellow beacon in the cold, black night.

Once inside with the engine off, a profound silence descended upon them. "Cool!" Leo said. "Like a hideout."

Irv chuckled. "Yeah! Cool!"

With a long-suffering sigh, Joey opened his door and stepped out. He got some bags out of the back, handing a couple to Irv. Leo insisted on helping, so they put him in charge of the cooler. Together, they trooped to the entrance of the house, where Joey had to use a credit card to get inside. This also turned on a number of lights throughout the house.

"Nice system," Joey said, nodding his approval.

"Nice house," Irv said admiringly.

Leo just stood there with his mouth agape. It was hard to impress a boy who had grown up in some pretty nice homes, himself, and an entire department store of goodies to play with, as well. But he was more than impressed. He was agog.

"This isn't a house," he managed to say at last. "This is a playground!"

He was sure there were plenty of things there for grown-ups, like a nice kitchen and lots of books and stuff. But all Leo could see at the moment was the home entertainment center, the focus of which was an enormous big-screen television complete with stereo surround sound. Attached to it were the usual tape and disc players, and a satellite tuner. But the best part was the most elaborate game system he'd ever seen. His little computer-friendly fingers itched to attach themselves to the controls.

Joey nudged Irv. "Look at that face," he whispered. "I told you. We don't have a thing to worry about. By the time the kid comes up for air, it'll all be over."

"Whatever you say, Joey." Irv glanced at his watch. "Hey, my favorite show's on! Dibs on the big screen!"

"No way!" Leo exclaimed, sprinting into the entertainment room. "I'm going to see if they've got Wolves of Doom."

"Kids," Joey said, chuckling.

Now that they were safe from prying eyes, he felt more relaxed. This would be a breeze. They had lots of food, and plenty to keep the kid occupied. The shipment of Arnies had to arrive at Lyon's dock sometime soon. And then it would be payback time.

"OF COURSE we're going to hand it over," Pop Lyon said.

Shannon was standing in Pop's office on the fourth floor, where she and several other employees, including Rick, had come to break the news to the old man. Much to their surprise, however, he already knew, having received a phone call just moments earlier.

Pop Lyon had good days and bad. This was obviously not one of his best, judging by the way his hands shook. But there was still fire in his pale blue eyes and in his voice as he spoke. Even at eighty, he was in control.

"We will comply with all their other demands, as well," he said, looking from one face to the other. As he spoke, he wheeled himself into a position to confront the group, to show them he meant business. "No word of this to the media. No outside intervention at all, including the police."

"But Pop," Paul objected. "That's not how it's done. I still have some friends down there. They'll know how to handle things without—"

"I said no!" Pop interrupted.

The effort made him cough. He had a nurse in attendance, and she brought him a glass of water. She glared at Paul, as did several others.

When he recovered, Pop continued vehemently. "I am not jeopardizing the welfare of my grandson for a crate of toys! That's all they want, and I'm happy to oblige. Let them have the damn things. I hope they choke on them."

"And if they don't give Leo back? What then?"

Pop turned his head sharply to see who had spoken. So did everyone else. Much to Shannon's dismay, it was Rick. As a newcomer, he was not as well versed in the fine points of handling Pop as the rest of them.

"Who are you?" Pop asked, wheeling himself closer to the man in the Santa Claus suit. "Do I know you?"

Rick shook his head. He had removed his beard and hat, but still felt conspicuous standing there in his red suit with its white fuzzy trim. The old man's intense scrutiny didn't help any. But he had to speak up.

"His name is Rick Hastings, Pop," Shannon interjected. "I hired him this afternoon, to fill in for Hans when he needs a break. Madge recommended him."

"I did not!" Madge exclaimed, emerging from the crowd just inside the office door. "I've never seen him before."

Shannon paled. "Isn't this your sister's cousin's nephew, or whatever?" she asked, suddenly feeling incredibly inept for even considering such a vague recommendation in the first place.

"No. Roger couldn't make it today. The storm stranded him in Vail. Or so he said."

"Then who..." Shannon trailed off, staring at Rick as if at some new species of bug. "You lied."

"I did no such thing," Rick told her. "You were the one going on about Roy Rogers and Madge. I just nodded." He shrugged. "So sue me. I needed the job."

There was general concerned muttering among the other employees. Pop rapped his cane on the floor for attention. He could walk, when he needed to, but arthritis made it quite painful for him. Everyone quieted down.

"What do you know about Leo's disappearance, young man?"

"Nothing more than anyone else," Rick replied. "I was only wondering if it's wise to be in such a rush to give away the shipment, when you can't be sure that whoever has Leo will give him back once they have it."

"But I *am* certain they'll release him," Pop returned. "Because after they have that shipment, there will no longer be any profit in keeping him. I'm also certain there will be no way of proving they had anything to do with it afterward, so I won't bother trying." He smiled grimly. "In return, I'm sure they're taking very good care of Leo. It's a little like honor among thieves, I suppose. That's the way the Bayers have always done business."

Those assembled gasped. Shannon was the first to voice what they were all obviously thinking. "Of course! The Bayers!"

"Hold it. Do you know for a fact it's the Bayers?" Rick demanded, his voice suddenly sharp. "Or is this merely supposition?"

Shannon was staring at Rick again. Was it her imagination, or had that coldness she'd seen in his eyes before increased? She didn't know what was going on, but since she was the one who had allowed him into their midst, she now felt responsible.

"Just who are you?" Shannon demanded. "What's your interest in this, anyway?"

"I have plenty at stake here," he returned, his voice cracking like a whip. Rick looked at Pop again. "Now, answer my question. How do you know it was the Bayers?"

"That's about enough of that, pal." Paul had stepped closer to Rick. "Pop doesn't need this stress."

With his bulk, Paul could be a very intimidating man. But then, Rick was a rather commanding presence, himself. At the moment, however, neither of them had a thing on Shannon. She put herself between them, glaring at Rick.

"Back off, Paul," she told him. "If anyone is going to get a piece of this guy, it's me."

Pop's cane thumped the floor again. "That's enough! All of you!" He, too, was looking at Rick. "In answer to your question, I have to admit I don't know for absolute certain that the Bayers are behind this. But after wrestling with them in the business arena for over fifty years, I know their style when I see it," he assured him. "Joe Bayer was just short of a common criminal. As far as I have been able to determine, his son Nathan *is* a criminal, a disgusting white-collar thief of the sneakiest kind."

Rick sighed. "That's putting it kindly."

"How do you know the Bayers?" Shannon asked suspiciously.

"Yes. I think it's time you explained yourself, young man," Pop agreed, staring at Rick through ancient, narrowed eyes. "What exactly is your connection to the Bayers? Did they send you to make sure the kidnapping of my grandson went smoothly?"

"I resent that more than you can possibly comprehend," Rick returned bitterly.

Shannon put her hand on his arm. "Rick—"

He cut her off. "Save it. Excuse me, I have things to do." The crowd parted for him as he stalked out the door.

"What the hell," Pop muttered.

Shannon was equally troubled by Rick's reaction. "He *is* connected, and we need to know how."

"I agree," Pop said, wheeling himself to his desk. "And I think I know who might know the answer."

While he made the call, Shannon sat down in one of the chairs near the old man's desk. It was a good thing, too, because Pop had his answer in minutes, and it was a shocker for them both.

"Rick was once married to Nathan Bayer's wife, Angela," Pop informed her. "Evidently, she and Nathan took everything from him, including his own flesh and blood. Chelsea Bayer is really Chelsea Hastings, Rick's daughter."

Chapter Six

Angela cursed. "It doesn't even ring!"

"It's the storm," Nathan told her. "The phone lines must be down." He patted the covers beside him, still warm from her body. "Come back to bed and stop worrying."

"Somebody has to worry. With those two idiots in on the deal, anything could happen."

He watched her cross the room. It had finally stopped snowing, and the clouds were beginning to move off. Moonlight streamed in through the window, illuminating her shapely form through her thin negligee. How such a lovely package could contain so much hostility was beyond him.

"Joey's okay," Nathan said. "Irv's dim but dependable, especially with Joey in charge."

Angela glanced at him, her beautiful face marred by a deep frown. "You don't suppose they'd have the brains between them to double-cross us, do you?"

"What?" He arched his eyebrows. "That's absurd."

"Is it? Think about it." She paced the floor, well aware of the effect her scanty attire was having on the man watching her. Let him suffer. "That shipment is worth a lot of money. And you, in your infinite wisdom, placed those two in complete control of the whole operation."

"Correction. *I* am in control, they're just following orders," Nathan objected. "And I did it this way because it leaves us completely out of harm's way."

"Unless old man Lyon decides to dig into the matter after he gets his precious little grandson back," Angela returned. "That's another thing. I can't understand why you think he'll just drop the matter once the boy is returned."

Nathan smiled. It was not a particularly nice sort of smile. "He'll drop it because he knows it's not worth the trouble I could cause him if he didn't. He also knows that dig as he might, the only link he'd find would be Joey and Irv, who would never let it go any further."

"So you say."

"They have proven themselves very trustworthy over a period of many years," Nathan said, his irritation with her growing. "I grew up with Joey, for heaven's sake! He was my father's right-hand man. As a matter of fact, I've known both him and Irv a lot longer than I've known you."

Angela looked at him sharply. "What's that supposed to mean, *dear?*"

"Nothing, *dear,*" he retorted. "Just that I know they won't cross me."

"And I would? Is that what you're getting at?"

Nathan paused, considering his words carefully. In fact, he was quite certain his pretty wife would be more than happy to stab him in the back, provided that it was of some advantage to her and that she could get away with it. But then, he supposed they were the same in that regard. Only a poisonous snake was comfortable sleeping with its own kind, after all.

"This is pointless, Angela," he said at last.

"Oh, really? What if Joey and Irv were to make a deal with someone who owed us one?"

"Like who?" Nathan asked.

"I'm not sure who," Angela replied. "I just have this strange feeling. Women's intuition, if you like. That's the trouble with unfinished business. It just sits there in your past, ready to surprise you, the way a bug you didn't squash completely always manages to crawl into your shoe to die."

SHANNON PULLED the collar of her fleece-lined overcoat up around her ears to protect them from the wind. She felt like some kind of spy, sneaking along the nearly deserted downtown streets in the snowy moonlight. It was profoundly cold, in the single digits, she was certain, turning the wind into a knife that poked its icy blade into any hole it could find in her meager defenses.

Rick was walking ahead of her, little more than a dark shape moving quickly through the shadows. She didn't really know why she had decided to follow him. It probably wasn't the smartest thing she'd ever done. There was the bitter cold to contend with, as well as the occasional seedy-looking inner-city denizen. But worst of all, she was following a man who was in a foul mood and conceivably dangerous.

Somehow, though, even if he was involved in something shady, Shannon didn't think Rick would harm her. It was Pop's accusation about him being involved in the kidnapping that had really set Rick off. And if Pop's information was correct, Rick had every reason to explode. Not only had Angela taken his child from him, she had even changed the girl's name. If Rick had been forced to give up total custody, he must almost consider himself to be the victim of a kidnapper of sorts, as well.

Shannon wanted to hear the rest of the story, but could well imagine what had happened. She came from a broken home, herself, and had painful memories of the terrible things her mother had said about Shannon's father in an effort to turn her against him. Much to her shame, she *had* turned against him, for a while, anyway. Unfortunately, by the time she was old enough to figure out what had really happened, her father had passed away.

Maybe that was why the loss she saw in Rick's eyes gave her such a strong desire to connect with him. She was well acquainted with loss.

So it seemed she wasn't being quite as altruistic in this quest through the cold and dark as she would like to think she was. Suddenly, she realized that, in a way, by helping Rick, she was seeking a form of absolution for herself.

There was also something else, perhaps nothing more than the hormones that had lured her into hiring a rather suspicious stranger in the first place. Whatever, some little voice inside told her that Rick could be a valuable ally right now. For one, he was apparently acquainted with the Bayers' way of doing things. For another, he held a very big grudge against them, a debt that might well be served by his helping her find Leo.

That she would undertake the search went without question. In many ways, Shannon considered Leo to be her own, and she had no intention of losing him, too. Pop's calm assurances aside, and whether Rick could help or not, she was determined to find the boy—before the shipment of toy spiders arrived, if possible. She didn't like going against Pop, but all this struck too close to home for her to ignore.

Somewhere, Shannon could hear people singing. The Union Station area, with its popular taverns, most likely. Fresh clean snow lay in a blanket all around, softening the city's edges. It was beautiful, in spite of the occasional sight of a decrepit building and the bitter cold. Here, Christmas lights blinked in most windows.

Soon, however, as she followed the form up ahead of her farther down toward the railroad tracks, those cheery windows gave way to ones that were boarded-up and dark. The snowy landscape now took on a forbidding, sinister dimension.

And then Rick disappeared. At least she hoped it was Rick. Shannon realized she had been so caught up in her own thoughts that it was possible she had lost sight of him and had started following another vague shape, instead. Fear welled up within her, making her almost sick to her stomach, and every doorway seemed alive with threatening shapes.

Suddenly, one of those shapes reached out and grabbed her. As she flailed her arms, trying to keep her balance, she was yanked roughly into a narrow crevice between two buildings by the collar of her coat. She struggled to stay on her feet in the frigid, near-total darkness. Just as she opened her mouth to scream, her attacker pushed her roughly backward through a door into one of the buildings. The bottom edge of the jamb caught her boot and she went down on her rear end, her coat providing little padding against the concrete.

A man's harsh whisper cut off the complaint that rose to her lips. "Hush!"

"Rick?"

"Who were you expecting, O'Shaughnessy?" he said in quiet, clipped tones. "The bogeyman? Well, down here, you might really have run into him."

"I—"

"Just stay there and keep your mouth shut."

Since he did not seem in the mood for any discussion just now, she did as she was told. Rick moved to the door, paused and then went back out into the cold, dark night. When he didn't return right away, Shannon decided he hadn't meant for her to literally stay where she was, so she got up from the floor and dusted herself off.

She seemed to be in a warehouse of some kind. With only the dim light filtering in from outside, it was hard to tell, but she could make out vague shapes that looked like crates. Lyon's occasionally used the storage facilities down here near the tracks when the store got a big shipment by rail. But Shannon didn't think she was acquainted with this particular building. Rick had little to worry about. She had no desire to wander around such a place in the dark.

But what was Rick doing down here? Why was he so jumpy? Shannon had to admit that was another reason she had followed him. He might not be shady, and probably didn't have anything to do with Leo's disappearance, but she felt certain Rick was up to something. His behavior just now seemed to confirm her suspicions.

Great. She had come to offer Rick solace, and instead had made him mad. That didn't put her in the best position to ask questions about what he was doing, or to ask for his help in finding Leo, either. To top it all off, she was cold, scared and her rear end hurt. This was turning into some Christmas.

Shannon jumped when Rick came back in and slammed the door. Then she heard him fiddling with what sounded like a heavy padlock.

"At least nobody followed *you*," he said, obviously relieved. "Sorry for being so rough, but you took me by surprise. I just assumed that anyone out walking on a night like this was either an idiot or dangerous, probably both. What are you doing down here?"

"Following you," Shannon confirmed defiantly. It was difficult to see his face in the dim light, but she thought she saw him smile. "What's so funny?"

He shook his head and chuckled. "Nothing. It's just that you really did give me a scare," Rick admitted.

"Good. That and your lame apology take some of the sting out of my... out of my pride. Now, what are *you* doing down here?"

"This is where I live."

"Oh." That revelation gave her pause. "Sorry."

"For what?" Rick asked. "My lot in life or for thinking I was up to no good?"

"Both, I suppose." Shannon wished she could see his face. "Can we have some lights?"

"This way." He moved closer and held his hand where she could see it. "I have a place in back. The situation isn't quite as dire as you seem to think."

"I didn't mean..." She trailed off with a sigh and took his hand. It was still cold. Cold hands, warm heart? "Look, if you don't want me here, just say the word."

"You followed me for a reason, didn't you?" Rick asked.

"I want to talk. About Leo. Among other things."

He squeezed her hand slightly. "That sounds promising. Come on. And watch your step."

That was difficult, since she couldn't even see her feet, but he led the way so confidently, it wasn't necessary. It was obvious he had made this trek in the dark before. Shannon had to assume there was a reason he did so without the aid of a flashlight. She doubted that reason had anything to do with not having the money to buy one. To her, it seemed as if Rick was a man with something to hide.

"We're not supposed to be in here, are we?" she asked.

Rick smiled mischievously. "Why? Does the idea of breaking and entering excite you?"

She had to admit it did, a little. Perhaps for the same reason Rick excited her. Hers was a fairly quiet life-style, and he offered the prospect of something different, maybe even a tad dangerous. Of course, she had no intention of telling him that. But somehow, she suspected he already knew.

"I was just asking," Shannon replied. "You know. In case the night watchman comes along. I'd like to know whether to wave hello or run."

"Relax. We're supposed to be here. Or at least I am," he added pointedly. "I just don't like to advertise my comings and goings. Seems safer that way, considering the neighborhood."

While Shannon pondered this information, Rick let go of her hand for a moment. She heard the jangle of keys in a lock and then he took her hand again, gently guiding her into what she could tell was some sort of smaller space. Finally, he turned on a light. Shannon blinked in surprise.

She found herself in makeshift living quarters, rather like a small, sparsely furnished motel room. There was a single bed on one side—neatly made, she noticed—as well as a nightstand and a chest of drawers. In the middle of the room sat a small table with two chairs. The opposite side was dominated by a large comfortable-looking armchair, behind which stood a reading lamp. That and the bedside lamp went on with the same switch Rick had turned on next to the now-closed door, bathing the room in a warm glow. Against the far wall, a little electric space heater purred to life, as well.

Though the furniture was old-fashioned, everything was clean and well taken care of, giving the little place a cozy, homespun ambience. In Shannon's opinion, it needed a few plants and some pictures on the walls. A window would also be nice. But under the circumstances, she decided to keep that opinion to herself.

"Nice," she said simply.

"Better than some places I've been in," Rick agreed.

He removed his snow-dampened coat and hung it on a peg near the door, then motioned for Shannon to do the same and hung hers up carefully, as well. He then had a seat at the table. Shannon joined him. Rick looked at her curiously.

"Well?" he asked.

Where to begin? Shannon wondered. "Who are you, Rick Hastings, and what are you doing working as a Santa Claus for Lyon's Department Store?"

"Who am I? That's a question I've been asking myself for the last three years," Rick replied, returning her appraising gaze. "I'm not entirely sure I know the answer yet. But I'm getting close. Why do you care, Shannon O'Shaughnessy?"

She smiled. "I did say I liked the direct approach, didn't I?" Shannon thought it over for a moment, and decided to be equally direct. "You don't have a corner on the pain market, okay? Maybe I think I can help you. Maybe I think you can help me. I don't know!" she exclaimed. "Maybe it's just good old-fashioned Christmas spirit. I followed you all the way down here in the cold, didn't I? That should tell you something."

"It tells me you're serious," Rick observed. "But about what remains to be seen. Didn't you say you wanted to talk about Leo?"

"I do," Shannon agreed. "Pop seems to think Leo is just fine. He's probably right. And I agree with him that this affair isn't worth going to the police and risking another war with the Bayers, either now or once Leo is home." She crossed her arms on her chest in a defiant gesture. "But I'm not going to just sit around. I want to find Leo and get him back. If possible, without handing over the Arnie shipment."

Rick was smiling slightly. "Why tell me this?"

"You know the Bayers and how they operate." His surprised expression pleased her. "Pop made a few calls after you left. He has contacts everywhere. But since I'm kind of going behind his back on this, I thought maybe you could give me some idea about where to start looking."

"I see," Rick said. He was gazing at her, obviously deep in thought. Finally, he seemed to come to a decision. "I can tell by the determination in those pretty green eyes of yours that you mean business, so I guess I'll have to level with you."

"Level with me?" she asked, confused.

"I don't intend to sit around and wait, either. I had already planned to go looking for Leo, as well as make sure that shipment ends up at Lyon's. But make no mistake," he told her in a quiet voice. "I *am* at war with the Bayers."

Shannon frowned. "Why do I get this feeling there's more to your involvement in this than meets the eye?"

She was astute, all right. Rick knew he would have to tread very carefully from now on, lest she ruin everything. But the path he was on now was very well traveled, and came easily to him.

"You probably get that feeling because it's true," Rick admitted. "And you're also right about it having something to do with why I'm working at Lyon's."

"I thought it might."

"Being a Santa is the perfect cover. I can be with the kids, and in the meantime keep track of the shipment."

"I see," Shannon said. But she didn't.

"Don't get me wrong, though," Rick added quickly. "I do need the money. The advertising blitz didn't come cheap and Arnie the Arachnid is being run on a very tight budget at the moment. I'm barely getting a salary."

Shannon's frown deepened. "I don't understand. Are you telling me you're an employee of the Arnie campaign?"

"Yes. I'm in Denver to watch over your shipment of Arnies," Rick explained. "There was word the Bayers were covertly trying to figure out where and when it would arrive. Since, as you noted, I am well acquainted with their ways, I came to interfere with any plans they might have had to sabotage the shipment. I had no idea they'd stoop to kidnapping, though."

Although this was far too much for Shannon to take in on such short notice, there was one thing she couldn't help grasping. In fact, she even reached out and grasped Rick's arm.

"Are they here?" she whispered, her eyes wide as she looked around to indicate the warehouse.

He laughed at her reaction. "Not yet."

"When?"

"I'm not at liberty to divulge that information."

Shannon let go of his arm and leaned back with a sigh of astonishment. "Whew! At the risk of perpetuating an age-old stereotype, I could do with a wee nip. Care to pop over to the local and join me?" Then she glanced at him and asked hesitantly, "Or am I putting temptation where I shouldn't?"

Rick laughed. "As I said, my situation isn't nearly as dire as you seem to think. You're on." He stood up and retrieved their coats, holding hers open for her. "Drink isn't responsible for my troubles, though there was a time when it could have been a contender, I suppose.''

"Then what is responsible?"

"Three people," Rick replied.

"Nathan Bayer and Angela I can guess. Who's the third?"

"Me."

Chapter Seven

Shannon didn't find the walk back toward the nearest pub nearly as cold, dark and scary, with Rick by her side. In fact, there was something cozy about the night now. She tentatively touched her gloved hand to his, and he surprised her by taking it. This was different from holding her hand while leading her through a dark warehouse. This was a gesture of warmth and companionship. When she glanced at his face, the small smile she saw there confirmed that he felt the same way.

The place Shannon had in mind was a boisterous watering hole directly across from Union Station called the Wynkoop Brewing Company. It had been among the first of what was now a wave of brew pubs sweeping the nation, so named because the proprietors brewed and served their own fresh beer right on the premises. Shannon liked the stout she could get there, which reminded her of a trip she'd taken to Ireland in her college days.

At this hour and particularly during this season, the pub was packed, loud and deliciously festive. Just the ticket to drive the chill from their bones and ease the telling of what Shannon thought might be a painful story for Rick.

It was also a great spot to lose oneself in the crowd, which they quickly did. After flagging down a server, they managed to squeeze themselves into a cranny far enough away from the main bar to allow a relatively quiet conversation. As Shannon had expected, Rick did seem more at ease here than he had in his little place at the warehouse.

So did she. For all its unusual ambience, it had been too intimate there by half. She sipped her stout, which looked and tasted more like sweet, black coffee than beer.

Rick had ordered the same. "Good," he said after a sip.

"So," Shannon prompted, "I believe you were about to tell me the story of your life?"

"That would only bore both of us to tears. I was born, raised and attended school in Arizona. It's a nice place, if you like sun, the desert and lots of quiet. But for the most part, the only people who find any of it truly fascinating are anthropologists, New Agers and white folks pretending to be Native Americans."

Shannon laughed. "A cynic. I like that in a man."

"Don't get me started," Rick warned. "I can do an hour on Elvis impersonators alone. But seriously, there isn't much to tell on that end. How about you? Colorado girl?"

"Sort of," she replied. "I was born in Nebraska. But after my parents divorced, my mother moved us here."

"How old were you?" he asked thoughtfully.

"Eight, the same as Leo."

Rick drank his beer, mulling over this fact. "And about the same as Chelsea was when Angela divorced me."

"I thought so," Shannon told him, nodding. "That seemed to be the age of the little girl who was the hardest for you to be around today. But also the one who seemed to have helped you the most."

He studied her face. "And so that's why you decided you might be able to help me?" he asked, obviously doubtful.

"Well, I don't know, Rick," Shannon replied, unable to keep an edge of sarcasm from her tone. "I was yanked away from my father at about the same age as your little girl, and grew up hearing a daily tirade about him and his evil ways. That might just give me some insight into your situation, don't you suppose?''

Rick realized that he had been so caught up in his own problems that he hadn't seen what was right in front of him. Shannon had been offering her help almost from the moment they met. She was right, of course. He didn't have a corner on the pain market.

"I'm sorry," he said. "I didn't know."

Shannon blew out a deep sigh. "I'm sorry, too. I don't have any cause to be snippy with you. It's just that hearing you talk about what happened to you has brought back some bad memories of those times."

They were both quiet for a moment. It was then that they appreciated their surroundings, for the way other conversations filled in the awkward silence in their own.

"Did you listen?" Rick finally asked.

"To the stories my mother used to tell about my father, you mean?" Shannon guessed.

He nodded.

"Well, I didn't have much choice, really. After all, she *is* my mother, and I was something of a captive audience."

"And did you tell any stories about him, yourself?"

Rick said this so quietly that Shannon wasn't sure she'd heard him correctly. She looked at him, but he was staring into his glass of stout, as if he might find some kind of answer in its black, velvety depths.

"I didn't repeat anything I heard her say," Shannon told him. "But I . . . I did believe her about some things. When I grew up, I found out what a liar she had been. But when I was little, and I saw how angry she was, I couldn't help blaming Daddy. It's one of the biggest regrets of my life that he died before I made up with him."

Rick looked into her eyes again, and saw that regret clearly in them. He reached across the table and took her hand. "Maybe you're right about us helping each other."

"Do you think so?"

"Just talking about it with someone who really understands is making me feel better," he said. "So let me ease your pain a little if I can. You may have blamed your father, but I'd bet my life he never blamed you in return."

"No?"

"No," Rick assured her. "I don't blame Chelsea. I may not understand the things she's done and said, but deep down inside, I know she doesn't mean to hurt me. I still love her and I always will. I'm sure your father felt the same way."

"Thanks, Rick," she told him.

"Anytime." He touched his glass to hers and they both had another warming sip of stout. "How's your relationship with your mother now?" he asked.

"Strained," Shannon admitted. "To be honest, I'm not sure I've ever really gotten to know her. She just never has had all that much time for me."

"Why not?"

"Business, mostly," Shannon replied with a sigh. "When we first moved here, she was in retail sales, but she worked her way up the ladder. She recently retired from a position as the main clothing buyer for a chain down in Florida. I got my start at Lyon's through one of her contacts, in fact." She smiled wryly. "Mom had a lot of contacts."

Rick had a pretty good idea what she meant. "Was one of them responsible for her moving here and divorcing your dad?"

"Exactly. I'm pretty sure she'd been seeing him for some time before the divorce. I don't know him very well, either," Shannon said. "Like Leo, I was basically raised by nannies. My mother and stepfather were both too busy with traveling and their careers.''

"Not too busy to jerk your father around concerning his visitation rights, though, I'll bet,'' Rick said. "I think that's the worst part. I lived for Chelsea. To Angela, I think she's a possession to be controlled, a big doll she can dress up and teach to be just like her.'' He scowled. "And she's doing a pretty good job of it.''

"The truth will out, Rick,'' Shannon said, trying to re-assure him in turn. "Someday, Chelsea will find out what a liar her mother is, too.''

His expression remained bleak. If only she knew just how far along Angela's conversion of their daughter really was. But there were things he could barely stand to think about, let alone speak of, even to this warm, lovely woman. Be-sides, it was too dangerous. In a few more days, maybe there would be blue sky above him again. But right now, there were still storm clouds hovering.

"I haven't really had much contact with the Bayers,'' Shannon continued. "We hardly run in the same social circles. But I've seen pictures of Angela in the newspaper. She's a very stunning woman.''

"In her case, beauty really is only skin-deep,'' Rick said with obvious disgust. He was glad to allow anger to re-place his self-pity. "It probably sounds like sour grapes, or something, but really, you can't imagine how awful An-gela is, Shannon. I haven't the words to describe her.''

If she was involved in this dirty little scheme to take over the Arnie shipment, Shannon was fully prepared to believe anything he said about the woman. But it didn't seem like a very productive thing to talk about. Venting anger only did so much good; beyond that, it was better to take a look at the source of that anger.

"There must have been something you liked about her once, though," Shannon said. "After all, you got married and had a child, and then raised that child together for eight years."

Rick sighed and slumped in his chair. "It's true. I lose sight of that fact sometimes," he admitted. "Probably because what happened afterward was so traumatic. But it wasn't a blissful eight years up until then, either."

"How did you meet?"

"It was a real classic, that's for sure. I wasn't long out of college and between jobs, so I started this fly-by-night pool-cleaning service in Phoenix for some quick cash."

"Hold on a second," Shannon interrupted, doing some quick math in her head. "Not long out of college? Wouldn't you have been almost thirty at the time?"

"Twenty-eight," he corrected. "It was my second degree."

Shannon's eyes widened. "Oh, really?"

Rick seemed suddenly uncomfortable. He looked away, scanning the crowd for a server. When he spotted one, he motioned for another round.

"Science was my first interest," he told her when at last he met her gaze again. "But I found I didn't like the sort of jobs available. So I went back to school and got a business-related degree."

"Uh-huh."

Science? Business-related? It was all a bit vague. But she could tell by the way he was again avoiding her eyes that it was unlikely she would be able to pin him down any further. It was probably difficult for him to admit how far he had fallen after the divorce. Shannon decided to let it be.

"Let's get back to the interesting part," she said. "I think I can see this one coming. One day you were cleaning a pool, and there was this ravishing woman baking in the hot Arizona sun, her body glistening with oil. You looked at her, she looked at you, one thing led to another and about nine months later Chelsea was born. Am I close?''

Rick laughed, breaking the tension. ''Very. I told you it was a classic. The details are that it was her rich daddy's house and that he did not much like a twenty-eight-year-old professional student turned pool cleaner consorting with his eighteen-year-old debutante daughter. When she turned up pregnant, he tried to arrange an abortion. Angela and I ran off that same day and got married as soon as the law allowed.''

''And Daddy?''

''Ranted, raved and threatened. When Chelsea was born, and he finally realized Angela had done it all mainly to spite him, as well as to get out from under his roof and his thumb, he disinherited her,'' Rick replied. ''Since I had come to those same conclusions about her myself by then, in many ways that was the beginning of the end for Angela and me, too.''

It was indeed a classic tale, with the usual sort of ending such tales often had, a messy divorce. In the middle, however, there apparently was a twist.

''Yet you stayed together until Chelsea was eight?''

''It's not that I didn't see the writing on the wall,'' Rick told her. ''But I loved her, or thought I did, and I already told you I doted on Chelsea. Ironically, though, it was Angela who held us together in the beginning.''

''Angela?'' Shannon asked, surprised.

''It's not what you think,'' Rick replied. ''Since there wasn't going to be any money coming from her father, she knew I was her only meal ticket, and I did have prospects. We hardly saw each other, anyway. By this time, my company had grown, and my employees and I were selling and installing pools as well as cleaning them. The business was starting to turn a good profit. In fact, we put in a pool of our own for Chelsea's sixth birthday."

At last, the server brought their refills. Since Shannon was a regular, the drinks were going on her tab, for which she was grateful. It had been her idea to come here and so this was her treat. For a moment, it occurred to her that Rick might not see it that way.

"Sounds like your business-school education paid off," she noted.

"I was making good money." Rick was shaking his head. "But Angela had been born and raised to spend money, and compared to what she was used to, what I made was chump change. However, it did enable her to start hanging out with some of her old crowd again, doing the Scottsdale circuit. That's how she met Nathan Bayer." He chuckled. "I never knew for certain just how it happened, but I'll bet she was sunning herself by a pool when he first saw her. Poor sucker."

"You really mean that, don't you?"

He nodded. "Don't get me wrong. I'd like to nail Nathan Bayer's hide to the wall for his part in what Angela proceeded to do to me. And this business with Leo and the shipment might just give me that opportunity," Rick said with obvious anticipation. "But a part of me feels sorry for the guy. I know what Angela is like. She'll do anything to get her own way. Absolutely anything."

Having pity for an enemy was the sign of a fairly well-evolved person, Shannon thought. Rick's high level of education combined with his common sense, made him the sort of man unlikely to quit the game of life easily. And yet, he apparently had done just that for a time, though it looked as if he might be on the mend now.

"I don't know what she did to you," Shannon said, "but I get the feeling it was more of a massacre than a divorce."

"Massacre is a pretty good description," Rick agreed. "Take Nathan Bayer's money and power, combine it with Angela's greed and total self-interest and add one highly paid lawyer."

"Sounds like a recipe for disaster, all right."

"I got the best representation I could afford, but it wasn't enough. They creamed me. Half of everything and then some. The house was gone, as well as part of the business. I was down, but good. So naturally they started kicking me."

Rick sipped his stout, but its alcohol content wasn't nearly high enough to blunt the memory. Not that he wanted it blunted. He wanted to remember, so that when payback time came, his victory would be all the sweeter.

"My visitation rights were the first to start eroding," Rick continued. "I tried to fight, but I didn't get much sympathy in Angela's carefully chosen legal arenas. It was already costing me quite a bit, traveling between Phoenix and Denver to visit Chelsea—when Angela let me see her, that is—and these little skirmishes just cost me more. Naturally, my business was suffering from my absence, too."

Shannon knew what was coming. She reached for his hand and he gladly let her take it in hers. "Then came the adoption proceedings?"

He sighed deeply and nodded. "It was Chelsea's idea."

"Oh, Rick! Your own daughter asked Nathan to adopt her?"

"Yes. I know Angela was behind it, manipulating her, as only Angela can. But it still came as quite a blow."

Rick looked away from her caring gaze for a moment. He was treading on dangerous ground now, and had to be careful. Still, he wanted, even needed to tell Shannon what he could.

"I went through the motions of objecting, but my heart wasn't in it. My own daughter didn't want me. Still, I felt I had to fight for her." He laughed bitterly. "A lot of good that did me. Nathan and his deep pockets made it viciously expensive. I took out a loan, using what was left of my business as collateral. Little did I know good old Nathan had an in at my bank. So when the dust settled, he bought the note, and I wasn't even given good-faith time to recuperate from the beating I'd taken. He and Angela offered to let me stay on, though. As a pool cleaner."

"Oh, Rick."

"I just walked out with the clothes on my back." Rick took a big gulp of stout, then put his glass on the table and pushed the rest away. "But I refused to give up all rights to my daughter. I never signed the papers to let him adopt her. Still, they managed to have her name changed, anyway, somehow. I doubt it was legal, but by then that was the least of my problems." He looked at her again. "Now you know why I'm at war with the Bayers."

Shannon thought she knew a lot more than that. "And you've been wandering around lost ever since, haven't you?"

He shrugged. "I told you it took three people to do this to me. I just stopped giving a damn about anything, except keeping a low profile in case Angela got bored and decided she wanted to punish me some more."

"But you *do* have a direction now," she said firmly.

"Yes, I do. And it almost seems like fate took a hand in this game," he told her thoughtfully. "I was working on the shipping dock of a toy company back East when I stumbled onto this Arnie thing. Intercepting Nathan's shady inquiries into the whereabouts of the shipments was also just a fluke. But now that I'm here, I don't care what Pop Lyon or anyone else says. If I can pin something on them, I will."

"And try to use it as leverage against them?"

"Exactly," Rick confirmed.

Shannon touched his hand. "Even if you can manage it, that won't undo the damage, Rick. At least not all of it. As I did about my father, Chelsea will have to come to her own conclusions about you. All you can do is let her know you're there for her, no matter what."

"Are you saying you wouldn't like to get the Bayers for this?" Rick asked. "If so, we'll be working at cross-purposes."

"What I want is Leo back, first and foremost," Shannon said pointedly. "My second priority is the shipment—it will bring a lot of money into the company, especially my department, and Lyon's has a very nice profit-sharing plan. But if I can accomplish both those things, then yes, I'd like to help you get the Bayers. I don't even know Angela and I dislike her."

"Good."

Shannon grinned. "That's why I followed you down here this evening, remember?"

"And I thought it was for the pleasure of my company."

"It *has* been nice," she told him.

They settled into a comfortable silence. A glow surrounded Shannon. It was Christmas time, she was warm, cozy and among happy people in a festive atmosphere. It was almost enough to make her forget Leo was missing.

"How would you like to come to my place tomorrow night for a late supper?" Shannon asked him suddenly.

The invitation gave Rick pause. There was no doubt they were attracted to each other. But what Shannon undoubtedly wanted, and deserved, was a relationship, not a one-night stand. And Rick had been through too much to enter something like that lightly.

"Well?" she prompted.

"A home-cooked meal sounds great," he said at last. "Of course, we have no idea what we'll be doing tomorrow, do we?"

"No. But whatever it is, we'll still have to eat."

"True," Rick agreed.

"Then it's a date?"

Rick smiled uneasily. "Right. A date."

Shannon could sense his reluctance, and understood it. Life had battered him around quite a bit. It hadn't been all that kind to her, either. All they could do was take things one step at a time.

"Where do you think we should start tomorrow?" she asked.

"I suppose we should make sure we're not missing anything obvious first," Rick replied, glad to move on to a different subject. "I assume there were employees around earlier in the day who you didn't get a chance to question this evening?"

"Good idea. I can do that in the morning," Shannon said. "I'll also have Paul check over the store again." She thought for a moment. "I'll have him talk to the cleaning crew, as well. You never know, something unusual might show up."

Rick shrugged. "And if nothing does, I guess we'll have to find a way to shake the Bayers' tree, in hopes that something or someone falls out that can give us a lead to Leo."

"We could go undercover!" Shannon exclaimed. "You know, snoop around their department store as customers." She snapped her fingers. "Or maybe even try to get hired on. The employees at Bayer's are notoriously un-happy. One of them might turn snitch.''

"Oh, I don't know, Shannon . . .''

"We'll talk to Pop," she continued, clearly excited about the idea. "He said no interference, but I'll bet if we tell him your side of the story, he'll come around. Pop is just pre-tending to go along with this quietly for Leo's sake. In-side, I know he's seething. The rivalry between the Lyons and Bayers goes way back. I've even heard that he once accused Nathan's father, Joe, of putting the moves on Sissy.''

"Sissy?" Rick asked.

"Pop's late wife."

Rick could tell that Shannon was determined to go through with this. In fact, it might not be such a bad idea, at that. But it would put him at great risk to be in a place where Angela or Chelsea might show up, so he would have to be very careful.

"I suppose I could see if they need a Santa," he said, thinking that if he stayed in costume, he'd be fine. "But I hate to leave Hans in a bind."

"It's been a dry year for Santas, so I'm sure Bayer's will need one," Shannon said. "As for Hans, we'll round up someone. Another employee, probably. They haven't been very cooperative so far, but we can have Pop ask them in person."

"Okay, then. I'm game."

She glanced at her watch. "If we're going to be asking Pop for favors in the morning, we should probably try to be on time, and that means getting an early start. I can't replace myself quite so easily."

Rick stood up. "I'll walk you to your car. Did you park in Lyon's lot?"

"Yes, but I think I'll just grab a taxi. It's been quite a long day for me, and that stout went right to my head."

Since it was getting near closing time, there were already a few cabs waiting outside. Rick hailed one and it pulled up to meet them, its tires scrunching in the fresh-fallen snow.

Shannon moved toward it. "Good night, Rick," she said. "See you tomorrow. Eight sharp."

"I'll be there." Rick touched her arm. "Shannon?"

She turned back toward him. "Yes?"

"Thanks. You were right. We *can* help each other."

Smiling, Shannon stepped up to him, her head tilted to look into his eyes. "I'm right about a lot of things. Hiring you, for instance. Even if it wasn't my head I was listening to when I made the decision."

"Then what?"

"Guess." She leaned close and kissed his cheek, slowly, savoring his warmth and the rich masculine smell of his skin. She whispered into his ear, adopting a sexy tone. "Didn't Leo tell you? I still believe in Santa Claus."

With that, she quickly turned to the cab, got in and gave the driver her address. Rick just stood on the curb and watched her go, wearing a stunned expression.

Chapter Eight

Leo woke up with the same feeling he had when sleeping over at his great-aunt Alice's—who really wasn't so great, in his opinion. It was that feeling of being in a strange place. But then his eyes focused and the feeling went away. Did it ever. This place might be strange, but it sure wasn't Great-Aunt Alice's house, no way. It was two in the morning and no one had even told him to go to bed!

He smiled, and with a big, comfortable sigh, stretched himself out full length on the leather sofa. Although his shoes were still on, there was no one to tell him to get his feet off the furniture. The television was tuned to the sort of trashy late-night movie his nannies always scolded him for watching if they caught him. He'd get a good scolding for leaving dirty dishes on the floor as he had tonight, too, especially sticky ones that had once contained about a gallon of ice cream with butterscotch caramel syrup. And he hadn't brushed his teeth, either.

But his nannies weren't there. Neither was Shannon, or Pop, or any of the other big people who were always telling him what to do for his own good. Adults. Go figure.

In fact, the only ones around at all were Joey and Irv. Joey did occasionally question Leo's behavior, but only when it was really stupid or something that might get them all in trouble, like building a snowman indoors. Besides, Joey had gone to bed an hour ago and had left Irv in charge.

Leo was coming to understand that Irv wasn't really an adult, or at least not the sort he was accustomed to being around. Irv liked to play video games while standing on his head. He belched out loud when he drank too much soda. Leo had even seen him spill some ice cream on the carpet and smoosh it in with his foot so it wouldn't show.

Of course, some of what Irv did made Joey really mad, so Leo could tell it wasn't stuff he should be doing. Irv just couldn't help it. Like right now, for instance. Instead of watching him like Joey said, Irv was fast asleep in one of the big leather recliners, snoring loudly, with a set of stereo headphones over his ears. Joey would yell at Irv for sure if he found him like that. Maybe Leo should wake him up soon.

First, though, he had to call Shannon. She was the only one he knew who wouldn't get mad at him for calling so late. He also really wanted to talk to her, because he didn't want her to worry, and he also sort of missed her. That was why he hadn't called earlier. He might accidentally say something mushy and he didn't want Irv to hear.

Leo grabbed his coat from where he'd dropped it beside the sofa earlier and dug around in one of the big side cargo pockets. It was there, right where he'd left it.

He hoped the batteries were still charged. When Pop had given him the cellular phone for his birthday, he had told Leo it wasn't a toy, and cautioned him to use it wisely. Pop had also made him promise not to let anyone else use it, except in an emergency, of course. Since Joey hadn't seemed too worried earlier about the phone lines being down, the calls he said he had to make must not be emergencies.

A little light came on when he activated the compact phone, indicating the batteries were still good and strong. Leo dialed Shannon's number from memory. He called her quite often, because she said he could, whenever he was feeling lonely or troubled.

Shannon would make a great mom. Sometimes Leo wished she really was his mom. But once, when he'd mentioned it, she had hugged him and cried a little, so he kept it to himself now.

When Shannon answered, her voice sounded funny, and Leo knew he'd awakened her. For a moment, he thought about just hanging up. But he knew that would only scare her.

"Hi," he said brightly.

Shannon sat bolt upright in bed, blinking her eyes in a futile attempt to focus in the dark. "Leo?" she managed to croak. "Leo, is that you?"

"Sure." He paused. "I'm sorry. I woke you up, huh? I'll call tomorrow or something, okay?"

"No! You stay on the line, Leo! Do you hear?"

"Yes, ma'am."

Shannon was suddenly wide-awake. She turned on her bedside lamp, then grabbed the glass of water she kept on the nightstand and took a sip to loosen up her sleepy throat.

"Leo?"

"Hi. Hey, this thing works great," he exclaimed. "I wasn't sure it would from this far away."

With his bright, happy tone, Leo sounded the way he always did, which puzzled Shannon no end. "Leo, are you okay?"

"Of course."

"Can you tell me where you are?" Shannon asked.

"Uh, not really."

Shannon closed her eyes for a moment. Naturally. The kidnappers were listening in. Any moment they would interrupt with some new, outrageous demand. But if she didn't press, maybe they would let her talk to him for a bit more.

"I really miss you, Leo. We all do."

"I miss you, too, Shannon. And Pop. I don't much miss the nannies, though. Well, maybe Mrs. Watkins. A little. She makes great brownies. But don't tell her, okay?"

"Okay." He sounded fine. And they were certainly letting him run on. What kind of kidnappers were these, anyway? "How are the, um, government agents?"

"Oh, they're great guys! Especially Irv. We made huge butterscotch caramel sundaes earlier, and played Wolves of Doom and—"

"Leo?" she interrupted.

"Yes, Shannon?"

This would probably do it, but she had to get some kind of information out of this call, and it didn't seem likely she was going to get it from Leo.

"Are you in any danger?"

"Huh?"

There was a moment of silence then, which Shannon was sure would be followed by a gruff voice telling her he was in lots of danger if that shipment of Arnies didn't come in soon.

Instead, it was Leo's voice. He was laughing.

"Cool! Are you watching television?" he asked.

"No, Leo. I was asleep," Shannon replied in measured, even tones. "And now I'm trying to talk to you."

"Oh. Sorry. I guess you don't get satellite, anyway. But there was this really great part on just now," he told her, still laughing. "This guy put straws up his nose, see, and pretended he was a walrus! Isn't that great?"

"Yes, Leo, that's just great."

What was going on? It was as if he didn't even know he'd been kidnapped!

At that thought, Shannon's eyes went wide. He *didn't* know! The kidnappers were keeping him in the dark about what was going on, continuing to feed him this line about saving the Arnie shipment and making him feel like part of some secret mission. And obviously treating him very well indeed. Maybe a little *too* well. Late-night television via satellite and butterscotch caramel sundaes, indeed! At this rate, he probably wouldn't want to come home at all.

But he was safe. And it seemed Pop was right. There wasn't any reason to worry about him. Or at least not yet.

That situation could change if the shipment was late or never came at all. Only Rick could answer that question, and he wouldn't. Or couldn't. He probably didn't know, either. Whichever, it really didn't matter. Shannon wanted Leo back, and she would get him—and the shipment if possible—without subjecting him to any more stress than she had to. If it was working for the kidnappers, who was she to mess things up?

"Have the agents had any luck finding the shipment yet, Leo?" Shannon asked him.

"Well, the real phone isn't working up here, so they haven't been talking to anyone. But they don't seem too worried. I bet if they had to, they could use some super secret radio."

Shannon frowned. What sort of operation was this? "Are you saying they don't know you're calling me?"

"No. I didn't want them to hear me." He paused for a moment. "I might, you know, say stuff."

"What sort of stuff?"

"Like I miss you...and I love you. Stuff like that," Leo replied quietly. He looked over at Irv, who was still sound asleep and snoring peacefully. "Irv would make fun of me. But it's okay, 'cause he's sleeping now."

Shannon couldn't believe her ears. They weren't even guarding him. The temptation to tell him to run away was very great. But she had no idea what his situation was, except that he was in the company of people who were evidently taking reasonable care of him. Wherever he might be, a small boy on his own could fare much worse.

Leo was laughing again. Irv had slipped sideways in his sleep, and a trickle of drool was running down his face. To Leo, this was every bit as funny as a guy with straws up his nose. By the time the trickle reached Irv's ear, Leo was practically howling.

The noise didn't wake Irv, but it certainly brought Joey out of a sound sleep. He came stumbling into the room, his eyes still half-closed.

"What's so funny, kid?" he asked, yawning. "And why aren't you in bed?"

Joey looked around sleepily. The first thing he noticed was Irv, snoring in the chair. Then he saw the cellular phone in Leo's hand. His eyes opened wide.

"Irv!" he bellowed. "Wake up! The kid's got a phone!"

Leo sighed. "Sorry, Shannon. I have to go. But don't worry, I'll be home for Christmas," he promised, and hung up.

"Give me that phone!" Joey demanded.

"Can't," Leo told him. "Pop told me not to unless it's an emergency."

"Why, you little . . . I'll show you an emergency."

Joey tried to look mean, but standing there in only his underwear, he looked more like a cranky bald bear. That started Leo laughing all over again. Irv wasn't any help. He woke up with a start and just looked around sleepily, yawning.

"Oh, for cripe's sake!" Joey exclaimed, then sat down on the sofa next to Leo with a weary sigh. "All right, kid. Who'd you call? The cops?"

"Nah." He held his phone at the ready. "I can if you want, though. Is the government in trouble?"

Joey looked befuddled for a brief moment, then the light dawned in his sleepy brain and he sighed again. "Oh, yeah."

"Cool! What kind of trouble? Can I have a gun?"

"No, you can't have a gun." He ran his hands over his face. "Just hold on a sec, okay? We're not in any trouble. At least I don't think so," he muttered. "Who did you call?"

"Just Shannon. I told you I wanted to, remember?"

Joey's eyes narrowed slightly. "What'd you tell her?"

"Nothing. You swore me to secrecy, remember?"

"Uh-huh. You didn't even tell her where we are?"

Leo frowned. "Well, she did ask."

"That's it!" Joey exclaimed, rising slowly to his feet. "We're dead. Irv, go start the car. I'll—"

"But Joey," Leo interrupted. "I didn't tell her anything. I don't even *know* where we are. I couldn't see from the back seat. I mean, we're in the mountains, but that's all I know, and I didn't even tell her that."

Joey sat down again with a huge sigh of relief. "Thanks, kid. But you should have told Irv or me that you had a phone. I do have an emergency call I need to make." He looked at Leo and smiled. "If that's okay with you?"

Leo gave him the cellular. "Sure."

Joey patted him on the head. "Thanks. Now, be a good boy and go get ready for bed. And brush those teeth."

"Aww!"

"Hey, you don't want 'em to rot, do you?" Joey asked. "Irv, show the kid what happens when you don't brush regular."

He pointed to Irv, who was still only half-awake and yawning. Leo could see that a piece of his removable bridgework had come loose in his sleep, leaving a comical gap in his front teeth.

Leo arched his eyebrows, then went to do as he was told.

"Hey, I was just a good example, huh, Joey?" Irv asked.

Joey watched as Irv put his bridgework right. "Yeah, Irv. A good negative example." He started dialing the phone number. "Now, go wash your face and teeth, too, okay? I gotta call the man."

Chapter Nine

Wednesday morning dawned bright, clear and cold. Two inches of new snow glistened beneath the winter sunlight. By noon, city life would turn the pristine white into obnoxious gray slush, so Shannon enjoyed the view while she could on her cab ride downtown. She felt wonderful, alive and refreshed, for her sleep after Leo's call had been deep and dreamless.

Well, maybe there had been one dream... When she saw Rick, who was already waiting for her at the back entrance to Lyon's, Shannon had this incredible urge to run into his arms and kiss him. But she refrained from giving in to it. At best, it would confuse him. At worst, it might change his mind about their dinner date tonight. After all, he had no idea of the starring role he'd played in that dream.

Rick held his hand out for her as she got out of the cab. Beneath her long black coat, she had on a white-and-black glen plaid woolen suit, with an emerald green silk knit tee and pale green hose. The skirt, modestly calf-length, had a side slit that displayed a generous portion of her thigh as she climbed from the cab, a view Rick enjoyed with arched eyebrows but no comment. Shannon smiled mischievously at him.

"Sleep well?" she asked.

Rick returned her smile, well aware she was baiting him. "Not bad, under the circumstances," he replied. Her kiss, though brief, had left him wanting more, as she no doubt knew it would. "You look fantastic this morning."

"Thank you. I slept well, too," Shannon informed him. "Especially after Leo called."

Rick frowned. "The kidnappers called you?"

"No. Just Leo."

She filled him in on the call as they made their way into the building. Rick came to much the same conclusion as Shannon had. Leo was safe enough, for now at least, and probably in no danger at all—perhaps suffering only a stomachache from eating too much junk food. He also agreed with her assessment of Leo's possible whereabouts, which she deduced from the few clues the boy had inadvertently dropped. But he still felt obliged to play devil's advocate.

"'Up here' could mean a more northern town or state, of course," Rick noted. "That's a fairly common idiom. 'This far away' could indicate the same thing."

"True," Shannon agreed. "But distance is relative to an eight-year-old. Come to that, if I were going to take one on a car trip, I'd want to make it as short as possible."

Rick chuckled. "Even ten miles is a major voyage."

"Right. And they have to bring him back, remember, to make the exchange for the shipment. So what they'd want would be a place close enough to be expedient, yet isolated at the same time. And Leo did say they had a satellite dish."

They both paused at one of the store's huge display windows. It faced the wide expanse of interlocking mountain ranges that served as Denver's western boundary.

"Up there," Shannon said, pointing out the window.

Rick nodded. "Somewhere."

While they stood pondering the vast area those mountains encompassed, Paul came up to them. Even for him, he seemed on edge.

"Heard the latest?" he asked.

Shannon filled him in on *her* latest first, which Paul absorbed with obvious puzzlement, and to which he summed up his reaction quite nicely in one word.

"Weird," he said. "Now read this."

Rick took the newspaper Paul gave him and held it so Shannon could see it, too. It wasn't front-page news, but had made a fairly big splash in the business section.

"Boy, eight, caught up in a web of intrigue surrounding Arnie the Arachnid," Shannon read aloud. "Retail tigers Lyon's and Bayer's at it again." She looked up at Paul. "Pop seen this?"

"You mean you didn't hear the windows rattling on your way inside?"

"Oh, brother," she muttered. "I wonder who leaked the story to the press."

Paul shrugged. "Who knows? The old man's pretty ticked about it, though. The thing is, I'm not so sure it's all bad."

"What do you mean?" Rick asked.

"The phones haven't stopped ringing this morning," Paul explained. "It's as if everyone is taking this personally. People want those spiders, and since Lyon's is where the Arnies are supposed to be, that's apparently where most folks want the Arnies to go. We've had offers of everything from legitimate legal help to vigilante search parties."

Rick leaned against the nearest wall and groaned. "In return for a guarantee they'll get an Arnie, of course."

"Oh, naturally," Paul returned. "But some people have even promised to do all their shopping at Lyon's. You'd think that would put a smile on Pop's face, wouldn't you?"

"Only if he can *keep* the Arnies," Shannon said pointedly. "If he has to give them away, those people will promise the same thing to Bayer's." She grasped Rick's hand and led him toward the elevator. "Which leads me to think he might be more receptive to what Rick and I have in mind."

Paul noticed the hand-holding, smiled and tactfully didn't mention it. "Okay, but I did warn you about his mood."

"Thanks. Oh, Paul?" Shannon said. "Would you talk to the cleaning crew before they leave? Just to see if they found anything unusual lying around."

"Sure thing."

It was quiet up on the fourth floor, where most of Lyon's business offices were. Everyone was walking as if on eggshells. When they saw Shannon and Rick heading for Pop's office, a good many decided to take an early coffee break. Pop's personal secretary, Carla, just raised her eyebrows and waved them on through, as if to say better them than her.

Pop's nurse was in attendance, taking his blood pressure. Although Shannon was pretty sure he would like what she had to say, she decided to wait until the reading had been taken.

But Pop beat her to it. "You saw the paper?" he asked perfunctorily, as if that were the only thing that mattered.

"Yes, Pop," Shannon replied.

"The media." He screwed up his wizened features as if the words left a bad taste in his mouth. "How dare those fiends call themselves journalists! All they want to see is blood! Blood to dip their poison pens in and play God with people's lives. But this time, they had help opening the vein." He looked at Shannon. "Do you know who told?"

She shook her head vehemently. "No, Pop."

Rick was next to be pinned by those stern, appraising eyes, and he was already shaking his head. "Don't look at me, Mr. Lyon," he said. "I have no idea who leaked the story. But I must say, I can't see why you're so upset about it."

Shannon's eyes went wide as she looked at Rick, then abruptly turned to Pop. "What he means is—"

"Tut!" Pop held up his hand to cut her off. He was still looking at Rick. "Mr. Hastings was perfectly capable of making himself and his meaning clear last night. I don't imagine that has changed. Go on, Mr. Hastings."

"I prefer Rick."

"And I prefer Pop," the older man told him. "Or I do when addressed by friends. Are you a friend, Mr. Hastings?"

Rick couldn't help smiling. "Well, I think I'll call you Pop, no matter what," he said. "Because it fits. You remind me of my father. He's a foul-tempered, crusty old curmudgeon with an ax to grind, too."

Shannon cringed and waited for the explosion. Instead, Pop chuckled. Then he laughed out loud.

"Sounds as if I might like your father, Rick," he said.

"You would, Pop," Rick assured him. "If you ever get to Las Vegas, look him up. He'll be the oldest old coot at any poker table with more interest in pinching the cocktail waitress than in who won the last hand."

"Like father, like son?" Shannon asked dryly.

Rick shrugged. "Ask me again when I'm seventy-five."

Pop dismissed his nurse, then motioned for them to have a seat on an old leather sofa near the window. He rolled his wheelchair closer to them so he could see better.

"So, Rick," Pop continued. "Tell me why you don't think I should be angry that someone leaked news of Leo's abduction."

"I didn't say that. Go ahead and be angry if you want," Rick said. "It won't get the story out of the paper or help you find out who the leak is, though. Nothing can do the first, and the latter doesn't really make any difference."

"No?"

"No. What's done is done. There is no such thing as bad publicity. When life hands you a lemon, make lemonade." Rick grinned. "I think I'll stop now. As the eldest here, the right to spout clichés is yours."

Pop glanced at Shannon. "Where did you find this guy?"

"He found me," Shannon replied. "And under somewhat erroneous circumstances, too, I might add."

"Tell me," the old man prompted.

"You already know that Rick was once married to Nathan Bayer's wife, Angela, and that their divorce was less than amicable," Shannon began.

"It was a creeping case of the plague," Rick inserted with a grimace. "And call that understatement."

"At any rate," Shannon continued, "I have heard enough about it now to be certain Rick owes nothing to the Bayers except the retribution they so richly deserve." She smiled at Pop's impatient frown. "In other words, he's on our side, Pop. I also found out something else last night."

Pop raised his bushy gray eyebrows. "Last night, eh?"

"Over a stout at the local pub, you dirty old man."

"At my age, young lady, that's a compliment. And it's what happened *after* the drink that has my filthy mind working overtime."

"Nothing," Shannon told him sternly.

Pop shook his head. "That's a shame. Life is precious, and our time on this earth so short." He looked at Rick and winked. "That's one of my best. How am I doing?"

"I'm taking notes," Rick assured him.

Shannon cleared her throat loudly. "Anyway, I found out that Rick is an agent for the Arachnid Arnie company."

"Arnie the Arachnid," Rick corrected. "It's patented."

"Whatever." Shannon was looking at Pop. He had a very unusual expression on his face. "What's wrong?"

"Hmm?" Pop blinked a few times. "Oh! Nothing, really. An old mind will wander, you know." He smiled at Rick. "So, you have a vested interest in this, eh? No wonder the story in the paper didn't bother you."

"It shouldn't bother you, either, Pop," Rick said. "I saw the Lyon's name right next to Arnie's in that article."

The morning sun streaming in through the office window caught Pop at the wrong angle, so he moved his wheelchair a bit. Shannon still thought she saw something odd in those pale blue eyes, but shrugged it off as her imagination. Just because Pop treated everyone in his company like part of the family, that didn't mean they knew his every little nuance.

"That's true, Rick," Pop agreed. "But the affiliation won't do Lyon's a lick of good if it's Bayer's that has the spiders, now, will it?"

"Which brings us to the reason we're here," Shannon said.

Pop held up his hand. "I'm sorry to keep cutting you off, Shannon. I know you're busting to tell me something and I promise I'll hear you out. But I want to ask our Arnie rep here something before I forget."

"Shoot," Rick told him, expecting the usual.

"Exactly why was Lyon's chosen as the sole supplier for the Denver area?"

The question took Rick by surprise. He smiled, his mind searching furiously for an answer any self-respecting field representative would have had on the tip of his tongue.

"The owner is a big fan," he said.

"Of Lyon's?"

Rick nodded. "Of you, too. And all toy makers. In fact, he has one of your original Leo the Lions in his collection."

"Does he now?" Pop's expressive gray eyebrows went up. "I'm touched. And what is this person's name?"

Rick had thought the old man was trying to trip him up, but now realized Pop was just being cagey. "I'm not at liberty to divulge that information," Rick replied with a grin.

"That's the same thing he said when I asked if he knew when the shipment was coming in," she told Pop.

Pop was still studying Rick intently. But salvation was at hand, and Rick grabbed it. "Actually, I have some news in that area," he announced. "In all the excitement this morning, I forgot to tell you."

Shannon spun her head toward him and leaned close. "The shipment arrived!" she exclaimed.

"No, not yet." Rick smiled at her sympathetically. "But I did get a report that delivery will be made in New York early this afternoon."

Pop was nodding his head. "And in Los Angeles at about the same time, correct?"

"That's right," Rick confirmed. "Allowing for the time difference, of course. How did you know?" he asked curiously.

"I didn't. It was just an experienced old retailer's guess," Pop returned. "I don't think anyone is going to have trouble selling out of Arnies, but that will be especially true on both coasts. Middle America has always been a harder sell, traditionally.''

Shannon agreed. "Will it play in Peoria?"

"Correct." Pop smiled at her like a proud father. "So, I imagine the shipments will be delivered in stages, in two waves, if you will, starting at the coasts and moving toward the center of the country. Probably meet up along or around the Mississippi River.'' He glanced at Rick. "Right?"

He cleared his throat. "You'll be hearing about it soon enough, so I guess I can tell you. That's exactly right."

And it was, or close. There would be a little glitch along the way, and he wouldn't put it past this wily veteran to figure that out, too. Maybe he already had.

"I thought so," Pop said. "That way, by the time Arnie reaches Peoria, so to speak, even reclusive farmers will have heard about him. Smart man, this employer of yours."

"You said it," Rick told him.

Pop smiled, then laughed. "Yes, I did, didn't I?" With one last twitch of his eyebrows, Pop turned his attention from Rick to Shannon. "Now, what's on your mind?"

Shannon was glad to comply. "Obviously, Rick isn't here by coincidence. There were indications the Bayers might try to interfere with or intercept our shipment, and since Rick has had dealings with them before, he was chosen to watch over it."

"By playing Santa Claus?"

"He's just moonlighting. Evidently, the Arnie campaign is on a budget," Shannon said before Rick could open his mouth. It couldn't be easy for him to keep explaining his situation.

"I can well imagine," Pop said, smiling slightly.

Shannon didn't know any other way to put this, so she just said it. "But now he wants to help me get Leo back."

Pop's smile disintegrated into a scowl. "I believe you know how I feel about that, young lady," he said sternly.

He sounded very much the perturbed parent. And Shannon felt like a high school girl trying to convince her father to let her use the car.

"But Pop, we have to at least try," she objected.

"Absolutely not! I forbid it!"

Rick was chuckling. "I bet if I were to light you a cigar and close my eyes, I wouldn't be able to tell the difference between you and my dad."

"Now, you listen to me, young man—"

"No, I won't," Rick interrupted happily. "Because I don't have to. You're not my father. In fact, you're only marginally my employer. I could go bounce boxes around for a lot more money than I'm getting here, so don't even bother threatening to fire me."

"I'll fire Shannon then. Just for subjecting me to you."

"One of your best managers?" Rick laughed. "Even you aren't that much of a curmudgeon. Besides, it's obvious you think of her as a daughter. No, you'll just have to listen to me, old man."

"I was afraid of that," Pop muttered.

"Whether you like it or not, I'm going to try to find Leo. In the process, I'll also try to pin the kidnapping on the Bayers. Failing that, I'll try to catch them in the act of unlawfully taking control of the Arnie shipment. One way or another, I intend to get something on Nathan and Angela."

Pop met Rick's defiant gaze without blinking. "They'll squash you like a bug."

"They tried that once before, and I came crawling back," Rick told him. "This time I'm going to sting them."

Pop turned his wheelchair so he could look out the window. He was silent for a long time. Finally, he appeared to come to a decision, and turned to face the pair on the couch. For Shannon, who knew him well, the sparkle in his eyes told the story.

"Go find my grandson, Rick," Pop said. "And do whatever damage you can to Nathan Bayer. I'm behind you all the way." He smiled at Shannon. "Both of you. Do you have a plan?"

"First, we're going to poke around Bayer's, maybe even go undercover there if we can," Shannon informed him. "Which means we'll need some time away from the store, I'm afraid."

Pop started to wheel himself toward his desk. Rick got off the couch and helped him. "Covering for Rick won't be easy," Pop agreed. "But if you hold off till lunchtime, I'll hit the cafeteria. The man who signs the Christmas bonus checks is a hard man to refuse a favor."

Pop handed her the note he had just scribbled out. "This authorizes a raise and advance for Rick. We can't expect a spy to make it on Santa Claus wages. And then take him to see Carl in Menswear." He eyed Rick's faded jeans. "If you want to fit in unobtrusively at Bayer's, you'll have to upgrade his wardrobe a notch."

"They are snooty. Isn't it nice to be one of the good guys?" She smiled. "Thanks, Pop. Great minds think alike."

"In that case, I wish you'd help me think of something to tell my next appointment," Pop said, grimacing.

"Who's that?"

"The police. They want to ask me why I didn't inform them of Leo's kidnapping."

"What are you going to tell them?" Rick wanted to know.

"Exactly what they want to hear, I suppose," Pop replied. "That the whole thing is just one big publicity stunt."

Chapter Ten

"It's ringing now," Angela said. "Finally. But they're not answering."

Nathan glared at her. "What do you mean, they're not answering? They have to be there."

"Listen for yourself." Angela dropped the phone in his lap and crossed his office to the built-in wet bar, where she poured herself a cup of coffee. She didn't offer him one. "I told you it was a bad idea to put them in charge."

"How many times do I have to tell you, Angela?" Nathan said. "They are not in charge. I am."

Angela sipped delicately at her coffee so as not to ruin her lipstick. As she did so, she looked at him over the rim of the cup, her expression one of boredom.

"Don't grit your teeth like that, darling," she told him. "You'll ruin your caps."

"To hell with my caps!"

"Nathan!" Angela's voice cracked like a whip, and she scowled at him ferociously. "How dare you swear in front of the child."

Chelsea was sitting primly in one of the office chairs nearest the window, where she could look out at the people passing by on the street below. If she heard her mother or Nathan, she didn't acknowledge them, so intent was she on the street scene being played out down there.

Like her mother, she had long, honey-blond hair, pulled back and tied to one side today, as was Angela's. They were dressed in similar outfits, as well, white knit suits with gold-buttoned jackets and knife-pleated skirts. But Chelsea had on thin-ribbed white tights rather than panty hose, and wore a cream-colored turtleneck, where her mother was showing plenty of cleavage at the low-scooped neckline of her jacket.

Still, they looked remarkably similar, and when they walked along together, they got plenty of attention, which was of course what Angela wanted.

At least for now. After all, Chelsea was only eleven. Once she hit puberty and started to turn heads for other reasons, which was a given, considering her genes, Angela probably wouldn't enjoy sharing the limelight quite as much.

Angela put a hand on her daughter's shoulder. "Chelsea, sweetie?"

She looked up, and it was then that the differences between them became more apparent. Where Angela's eyes were a pale, almost reptilian gray, Chelsea's were soft brown and soulful, like her father's. She had her father's nose, too, for better or worse. At eleven, her small face didn't do it justice; by her teens, however, the Roman contours would give her a proud, regal air to Angela's pert and perky.

Not that it would be given the chance. Angela had already planned to correct what she perceived as a flaw. There wasn't much she could do about the eyes. Yet. She was keeping tabs on the technology.

"Yes, Momma?" Chelsea asked politely.

"Your daddy and I have some business to discuss. Would you like to go down and see the new line of scarves I had Mrs. Terret order in?"

Chelsea frowned. "I'd rather go look at the toys."

"Very well, if you must." Angela tapped her finger on the bridge of Chelsea's nose. "And don't scowl, dear. We don't want to wrinkle, do we?"

"For pity's sake, Angela," Nathan exclaimed. "Eleven-year-old skin doesn't wrinkle. Let the girl be."

Angela whipped her head around to pin Nathan with her snakelike gaze. "It's a bad habit that I don't want her to continue. Just like your bad habit of telling me how to raise her," she said caustically. And then, quick as a wink, her voice returned to its former soft lilt as she addressed her daughter. "Go on now, honey. I'll be down in a little while and we'll go to lunch."

"Yes, Momma."

When Chelsea was gone, Angela's entire demeanor changed yet again. She came to stand in front of Nathan's desk, arms folded over her breasts, a very deep wrinkle of her own in evidence between her perfectly plucked eyebrows.

"Don't you ever interrupt me again when I'm correcting my child, Nathan. Todd is your concern, but Chelsea is all mine. I mean it."

Nathan had no doubt about that. And normally he wouldn't pursue the matter further. But he was in a lousy mood this morning. Right off the bat, the newspaper had all but accused him of kidnapping. He had an appointment with his lawyers for that afternoon to discuss a libel suit. The mountain phone lines were back in operation, but Joey still hadn't called. Worse, he wasn't even answering the phone at the lodge. It all had Nathan so ticked off, he didn't care who he tied into.

"Chelsea is my child now, too," he reminded her. "She carries the Bayer name. And if I have something to say about her behavior or yours, I'll say it."

"You know perfectly well why I had her name changed, and it had nothing to do with needing your parenting help."

"Yes, Angela, I do know why you did it," Nathan agreed quietly. "Sheer, unmitigated venom."

In fact, after what she had done—and eventually forced him to do—to that poor sap Hastings, it was amazing Nathan had the guts to stand up to her like this. If she were to decide to come after him with a divorce lawyer, he'd probably shoot himself just to get it over with quickly.

Angela had started tapping her foot. It scarcely made any noise on the thick carpeting, but it was something she knew annoyed Nathan, so she did it, anyway.

"So, Mr. Big Shot. Woke up cranky today, did you? We'll see how you are tomorrow morning after waking up alone!"

Nathan sighed. "Angela, just sit down and shut up, will you? I have a headache."

"So will I." Angela smirked. She sat down and crossed her legs, the whisper of nylon audible in the quiet office. "A bad one. Might even last the rest of the year."

"Enough!" Nathan looked at her perfect legs and had to close his eyes for a moment. It was no use. He looked her in the eye and capitulated. "I'm sorry, all right? I'm on edge. Where are those two idiots?"

Angela wasn't quite through making him squirm. "How should I know? They're *your* idiots. *You're* the one in charge, right? Or so you keep telling me."

Nathan started to say something, but stopped himself just in time. He remembered when he was a boy, sitting right here in this office, watching his father. The old man blustered at everything and everyone that got in his way.

There wasn't a definite link between his behavior and the aneurysm that stilled his nearly endless tirade at sixty-two. But it had to have been a factor. All that yelling and all those bulging veins. It didn't take a doctor to figure out that wasn't good for a person.

The manner of his father's death was a lesson Nathan had taken to heart, literally. Exercise, a low-fat diet and stress reduction were the order of the day. He had also long ago removed the gun his father had always kept in the top right-hand desk drawer.

And now, looking at Angela's smug, perfect face, Nathan was very glad it wasn't there. "They'll call," he assured her in quiet, clipped tones. "They're probably just out for a walk. Kids get restless, you know."

Angela was checking her nails. They were perfect. "I say they've made another deal."

"Who with?"

"I wouldn't know. Another retailer maybe," she said. "Or maybe even old Pop Lyon himself."

Nathan's eyes narrowed. "Joey wouldn't do that."

"Wouldn't he?" Angela glared at him. "You pay him peanuts and treat him like dirt, Nathan, the same as all your employees."

"But he has complete job security," Nathan said.

"Well, whoopee!" Angela exclaimed sarcastically. "Did you ever stop to think he might aspire to something better?"

Nathan laughed. "Joey? Come on."

The phone rang. It was Nathan's private line. He gave Angela an I-told-you-so smile and picked up the receiver.

"That better be you, Joey," he said gruffly.

"Sorry I didn't call earlier. The phones were out."

"But they had them fixed by nine this morning, Joey," Nathan said. "I've been calling the lodge since then."

"What can I tell you, Nathan? We've been right here the whole time. Maybe they've got the lines crossed, or something."

Nathan scowled. "Maybe. Everything okay?"

"What could be wrong?" Joey asked.

"Nothing." Nathan leaned back in his chair with a sigh of relief. Same old Joey. "Kid okay?"

"I should feel so good. Any word on the shipment?"

"Not the one we're after. But it won't be long now," Nathan said. "They hit both coasts at the same time about an hour ago. It's wild. You ought to see those crowds snappin' 'em up."

"Yeah, well, maybe there's something on the radio."

"Maybe." Nathan grinned at Angela. "Anyway, you hang tight, Joey. Call me if there's any trouble."

"Relax, Nathan. Everything is going according to plan."

Chapter Eleven

Shannon had decided to try the undercover shopper route first, with the intent of asking seemingly innocent questions about the Bayers and their life-style, particularly any mountain property they might own. So far, however, all the sales clerks she had spoken to didn't know, didn't want to know and, furthermore, couldn't care less how the Bayers lived.

In fact, given the dour, elitist attitudes exhibited by everyone in the entire store—including quite a few of the customers—she wasn't at all enthusiastic about the prospect of becoming a Bayer's employee, even of the temporary variety.

Rick wasn't enthusiastic about being there, period. He had argued against this approach, suggested alternatives and in general had dragged his heels the entire time. He was acting strangely in other ways, as well, nervous and jumpy, as if he expected to be caught at any moment.

"Would you relax?" she urged.

"I *am* relaxed."

"Is that a fact?" Shannon grinned. "Then I can hardly wait to see what you're like when you're tense."

Rick managed a small, crooked smile. "I just think this is a total waste of time, that's all. We could accomplish the same thing by going down to city hall and checking property records.''

"Maybe," Shannon said. "But in the first place, I've found that bureaucracies don't function all that well this close to a major holiday. Second, you know as well as I do that the rich have ways of keeping their names off any lists that might cause them to pay their fair share of taxes. And third, that's not the only thing we're trying to find out. We have that one name I remembered Leo mentioned, too. Irv, wasn't it?''

Rick sighed, disgusted. "Right. Irv. And what have we gotten when we drop that name, Shannon?''

"So far, blank stares," she admitted. "But hope springs eternal. While we're here, shall we look at ties?''

"Yeah, sure.''

Though he was being a grump, Rick looked sharp in his dark blue wool trousers and coordinating Harris tweed jacket. His shirt, in a shade Lyon's menswear maven Carl had described as chamomile, was open at the throat, since Rick had absolutely refused to wear the tie Carl had also picked out.

As they browsed for one he could stand, they heard a flurry of excitement coming from the electronics department and went to investigate. Rather than discover that some kind of special sale was in progress, however, they found that a large crowd had gathered around the wall-size bank of televisions. And every one of them showed the same thing.

Arnie the Arachnid had arrived in New York. He was taking Manhattan, the Bronx and Staten Island, too. So far, the crowds were manageable and restrained, even festive. The lacquer-haired newsperson, of course, predicted, darkly, that such behavior would only last as long as the Arnies did. And of course, no matter what sort of mayhem ensued, viewers could rest assured that her station's cameras would be there to film it all.

Shannon glanced at Rick. "That's a rather enigmatic smile you have on your face," she observed. "Bemused, even."

"It's just that..." He trailed off, and turned to look at her. "So much has gone into this moment. Now that it's started, I'm...I don't know. Overwhelmed, I guess." He leaned close to whisper in her ear. "Can you keep a secret?"

Her eyes widened. "To the grave. What is it?"

"Those things are ridiculously cheap to make."

"And they sell for ten bucks a pop," Shannon remarked, her eyes opening wider still. "I take it there is some sort of profit sharing at good old Arnie Inc."

Rick nodded. "Something like that."

"In other words, you may not need to moonlight anymore."

"Don't worry," he assured her. "I can't turn in my Santa suit just yet. It'll be a while before I see any money."

"Good," Shannon said.

"Thanks!" he said indignantly.

"You know what I mean." She linked her arm through his. "Come on. I want to get a look at their toy department."

They strolled around Bayer's centerpiece indoor fountain, with its gaily splashing water, tinted green in honor of the season. In contrast to Lyon's almost art deco interior, Bayer's had been originally designed to look flamboyantly rich—not unlike its customary clientele.

In fact, Pop had once accused Joe Bayer of lifting the decor from a Las Vegas casino. Although the display areas had been updated over the years, those roots still showed in the store's white marble columns, gleaming brass railings and high, domed ceilings.

Bayer's wasn't nearly as big as Lyon's, but made up for the lack of space by careful selection of merchandise. But often, the value of this merchandise was implied rather than real, by virtue of its brand name or celebrity endorsement. That there were those who put such things above price, however, was evident. Lyon's had only the one downtown location, while Bayer's had that and space in every Denver mall, as well.

Still, Lyon's did more than survive, it prospered, in part because of its loyal customer base. A product bought at Lyon's came with a guarantee beyond that of the manufacturer. Pop was fond of saying that it was a difference in philosophy.

But where Arnies were concerned, loyalty and philosophy seemed to have gone out the window. So, evidently, had decency.

"Oh, brother!" Shannon exclaimed quietly. "Look at that."

Rick had already spotted the sign hung prominently over the toy department sales counter. He read it aloud. "If it's an Arnie you need, for Timmy or Sue, by hook or by crook, Bayer's will get one for you."

"I guess that article didn't faze them," Shannon said.

"Hardly." Rick shook his head in disbelief. "And Pop wondered why Lyon's was chosen as the sole distributor. Man! That steams me! It's like they're thumbing their noses at us."

"They are. And unless we can find Leo, we'll have to pucker up." Shannon was looking around the toy department, checking out the competition. Suddenly, she grabbed Rick's arm. "I think we just got the break we're looking for."

"What?"

"Who," she corrected. "That clerk. He did some part-time work for me a while back. But he needed a full-time job and I just didn't have an opening for him. Shame, too. He's a real nice guy."

Rick was still perturbed by the sign. "Then what's he doing working in a garbage dump like this?"

"Making a living," Shannon returned dryly. "But I'll bet he'll be more open about this dump than those other stiffs. Maybe you'd better look around, or something, divert attention from me while I have a word with him."

"That's me, just a momentary diversion. How big a fire do you want me to start?"

"Tempting," Shannon said. "But just ask that other clerk to show you a slime gun, or something."

She left him to his own devices and went to talk to her former employee. Rick didn't want to see another slime gun, but there were some very interesting dolls in a locked glass case that he wanted to get a better look at.

He always sent a gift to Chelsea on her birthday and for Christmas. Angela probably just threw the presents away, or told her they were from someone else, so Rick knew he was really doing it more for himself than his daughter. But he had to try to stay in contact somehow, even if Chelsea didn't know about it.

Pop was right to make him get some fancier clothes. If he'd been wearing his faded jeans, he doubted the clerk would have let him near the expensive, computer-controlled doll. As it was, the man opened the case, handed Rick one, then went to help someone else. Since the clerk wasn't paying any attention to Shannon and the other salesperson, Rick figured he had diverted as much attention as was necessary, and turned his to checking out the doll.

It was okay, he supposed, but in his opinion, over-wrought. Turn it on and it behaved as much like a real baby as was technologically possible at the moment. Not much had been left up to the imagination. Educational toys were great, but this one seemed more like a simulator. Where was the play value? Where was the fun?

Maybe it was just something he couldn't understand. He decided to go to the source, and looked around for a little girl to ask.

That's when he saw her. For the first time in a little over three years. She had grown, in so many ways that at first he couldn't take them all in, and he realized with a sharp pang of grief that those past three years had been important ones for Chelsea.

Though he knew he should turn around and walk away, for a moment, Rick could only stand and stare. There was just so much *more* of her. She was taller. Her hair was longer. That nose, *his* nose, still didn't quite fit, but it wouldn't be too long now. In another three years, she would be on the verge of young womanhood. Two more after that and she'd want her own car. A few more and...what? Her own children, perhaps? It all passed so quickly.

And it was passing without him. All the bitterness and rage that he had spent three years putting behind him sud-denly came boiling up in a dizzying rush.

But then she looked at him, and in an instant all the an-ger was gone. Her sweet smile was like a balm to his wounded heart. At least some things hadn't changed. Those big, brown eyes. And she was holding a plastic model of a horse. He remembered horses had been an obsession of hers since she was four or five.

When she turned back to studying the little horse, Rick realized he'd been fooling himself. She had changed, but so had he. There were fewer pounds around his middle, and a few more gray hairs on his head. His face hadn't escaped the effects of time, either, especially when combined with too much anger and not enough understanding—from both himself and the one person he cared more about than any other.

Chelsea didn't recognize him. His own daughter had forgotten who he was. And Rick simply couldn't bear it.

All the things he had been working for suddenly didn't seem to make any difference. Putting the doll he still held in his hand down on a nearby counter, he did the one thing that could bring those hopes crashing down around his ears.

He approached his own child. "Hi, Chelsea."

"Hello," she said distractedly. She was focused on the model horse, and her reply was mainly a reflex action.

But at the sound of his voice, a connection that had already started to form in the young girl's mind was completed at last, and she looked up at Rick. Her sweet, tentative smile wavered, then melted into a frown. Slowly, that frown turned into something even uglier.

He saw that Chelsea recognized him now. And that she was afraid of him.

"Momma says you're supposed to stay away from us."

Rick didn't know which hurt worse, the look on her face or the way her voice had quavered when she'd said those words.

"Chelsea, honey—"

"Momma says you're not supposed to talk to us, either," she told him. "She says you'll be mean."

"I'm sure your mother has said a lot of things about me, Chelsea," Rick said, struggling to keep his voice calm. What he wanted to do was grab her, hug her, somehow communicate all the love he had inside for her.

However, Angela had done her dirty work well; his own flesh and blood was backing away from him. "But you have to believe me, Chelsea. I never hurt your mother. And I would never, ever hurt you."

"She cried. Her eye was all purple and black."

Rick felt his stomach knot up. What could he say? Call her mother a liar? Down that path lay certain defeat. Rant and rave about a judge who had accepted her word against his? Chelsea wouldn't understand that. *He* didn't understand that. All he knew was that he had been mangled by a legal system gone astray, the best justice money could buy.

And all he could do was continue to plead his own case. "It wasn't me, Chelsea. I don't know what happened to your mother, but it wasn't me. I love you, honey. And I'm so very sorry about all this mess."

For a brief, glorious instant, the fear on the little girl's face went away. "Is that true, Daddy?"

It was just four words, but they meant the world to Rick. In them he could hear her confusion. Her mind was not yet totally made up against him. And in her suddenly teary eyes he could see a question, a need not unlike his own.

He bent down on one knee and opened his arms to her. "I know we're not supposed to, Chelsea. But I could really use a hug right now."

She took one hesitant step toward her father. It was as far as she got. "Chelsea!" her mother yelled. "Stop!"

Again, fear marred Chelsea's sweet features as Angela came striding up behind her and grabbed the child's arm, pulling her backward. Rick took one look at his former wife's face and saw all he needed to. He was in big trouble. As he turned around, hoping against hope that it wasn't too late, his gut feeling was confirmed.

There were two of them, large-size males, and they didn't look in the mood for resistance of any sort. Rick had no intention of offering any. The moment he had seen Chelsea, he knew that what was about to happen was a very definite possibility. When he hadn't left her vicinity immediately, he had broken the law.

"Are you Rick Hastings?" one of the police officers asked.

Rick nodded. "I am."

"Mr. Hastings, you have violated a restraining order that was obtained against you by your former spouse for her own protection and that of her child, Chelsea Bayer. At this time, I am going to place you under arrest."

Even with his fine new clothes, the officers weren't taking any chances with Rick. While one continued the legal spiel and kept a wary eye peeled, the other got out his handcuffs. As he maneuvered Rick into position and snapped them around his wrists, Shannon pushed her way through the crowd that had started to gather.

"What's going on?" she demanded. "Rick? What is this?"

"Stay out of it, Shannon," he said curtly.

"Please step back, ma'am," one policeman told her in a no-nonsense tone. "Mr. Hastings is under arrest."

"What!" Shannon cried. "What did he do?"

"For heaven's sake, Shannon!" Rick exclaimed. "Do what they tell you and keep away!"

She tried to move closer, and the officer physically prevented her. "Mr. Hastings has violated a restraining order. If you have an interest in this case, you can come to this precinct and inquire through proper channels," he told her, handing her a card that he whipped out of his uniform pocket. "Now stay back, or I'll be forced to arrest you for interfering with us and you'll be coming along with him right now. Have I made myself clear?"

Shannon nodded. She knew that domestic disputes were one of the most dangerous situations a police officer encountered. Besides, she knew this wasn't their fault. As they led Rick away, Shannon turned to glare at the woman she suspected was responsible.

There was a smug little grin of victory on her pretty face and Shannon had the sudden urge to claw it right off. But then, Angela noticed her, and Shannon realized such a thing wouldn't be easy. Never in her life had she seen such a fierce, almost blood-thirsty expression on a woman. It made her own blood run cold in her veins.

From somewhere, however, she summoned the courage to approach Angela, anyway. It was quite clear to her that the other woman expected, even relished, confrontation.

And the first shot fired was hers. "Well. Isn't this touching," Angela said in a cool, snobbish tone. "It looks like Rick found himself a little redhead to fight his battles for him."

Shannon had to admit there was something imposing about Angela. She seemed larger than life, like an animated statue sculpted by an oversexed perfectionist out of pink alabaster, rather than a real woman of flesh and bone.

But then, there was a reason Leo referred to Shannon as the Amazon. She highly resented being called little and had a fiery temper in keeping with both her hair color and her ancestry.

There was, however, a problem. Chelsea. The girl was alarmed, afraid and huddled close to her mother for protection. Suddenly, it occurred to Shannon that it was the other way around. Angela was actually hiding behind Chelsea.

If the child hadn't been there, Shannon would have really torn into the other woman—verbally, of course. Still, there were some things that needed to be said, and Chelsea might as well hear them, too.

"My name, Mrs. Bayer, is Shannon O'Shaughnessy," she told her in a low, clipped voice. "I am the toy department manager for Lyon's, where Rick is presently employed as a Santa Claus. He came here with me on an errand for Mr. Lyon and I assume full responsibility for his actions."

"Rick? A department store Santa Claus?" Angela laughed derisively. "I suppose it fits Lyon's style, though. Leave it to you people to hire a thug for such a sensitive position."

"If anyone can be accused of hiring thugs, it's Bayer's," Shannon objected, just managing to keep her cool. She pointed to the sign over the sales counter. "By hook or by *crook?*"

Angela looked bored. "It's a joke, dear."

"If we find Leo before the shipment arrives—and we will find him—the joke will be on you. *Dear,*" Shannon retorted curtly. "And then we'll see who winds up in jail."

"That sounds like a threat."

"It's a promise," Shannon assured her.

"I hope you're not accusing us of kidnapping," Angela warned. "We're already planning on suing the newspaper for that mistake. We'd be happy to include Lyon's, as well."

"I'm not accusing you of anything. Yet," Shannon said, frowning, "I am curious about one thing. Since Rick never signed any adoption papers, how did you and Nathan manage to change Chelsea's surname?"

Angela's eyes narrowed as her expression changed from hostile to wary. "I hope all that loyalty isn't for Rick, Ms. O'Shaughnessy. He's a dangerous man. And a pathological liar."

While it was true that all Shannon had was Rick's side of the story, she was inclined to believe him, and what had just happened was strong evidence to support that belief.

"My loyalty is for an eight-year-old boy who is being held hostage for commercial gain, no matter how elaborate or comfortable his circumstances might be at the moment," Shannon returned. "As for Rick, I scarcely know him. But I know what I saw here today. If you truly believed Chelsea to be in danger, why did you wait until the police arrived before you came to save her from such a supposedly dangerous individual?"

Angela put her hand on Chelsea's shoulder. "I'm sure I don't know what you mean."

"No? Then let me spell it out. To me, it seems as if you used your own child as bait."

"How dare you!"

Angela was looking around for assistance. "That's it!" she said stridently. "I've heard enough. If you don't leave right now, I'll have security forcibly eject you."

"Don't bother. I'll leave. But understand this." She met Angela's hate-filled reptilian gaze. "I am going to redouble my efforts to get Leo back. And if I do find that you are somehow involved, I will take great personal pleasure in seeing your pert, perfect little butt behind bars!"

"Security!" Angela yelped.

Shannon turned to go. On a whim, she turned back and gently touched Chelsea's cheek. "If you ever want to talk to a real adult, honey, come see me at Lyon's. I'll buy you a hot chocolate."

She then strode out of the store, feeling rather proud of herself. Except for Rick's getting carted off to jail, it had been a good day so far. Her former employee had given her a clue to follow up on, and she had insulted a Bayer.

No wonder Rick had been so jumpy. Worse than his going and getting himself arrested, though, at least as far as Shannon was concerned, was that he hadn't trusted her enough to tell her about the restraining order—and whatever incident had prompted Angela to acquire it. She had thought all along that there were things he was hiding from her.

What other surprises sat waiting to jump out at her? Shannon was tempted to leave him behind bars until he told her every last one of his secrets. In fact, she might not have any choice. At this time of year, it could take a while for her to arrange bail for him, especially considering she had never done such a thing before.

Paul would know how, though. He might even be pressed into accompanying her to the police station, if he wasn't already standing in for Rick on Santa duty, that is. Regardless, she would have to touch base with her department and let them know where she would be.

That would be fun. She could see it all now. "Hello, everyone. I'm off to get Santa out of jail. Don't wait up."

Chapter Twelve

To call any big-city police precinct house a zoo was to do a disservice to animals everywhere. Its human counterpart was much less civilized, even at Christmastime.

Although the experience was depressing, it made Shannon see her own situation in a different light. No matter how badly things were going, they could always get worse. She thanked her lucky stars for what was a far better life than many people would ever know.

Paul hadn't been able to leave the store, but he had helped all he could, putting Shannon in contact with some police friends of his and a good bail bondsman. Even then, it was nearing five and dark outside when Rick emerged from the holding-cell area. He signed for his belongings, had a short conversation with the bondsman, then approached Shannon where she stood waiting for him in the precinct lobby.

The first thing Shannon noticed was that there was a bruise on his right cheekbone and a cut on his lip. Some blood from that cut had dried on the lapel of his chamomile-colored shirt. He looked tired and dispirited.

"Good Lord! What happened to you?"

Rick managed a small smile. "One of my cell mates took exception to this prissy yellow shirt," he replied. "He thought it might mean I would be an easy target. He was wrong." He held up his right hand, which had gauze wrapped around the knuckles. "As the saying goes, you should see the other guy. Luckily, the guard didn't cite me for fighting or I'd still be in that cell."

"Come on," she said. "Let's get out of here."

"My thoughts exactly."

Shannon had parked her car in a nearby lot. She led the way in silence. Obviously, Rick was capable of violence. But that came as no surprise to her; most human beings were, given the right set of circumstances. And defending oneself against a jailhouse bully certainly qualified.

When they got to the car, Shannon stopped, then suddenly turned and gave Rick a big hug. It surprised him totally at first, but then he wrapped his arms around her and hugged her, sighing deeply. Finally, she let him go.

"What was that for?" he asked.

"I just felt like it," Shannon replied. "Now, stand still, because I also feel like smacking you on the nose."

Rick held his hands up in front of his face, palms out. "Pass," he said. "I've taken enough cheap shots for one day, thank you very much."

"This one is well deserved. Why didn't you tell me she had a restraining order against you?"

His shoulders sagged. "Because then I'd have to explain, and I just didn't want to do that," Rick replied. "Listen, could we discuss this in the car? This suit coat isn't cutting it. I'm freezing."

Shannon unlocked the passenger door, then went around and unlocked her own. She started the car, but the engine was cold and there wasn't any heat yet. Rather than sit there, she pulled out of the parking lot and headed for her place.

"So you'll know the day wasn't a total loss, I did get a lead from that former employee of mine," she told him. "The Bayers have a time-share interest in a ski lodge up near Vail. He gave me directions, but we'll have to wait until daylight to go looking. I guess it's a real hideaway."

"Just as well," Rick said. "I'm pretty beat." He gently touched his cut lip. "And beat-up."

"Did they feed you?" she asked.

"No. I had just missed lunch and got out right before dinner," Rick replied, shivering with more than the cold. "I'll grab a burger, or something."

"I'm cooking, remember? That is, if you can wait that long. It'll take about an hour—after we get there, that is."

Rick nodded. "It'll take at least that for me to regain my appetite." He was silent for a moment. "If you want to change your mind about having me over, I'll understand."

"Just because you got arrested?" Shannon glanced over at him. "I realize we only met yesterday, but you should know me better than that by now. I'm not exactly sending out mixed signals, now, am I?"

"I...I'm not so hot at reading those kinds of signals anymore, Shannon. Maybe I never was. In case you haven't noticed, there are only two females in my life. One of them hates my guts and the other is scared to death of me."

Traffic was heavy, and for a moment Shannon had all she could handle just getting into the proper lane. Once she had that accomplished, she breathed a sigh of relief and chuckled.

"That Angela is a piece of work," she said. "I only talked to her for about a minute and I'm pretty sure she hates my guts, too. Chelsea..." She trailed off with a shrug. "Chelsea is young, even for eleven. I think she's scared of just about everything right now. But that can be changed, if you work on it."

"If I'm *allowed* to work on it," Rick corrected. "You saw what happened when I tried. It's the reason I've stayed away from her for this long. Angela has me where she wants me."

"That can be changed, too. Believe me, I am very much in the mood to help you take that woman on."

He studied Shannon's face in the headlights of passing cars. "So, you talked to Angela?"

"I'm the astute one, remember?" Shannon reminded him. "Don't pussyfoot. If you have a question, ask it."

"Did she tell you how she got that restraining order?"

"She said you're a very dangerous man. And a liar." When they stopped at a red light, Shannon looked at him. "Did you hit her? Or Chelsea?"

"No! Never!" He slapped the dashboard with his bandaged hand and winced. "Now do you see why I didn't tell you?"

Shannon touched his sore hand. "Sorry, but I had to ask. It does happen, even in the best of families."

"It didn't in mine. If anyone had ever laid a finger on Chelsea, so help me..." Rick paused, getting control of the anger within him. "Someone did hit Angela, though."

"What do you mean? Who?"

"I don't know who," he replied. "All I know is that I walked into a courtroom one day for what I thought was going to be a preliminary custody hearing, and there sat Angela with a great big shiner. She said I did it. The judge believed her. That was the turning point for the rest of my dealings with the courts. From that day on, I didn't stand a chance."

The light turned green and Shannon accelerated quickly before the car behind her ran up her tail pipe. Good reflexes and a fast car were a must for driving in Denver, especially during rush hour.

"Are you telling me she had someone hit her so she could set you up?" Shannon asked incredulously.

"Maybe. Maybe she hit herself, I don't know. I told you the woman is capable of anything."

Shannon didn't live far from the downtown area as the crow flies, but the only streets that took anywhere near that straight a path were virtual parking lots at this hour, so she chose a less traveled route. Even that was busy, however, and of the roller-coaster variety common to Denver. At least the car heater finally kicked in, making the drive more tolerable. Rick lapsed into a comfortable silence, which was fine with Shannon. He actually seemed to relax a bit, too.

So did she. Besides its being the lesser of two evils, this route featured Christmas lights and decorations all along the way, making it relatively pleasant to traverse. And the lack of clouds allowed them to see the moon and stars. Looking back the way they had come, they could see even the downtown area was like a giant centerpiece decorating the twinkling city itself.

Gradually, the last of the major commercial structures gave way to the suburbs, with its mix of residences and the ubiquitous strip malls and corner convenience stores.

Upon arrival at Shannon's place, they had to brave the cold night air again. She had a garage, but the driveway leading up to it was on a slant, and she hadn't had time to shovel it after the last snow. It was therefore too icy for her car to climb.

"I'll have to get a four-by-four one of these days," she muttered as she led the way to her door.

"Can you afford one?" Rick asked. Although her home was a modest trilevel, it was in a pretty, well-tended neighborhood close to the Cherry Creek reservoir. "After making your house payments, I mean?"

"Actually, I don't have any house payments per se. This was an investment property of my stepfather's, and after the depreciation on it ran out, he pretty much gave it to me," Shannon explained. "I paid the closing costs, that's all."

"Nice of him."

"Very," she agreed. A motion sensor turned on her porch light as they approached. "Surprising, too. He's not really the type to put family before business. But this was after my divorce, and I guess he felt sorry for me for once." She put her key in the lock. "Still, there are the utilities and insurance to pay for. And the taxes aren't cheap. But I do okay."

They entered and Shannon turned on the lights. It was a standard trilevel floor plan, with kitchen, living room and other so-called public areas on the main level, utility and recreation areas downstairs and bedrooms upstairs. All but the bedrooms were more or less visible from where they stood in the entry hall.

As Rick had somehow expected, she had the place fully decked out for the holidays. A Christmas tree stood in one corner of the living room, done up in little white lights and with tiny stuffed animals for ornaments. Everywhere he looked, there were touches of the season, from the pretty cards lining the mantel over her fireplace to a little crèche on one shelf of her combination stereo cabinet and bookcase.

Oddly, though, he didn't see a garland or so much as a single strand of tinsel anywhere. He had only been standing there for a few moments, when he found out why.

First, something bumped the back of his leg. Hard. He was forced to take a step forward and flail his arms to keep his balance. Then, out of the corner of his eye, he saw what looked like a shiny black bowling ball streak past him.

"What the—"

"Phil!" Shannon chastised. "Kindly wait until you've been introduced before you try to kill the man."

Rick was looking around warily. "I'd prefer Phil didn't try to kill me at all, thank you very much."

"Just kidding. But he does tend to throw his weight around, and seventeen pounds' worth of muscle-bound cat can pack quite a wallop." She glanced fretfully at him as she put her coat in the hall closet. "You're not allergic, are you?"

"No. Actually, I like cats," Rick told her. He studied the black feline in question, which was now sitting in the doorway leading to the kitchen. "That is just a house cat, right?"

Shannon laughed. "Supposedly."

Phil was huge, much bigger than the other cat that came crawling out from under the sofa and rubbed Rick's leg. This one was mostly white with a few brush strokes of gray. Rick bent down and scratched him behind the ear.

"Meet Buttons, he got all the brains." Shannon headed for the kitchen. "I'll feed the boys and then start dinner." She filled the bowls on the floor, then put away the cat food and went to the refrigerator. "Care for a drink? I have soda, beer or wine."

"I trust your taste in beer."

"'Tis a wise man you are," she told him in her best Irish brogue, which was very good indeed. "I'll have one while I cook."

She poured them each a glass and handed Rick one. He took a long, appreciative swallow of his and sighed. "You don't have to hurry supper on my account."

"I'm hurrying on my account," Shannon said. She was already assembling ingredients on the counter near the stove. "I'm famished. I missed lunch, too."

Rick leaned on the counter near her. "You could have left me in jail. Actually, I'm still surprised you didn't."

"Why?" she asked, glancing at him curiously as she washed some vegetables in the sink.

He thought about that for a moment. "Because I don't deserve it, I suppose. I wasn't being truthful with you. In some ways, I'm still not," he admitted.

Shannon smiled slightly. "Don't you think I know that?"

Rick studied her face. That enigmatic smile bothered him. She was one of the most intuitive women he had ever met. But more to the point, she was starting to get under his skin, and by the end of this evening, he could very well find himself telling her more than he should.

He wanted, even needed to trust her. And she was doing everything in her power to show him she deserved that trust. But there was only so much of himself that his battered spirit would allow him to reveal just yet. This time around, if anything were to happen, it would have to happen for real.

Shannon O'Shaughnessy was quickly making herself an indispensable fixture in his life. He couldn't imagine not seeing her tomorrow. For a man who didn't know what tomorrow would bring, that was scary.

"Thanks for doing all this," he told her. "I want you to know I really appreciate it."

"Don't you think you're worth it?"

"I don't know what you mean."

"I mean, has Angela beaten you down so far that you've lost your self-esteem?" she returned.

"No! I may be bloody, but I'm not beaten."

Shannon nodded. She was happy to hear it. A man without spirit wasn't much of a man. "Good. But speaking of bloody, that's just what you are. Why don't you go wash up while..."

Suddenly, the room was cloaked in darkness.

"Buttons! Turn that light back on right now," Shannon ordered.

Rick laughed. "A cat that turns lights off and on? You're kidding, right?"

The lights in the kitchen came back on. Buttons was sitting on the counter near the switch looking smug.

"You keep that up and you won't get any treats," Shannon threatened. The lights promptly went out again. "I mean it, fuzzball! This is no time to show off your little fetish."

"The Christmas lights in the living room are out, too," Rick told her, still chuckling. "Maybe it really is a power failure this time."

Shannon put down her beer glass and glanced out the kitchen window over the sink. "It's possible, but my neighbors in that direction have lights. I wonder if the houses across the street do? Let's look out the front."

She started out of the kitchen and stumbled. Rick grabbed her, keeping her upright. "You okay?"

"Cats! Phil just sideswiped me."

Rick held her hand as she led them through the darkness to the front picture window. Colorful lights were twinkling merrily back at them from across the street.

"Probably just overloaded a circuit," Rick muttered. "Where's your fuse box?"

"In the garage. It's this—"

A thumping noise stopped her in midsentence.

"Was that one of your cats?" Rick asked.

Shannon tightened her grip on his hand. "I don't think so. They can't get in the garage and that's where that noise came from."

Another thump sounded eerily loud in the quiet room. No doubt about it. They were no longer alone in the house.

Chapter Thirteen

"Do you have a flashlight?" Rick asked softly.

"You can't go in there." Shannon tugged on his hand, trying to hold him back. "I'll call the police and we'll wait for them to arrive."

Her urgent whispers didn't deter him. "I've had enough police for one day."

"It's a different police station."

"No."

Shannon pinched his wrist in frustration. "What if they're armed burglars?"

"After the day I've had, I'm in the right mood to tangle with them," Rick assured her calmly. "Besides, with all the noise they've made, I don't think they're professional thieves. But if we argue long enough, maybe they'll escape."

"Wait here till I get the flashlight."

The room was dark but Rick's eyes had adjusted to the dim light and he watched her silhouetted form moving through the house. Shannon was back in a moment with a huge flashlight.

"What is that? A secret weapon?"

She handed him the long black wand. "Solid metal."

He liked the weight of the instrument. Almost as good as a baseball bat. "How many ways into the garage?"

"Three," Shannon replied. "One door from the kitchen, the other in the backyard and the last from the driveway."

Rick nodded. "Stay here."

"No way. In every movie I've seen, the woman gets it as soon as she's separated from the guy. Besides, there's an easy way out of this mess."

Shannon grabbed their coats from the hall entry closet and picked up her ring of keys from a nearby table.

"That's your plan?" Rick asked, taking his coat. "We run away?"

"No. I have an automatic garage-door opener in the car," she explained patiently. "If we take a flying run at the hill with the car we can run them down."

Rick was shocked. "Run them down!"

"Well, I don't mean hit them, exactly. Just scare them into running away. It's almost Christmas. We don't want them to spend it in jail."

"We don't?"

"May I remind you of your own recent incarceration?"

"Oh. Right." He followed her outside. "In that case, why don't we just open the garage door and let them leave."

Shannon frowned. "If that's what they want to do, they'll do it when they hear me start the car. If not, then I'll sure scare them into wanting to leave. Besides, my plan makes more sense than yours. Walking into a dark garage unarmed is dangerous."

He was facing one determined woman. "Just in case your plan doesn't work, I'll wait here on the porch. Hit that door opener before you make your run," Rick suggested. "Otherwise, you might wreck your own garage."

"Oh, ye of little faith."

If her car even made it up that icy hill, Rick was ready to follow it into the garage. The garage door was rumbling upward as Shannon gunned the engine of her car and pressed the gas pedal to the floor. As she hit the icy driveway, the rear end slipped sideways but she straightened the wheels, correcting them just enough to enter the wide opening without a scratch.

The brakes squealed as she slammed her foot on the pedal, the dry pavement allowing her to lurch to a sudden halt. Two men stood frozen against the back wall, like deer caught in her headlights. Their empty hands were held high over their heads in surrender. Rick had been right; these were definitely not pros.

He came running into the garage as Shannon got out of the car. "What are you doing in my garage?" she demanded of the intruders.

The pair were clad in similar dark clothing. Both were also dark-haired and appeared to be in their early twenties. "Don't shoot," the tallest one pleaded. "We're not armed."

Shannon almost laughed. She hadn't given them even the slightest indication she was armed, herself. Still, it didn't seem wise to clue them in to that fact. She looked around the garage. Boxes were everywhere, their contents upended.

"This place is a mess!" Shannon exclaimed. The men looked sheepish, but the woman facing them was furious, more for their interruption of a promising evening than anything else. "What were you after?"

"Listen, lady, we didn't mean any harm."

Rick found the fuse box and flipped some switches. The garage was instantly flooded with light. "Tell us what you were after or we're calling the police," he threatened.

"No! Don't do that!" The tall one looked at the ground and shuffled his feet. "We . . . we were just looking for Arnies."

"What?" Shannon cried.

"We followed you home," the short one admitted quickly. "From Lyon's. We thought you might have the spiders stored here. Our kids want them real bad."

"You were going to steal the shipment?" Rick asked softly.

"No, no," they both hastened to assure him. "We only wanted five," the tall one replied. "Two for my kids and three for his."

"Just five, huh?" Shannon shook with frustration. "Well, I don't have *any* blasted Arnies," she screamed. "In fact, I wish I'd never even heard of the damn things!"

"Uh, guys, I suggest you leave," Rick told them. "Before she *really* loses her temper and takes it out on you."

The men skirted the other side of the car, staying far away from her. Rick spoke with them briefly before they ran down the hill into the street. Shannon didn't notice; she was busy rummaging around in her things.

Rick returned to the garage, found the switch and brought the door rumbling down. "Shannon, it's freezing out here. We can clean this up later."

"If I ever get my hands on the man who invented those Arnies, I'm going to strangle him. Those spiders have been nothing but grief."

Rick took her keys and let them into the house, ushering her into the kitchen. "Still hungry?"

"No! What I need is a drink!" Shannon exclaimed, grabbing a bottle of Irish whiskey and two small, long-stemmed cordial glasses from a cupboard. "Join me?"

Rick laughed. "Of course," he answered, though it hadn't really been a question. Shannon was passionately furious and he found her anger exciting.

They adjourned to the living room, where Shannon touched a button near the fireplace mantel. Flames leapt to life, licking realistic-looking ceramic logs. She then poured a small whiskey for each of them and put the glasses on a low, glass-top coffee table, then settled in on the couch.

Shannon took a long sip of her drink. It had a warming effect she could feel from her head all the way down to the very tips of her toes.

"Arnies!" she said hotly, still fuming. "I'd like to take one of those toy spiders and rip its rubbery legs off one by one, and then make the inventor eat them."

Rick had a seat beside her and sipped at his own glass. He could think of better ways of letting her vent the heady emotions running through her. He suddenly turned toward her and covered her mouth with his own. To his delight, Shannon wrapped her arms around his neck, kissing him back.

Still, when he lifted his head, Shannon seemed stunned by the kiss. "Rick! What was that for?"

"Took your mind off spiders, didn't it?"

And everything else. The kiss had been sensual, erotic and mind-shattering. Shannon was quite willing to admit to herself that seducing Rick had been her original intention for this evening. Maybe it still was. But now that it seemed quite clear he had ideas of his own in that direction, she wasn't sure she knew how to deal with him anymore.

To be honest, she was scared. It had been a long time since she had gotten this close to a man, especially a man she actually cared about. And she did care about Rick. A lot. That scared her, too. Still, the thought of making love with him made her insides tingle.

Combined with the heat of the fire, Rick's body close to hers and the smoldering desire she felt for him deep inside, she was suddenly much too hot for the wool suit she was wearing.

"Would you excuse me for a moment?" she said. "I think I'll go change."

"Into something more comfortable?" Rick asked.

"Rick!" she chastised. But this time, he did not look away or apologize for the wicked sparkle in his eyes. "I'm too warm, that's all."

"I can well imagine."

Shannon turned and went upstairs, suddenly feeling as if she had created a monster. Just who was seducing whom?

"Relax," she urged herself quietly. "He won't bite."

At least not hard. The thought made her insides tingle again and yet gave her a fit of the giggles at the same time. She poked through her closet and drawers, trying to find the right look. Finally, she settled on an oversize, cream-colored cotton sweater with gray piping over a pair of ribbed gray cotton spandex leggings and gray suede ballet slippers.

Shannon looked in the mirror and nodded, satisfied. She was comfortable, but not in a take-me-I'm-yours way. It was rather a soft, cuddly, let's-see-what-happens sort of way.

When she returned to the living room, however, Rick gave her a look that made it clear his mind wasn't on what she was wearing. In fact, she suddenly felt completely naked.

As she sat down nervously beside him, Rick settled himself more comfortably against the back of the couch. He then reached over and gently stroked her copper-red hair.

"I don't think I've had the opportunity to tell you what a stunningly beautiful woman you are, Shannon."

"Compared to Angela? Hah!"

"In the first place, the only one who's comparing you to Angela is you," Rick assured her. He ran his fingertip along the line of her jaw. "Even then, you're miles ahead. She only thinks she's smart. You really are. And you have a good heart."

Shannon rolled her eyes. "Oh, yes. Inner beauty."

"Don't sell it short. You saw some of Angela's inner ugliness earlier today, and you can't tell me it doesn't mar her seemingly perfect features."

She thought of that murderous glare Angela had given her that afternoon in Bayer's toy department. "Well, I suppose that's true, but—"

Rick touched her lips with his fingers. "Your warmth and caring show on your face the same way." He turned toward her slightly. She had her legs tucked up underneath her, and he put his hand on the curve of her hip. "And if you'll excuse me for being blunt, Shannon, you have the kind of body that men dream about. I certainly did last night."

Shannon could no longer look him in the eyes, so strong was the passion she saw there. "I dreamed about you, too."

"Did you?" Rick touched her cheek, and softly urged her to look at him again. "Mine started like this."

Rick kissed her, just once, and so gently it felt like a mere whisper of a touch on her sensitive lips. His eyes were open, gazing deeply into hers, as if to reassure himself that this was not a dream. Then he dipped his head and kissed her again, more forcefully, his sore lip forgotten now as he communicated a tiny bit of the raging need he felt for her.

Shannon met it with a need of her own. She was surprised by the ferocity of her feelings, even a little frightened of them, but they would not be denied. Her mouth opened to his and she felt the velvety smoothness of his tongue glide between her lips, tasting of strong Irish whiskey, almost as potent as his own, sheer masculine tang.

They were both left momentarily breathless by the power of their mutual desire, and their lips parted, but even this slight respite was too much for them to bear. Rick's tongue plunged into her mouth again, dueling with hers, and at the same time he pulled her legs around over his so that she was almost sitting in his lap.

The position afforded him access to all her curves, and he plundered them without mercy, running his hand along the warm length of her thigh and up under her sweater to the even more tempting heat of her bare skin. Shannon groaned with pleasure at his touch, and entwined her fingers in his hair, encouraging him to explore further.

But Rick needed no such encouragement. His fingertips sought and found the catch to her bra and released it deftly. Her breasts came free and he cherished their sweet weight and softness in the palm of his hand.

"Shannon," he whispered, his voice a low moan of need and desire. "I want you. Now. If that isn't what you had in mind, you'd better—"

Shannon cut him off by putting both hands on his face and pulling him back into her embrace, the thrust of her tongue against his leaving him in no doubt. Just in case, she let him up for air and met his passionate gaze with the emerald fire of her own.

"I don't know about your dream," she said, her sultry voice hoarse with desire. "But mine didn't stop here."

"Mine didn't stop at all."

"Don't tell me." Shannon lay back on the couch and beckoned to him. "Show me."

Rick was more than happy to oblige. He stretched out beside her and rediscovered the depths of her sensuous mouth all over again, until she was gasping for breath. Then he left a trail of kisses across her cheek, down her throat, and into the valley formed between her breasts at the neck of her sweater. When that was not enough, he helped her remove it, removing his shirt at the same time, and they pressed their bodies together, reveling in the shared heat.

At last, Rick could stand no more, and slipped lower to bury his face in the twin pillows of her breasts. They were highly sensitive, and the large, rose-colored areolae responded instantly to the delicate touch of his tongue, turning hard as cherry stones as he tasted each one in turn.

Shannon gasped as he moved lower still, drawing a line with his artful tongue from beneath her breasts down over the delicate curve of her stomach. He paused momentarily at the waistband of her leggings, kissed her belly, then raised himself and removed them in one smooth motion.

For a moment, Shannon felt shy again, and couldn't meet his gaze. She looked at the fire instead, glad its glow hid the blush she could feel warming her already heated skin. But then she realized he was settling down beside her, and that he had removed the rest of his clothing, as well. Her eyes roved over him, widening at the strong, hard muscles she had only surmised were there before.

His arms were thick, their muscles sharply defined, and his chest broad and well developed. It tapered to a slender waist, and the sort of taut belly that her former husband had left behind almost from the day they were married. His legs showed the same kind of development, the kind that came from hours of hard labor, and not in the luxury of a fancy gym with mirrors on the walls, either.

Shannon nipped delicately at the taut skin of his male nipples, enjoying the way her touch made his marvelous stomach muscles tighten. She meandered her way down to those muscles along a path that crossed the peaks and valleys of his body. After pausing for a moment to savor his firm belly, she glanced up at him, grinning at the look of anticipation she saw in his smoldering brown eyes.

Rick moaned with pleasure as her mouth surrounded him. Shannon moaned, too, for the sheer pleasure of fulfilling his carnal needs. She ran her hand along his spine, then clasped his taut buttocks, marveling at his splendid conditioning.

"Is this anything like your dream?" Shannon asked, retracing her steps up to his throat, where she nuzzled her face against him before gazing into his eyes.

"*You're* a dream," he muttered, then pulled her down against him once again.

Shannon could feel his manhood throbbing against her, the beat of his heart matching her own. She had no idea where his dream went from there, but she knew where hers had gone, and she knew what she wanted.

Rick certainly did not object as she placed her hands on his broad chest and straddled him, the silky skin of her thighs against his hips making him gasp. In the light of the fire, her eyes glimmered, and her hair was like a fiery aura surrounding her face.

As she lowered herself slowly upon him, Shannon closed her eyes and uttered a low, wanton moan of satisfaction. When he filled her to the very core, she stopped, and her eyes fluttered open. She looked at him and licked her parched lips.

"Is this a dream?" she asked in a sensual whisper.

Rick ran his hands up along her perspiration-slick sides and cupped her swollen breasts. "It must be. Reality never felt this good, at least not for me."

"Nor me." Shannon started to move her hips. "If it is a dream, don't wake me."

Rick could only moan and shake his head. She was a strong woman, with powerful muscles of her own and an even more powerful need. It had been a very long time for both of them, and they abandoned themselves completely to the ecstasy of sheer physical contact. Their only conscious thought was that this had been inevitable from the moment their eyes had first met. It seemed like destiny, and that made it all the sweeter.

Shannon's climax came so quickly, it surprised them both, and the ferocity of it carried Rick over the edge into his own. Wave after wave of release poured over their intertwined bodies until they lay together on the couch in a damp, panting heap. When they had sufficiently recovered, they looked at each other and laughed.

"That's not how my dream ended," Rick said.

Shannon snuggled against him, still chuckling. She drew lazy circles on his chest with her fingertip. "No?" she asked.

Rick shook his head. "No. Shall I show you?"

Rick's dream hadn't taken place in front of a fireplace, but he made do quite nicely. Shannon wasn't sure about her own response rate at first, but as he lowered himself atop her, those doubts disappeared. He slipped within her, and the power of his deep, rhythmic thrusts soon had her writhing beneath him in pleasure. This time, it was a much slower climb to the apex of their desires, but the passionate effort was more than repaid in intensity.

Afterward, they lay facing the fire, nested like spoons in a drawer, with Shannon in front and Rick behind, his arm wrapped protectively over her.

"I think we scared the cats that time," she said softly.

"That's what they get for watching."

"True." Shannon was quiet for a moment, listening to the hiss of the fire and feeling the steady pressure of Rick's chest against her back as he breathed. "Rick?"

"Yes, Shannon."

"I didn't mention this before, and I suppose it's a bit late to do so now, but I never intended for you to go home tonight."

Rick kissed the nape of her neck. "Thanks for the invitation. But you couldn't get rid of me now if you tried."

"I won't be trying anytime soon." She sighed. "This has been a very nice day."

"Well, it ended nicely, anyway," Rick agreed.

"And tomorrow, we'll find Leo."

"I hope so, Shannon," he said, glad that she couldn't see the frown on his face. "I really do."

Chapter Fourteen

"Face it, Nathan. I was right all along," Angela told him over the phone in her very best I-told-you-so voice. "The three of them were never even here."

"How can you tell?"

"Because it's clean," she replied. "It looks just the way the service left it after our Thanksgiving weekend."

From where Angela stood using the phone near the massive stone fireplace, she could see almost the entire lodge, with its exposed-beam cathedral ceiling, sleeping loft and rustic knotty-pine-paneled walls. She abhorred the place, actually, and the whole après-ski atmosphere it exuded from every smoke-scented crevice. But it had its uses, she supposed.

Right now, it was giving her a much-needed break from Nathan and Chelsea. Seeing Rick had aroused her suspicions, as had the continued lack of a response when she dialed this number. But Nathan had business to attend to, so she had summoned the chauffeur and come up to the mountains to see for herself.

Crossed wires indeed! Double-cross was more like it. Was Rick behind all this? She couldn't think of many other reasons he would show up in Denver now, after all these years, and looking much too self-assured for her liking.

He was up to something, she was sure. And what with Nathan whining about all the money he should be making on Arnies and Chelsea carrying on about seeing her father again, not to mention baby Todd, it had gotten too hard to think back in the city. A night away would do her good, even in these unrefined surroundings.

But she was beginning to wish the phone lines were still out. Nathan was unconvinced, thus giving him something else to whine about.

"So it's clean," he said. "So what? Maybe they just went to get something and will be right back. Did you think about that, Angela?"

"You think about it, idiot," she returned sarcastically. "Do you suppose Joey, Irv and an eight-year-old boy could have spent a night and a day here without making a mess?"

"Maybe they cleaned up after themselves."

Angela yawned. "I repeat, Nathan. Joey, Irv and an eight-year-old boy. Get the picture?"

"I suppose you're right." He cursed. "Where are they?"

"Somewhere *else*, dear. Because they made a deal with some*one* else. Maybe Rick. Or Lyon's. I suppose it's even within the realm of possibility that they dreamed up this scheme all by themselves. But they are most definitely not here."

Nathan cursed again, loudly and at length. Angela held the receiver away from her ear until he calmed down. At last, he started speaking in a normal tone.

"What did you say?" she asked. "I didn't catch that."

"I said, have that little weirdo drive you back down here as quickly as possible," Nathan returned. "I'm lonely."

"Well, tough. It's late, I'm tired and the roads are still icy in spots. Emilio and I are spending the night here," Angela informed him tersely. That caused Nathan to mutter an even more politically incorrect term for the chauffeur. Angela just sighed. "Let's not fight, Nathan. It's no fun over the phone. I can't see the blood vessels in your neck bulge this way."

"That was cruel, Angela."

"Good night, Nathan. I'll see you tomorrow."

She hung up without waiting for him to reply. Then, as an afterthought, she took the phone off the hook, as well. That would really get Nathan's goat.

There was a loud pop, and Angela turned toward the sound, her eyes dancing with anticipation. She accepted the glass of champagne Emilio offered her and took a delicate sip, then sank into the softness of the comfortable fireside couch. He sat down beside her with his own glass, and the rest of the bottle close at hand.

"You should have heard what Nathan called you," she said.

Emilio shrugged his broad shoulders. Although he was shorter than Nathan, there was really nothing all that little about him. The son of a once-proud family that had fallen on hard times, he had the aristocratic bearing and an insider's knowledge of the rich that had served him well in his chosen profession. His rough-and-tumble childhood had also given him a few useful tools, such as a way with cars, locks and the less savory members of society. In other words, he had once made his living as a thief. He also possessed a quick and very nasty temper.

Angela had met Emilio four years ago, when her breakup with Rick was well under way, and she had already begun dating Nathan. Luckily, she managed to convince him to hire Emilio as a bodyguard and chauffeur. Of course, it would never have happened except for another of the gorgeous, raven-haired young man's talents—his tremendous acting ability.

"To me, Nathan is nothing but a joke. He calls me names, he thinks he is better than me and all the while I am making love to his wife." Emilio finished his champagne, then poured more for them both. "It's funny. But sometimes he also makes me mad."

"I know. He makes me mad, too. Unfortunately, he pays the bills, so we'll just have to put up with him. For now," she added thoughtfully. "Tomorrow, I think we may try to find a way to get those spiders for ourselves."

"How?"

She grinned wickedly. "I think we'll start by asking Rick."

"Ah! So that's why you asked me to have him watched," Emilio said, his dark eyes flashing. Their glasses clinked in a toast. "To our future."

"THAT'LL BE fifteen hundred dollars."

"What? You're crazy!" Joey cried.

Leo shook his head. "Park Place with a hotel, fifteen hundred simoleons. Fork it over."

"Leo's right, Joey," Irv confirmed. "He's really good at this, huh?"

"Yeah," Joey muttered. "Kid's going to be a real tycoon someday." He continued to grumble, but peeled off the money from his dwindling stack and handed it to Leo. "There you go, Leo, and I hope you choke."

Leo just laughed. He liked Joey. Even though he said stuff like that a lot, he was a nice man. Last night, when he thought Leo was asleep, he'd even tucked him into bed. He had also told Leo he knew what it was like to grow up without a father, and to hang tough, because it got easier.

They were all three sprawled out on the floor of the safe house, playing Monopoly. Leo loved the game, and was very good at it. To him, it was the perfect way to end an almost-perfect day. Because he was a little more homesick today than yesterday, for it to be perfect, he'd have to call Pop or Shannon. But Joey still had Leo's cellular, because he said he was waiting for an important government call.

But there was no harm in asking. "Joey?"

"Yeah, kid."

"Would it be all right if I called Shannon now? I promise I won't talk long," Leo told him.

Joey looked at Irv, who just made a face and scratched his head. "I don't know, Leo," Joey said after a long pause. "You know I'm waiting for that important call."

"But the other phone works now, right?" Leo persisted.

"Uh, right. But—"

Irv interrupted him. "Oh, let him call her, Joey. We're sitting right here, so we can, you know, screen it for secret information, or anything."

Joey gave an exasperated sigh. "Yeah. Okay. At least, this way I can quit the game before I lose my last ten bucks. But use the cellular." He handed it to Leo and winked. "Harder for the spies to trace the call."

Leo gleefully pressed in Shannon's number and waited for her to answer. When she did, it sounded as if her cats were playing with the phone, or something. There was a lot of fumbling and even a loud thump, like it bounced on the floor.

"Hello?"

"Shannon?" Leo asked, frowning. "Do you have a cold?"

"Leo!" she exclaimed. "No, honey, I'm just fine. How are you?" This time, she decided to cut the folderol. "*Where* are you?" she asked.

"I still don't know. But guess what?"

"Leo—"

"There's a pool in the basement," he continued.

Shannon cleared her throat. "A pool?"

"It's some kind of special one, made for swimming laps while you stay in one place. But it's great for playing in, too! We played in it all day."

"You and Irv?" Shannon asked.

"And Joey, too."

At this exchange, Joey's eyes opened wide and he started to reach for the phone. "Jeez, kid!"

Leo was genuinely alarmed, but he realized his mistake and quickly corrected it. "Oh, that's not their real names."

"Oh. Well, that explains a lot," Shannon said. "Leo, honey, I know you're having fun, and all, but we're a little worried about you."

"Why? This was the best day I ever had." he assured her. "Well, since Mom and Dad . . . you know."

"Yes, dear." Obviously, there was still nothing to worry about. And it was so good to hear his voice. "Tell me about it. What did you do? Besides swim, I mean."

"Well, first, while Joey slept, Irv made breakfast. We had waffles, with ice cream and hot blueberry syrup. Both of us spilled it on the white rug in the entertainment room, and nobody even yelled at us."

"No one?"

"Well, Joey did, a little," he replied. "Anyway, we found a channel on the satellite that played nothing but cartoons, and watched until Joey got up around noon and made us stop because he was afraid we were rotting our brains. But then we found the pool, so it was okay."

Shannon frowned. This had to be the oddest kidnapping in the history of the crime. And the oddest pair of perpetrators, as well. "Just how old is this Irv, Leo?"

"Irv? I don't know. He doesn't have any gray hair yet, like Pop, but he's older than me. Fifty, I guess." Leo looked at Joey, who was again signaling him wildly. "Uh, I think I'm going to have to get off the phone now. Joey is waiting for an important call."

"About the Arnies?" Shannon asked.

"Yeah. Did you see 'em on TV? Wasn't that cool?"

"Yes, Leo. It was cool. You tell Joey we don't have ours yet, but we should soon, okay?"

"But what about the spies?"

"Just tell him what I said, Leo," Shannon said calmly.

"Okay."

Leo relayed the information to Joey. Joey just nodded his head. "I know, kid. You tell her I know all about the marketing waves. And then you'd better hang up. Those spies have ways of tracing cellular calls, too."

"Shannon? He says he knows about the waves. And I have to go now, so they don't trace the call."

"All right, Leo. You just continue to do what Joey says and have a good time. I love you."

"I love you, too. And Pop. See you soon."

"Yes, Leo," Shannon assured him. "Very soon."

Leo pushed the disconnect button. He looked at Joey. "I'm sorry, Joey. I didn't mean to mess anything up. Did I do okay covering for you?"

Joey seemed deep in thought. "You did just fine, kid. I'm the one who may have messed up." He shrugged. "Oh, well. No big deal, I suppose." He looked at Irv, who had the oddest expression on his face. "What's eating you?"

"I'm only twenty-eight, Joey!" Irv exclaimed. "I don't really look fifty like Leo said, do I? Huh?"

Both Joey and Leo started laughing. "No, Irv," Joey said. "I'd say you don't look a day over thirty-five or forty, tops."

"What!"

Joey just grinned. "Go get the cards, Leo. It's time you learned a real game. Maybe I can take some of that play money back from you."

"You mean poker?" Leo asked. "Pop and I play that all the time, too."

"Oh, brother," Joey said with a sigh. "I think I'm in for a bumpy night."

Chapter Fifteen

Shannon awoke just before her alarm went off at six in the morning. Rick was in bed beside her, already awake and watching her, his eyes full of a tenderness that made her feel warm all over.

"Good morning," he said.

"Morning." She kissed him sleepily. "I should warn you, I'm not worth a hoot until I've had a hot shower."

"For me it's coffee," Rick told her. He kissed her again and got out of bed. "Shall I bring you a cup when it's ready?"

Shannon yawned. "That would be lovely, thank you."

She watched him pull on his pants, her eyes opening wider and a big smile spreading across her face as she remembered becoming intimately acquainted with almost every inch of his tanned, well-toned skin last night.

When he left the room, she got out of bed, then grabbed her robe and went to take a shower. The hot, stinging spray felt wonderful against her muscles, a few of which were sore from not having been used in quite some time, and perhaps never so vigorously. Rick was an attentive, gentle lover, but keeping up with his strong body had been a challenge. Each and every little muscle twinge, however, was a joyful reminder of the ecstasy they had shared.

The smell of fresh coffee reached her after she had washed her hair, causing her to hurry through the rest of her ablutions. The lights went out just as she was rinsing off the soap suds.

"Buttons, darn you! Turn those back on." When they did come back on, she gasped in amazement. "Why, Buttons! That's quite a trick! Who taught you that?"

But when the shower door opened and Rick stepped into the shower with her, she knew she'd been fooled. He handed her a steaming cup of coffee, careful to keep it out of the spray.

"Actually, Buttons taught it to me," he said.

While Shannon sipped at the hot, black liquid, Rick drank in her shimmering beauty with every bit as much enjoyment. At last, she put the cup aside, a wicked gleam in her eyes.

"My, such talent," she murmured, running her fingertips over his glistening chest. "Turning lights on and off. Making and fetching coffee. And good coffee, at that."

"I can do other tricks, as well," Rick assured her.

Shannon pressed herself against him. "Mmm. Show me."

Rick proceeded to do just that, his strength again an asset in the small, steamy confines of the shower stall. He grasped her hips and lifted her up, taking his fill of her slippery breasts when they were level with his mouth. Then he slowly lowered her back down. She gasped as he entered her, surprised and wildly thrilled. This was a first for her.

She covered his mouth with her own, communicating her excitement with her tongue. Since it was new to her, she had no idea what to do, then found that there was very little she *could* do. In this position, she was almost totally at his mercy. That thrilled her, too, but only because she now trusted him completely—at least in carnal matters.

Shannon pulled back and looked into his eyes. "I like this trick," she whispered hoarsely. "I've never done it this way before."

"I thought not," Rick gasped out.

"Why? Am I doing something wrong?"

He chuckled. "No! It's just that this is very much ladies first. I'm not *that* strong. And the way you're squeezing me, I won't last another minute."

"Oh!" Shannon made a conscious effort to relax those muscles. The expression on Rick's face went from imminent explosion to relaxed pleasure. "Better?"

"Much."

By lifting her with his hands under her buttocks and making small movements with his powerful hips, Rick began to move deep within her. Combined with the motion of his hard, slick belly against hers and the water cascading over them both, it produced a sensation that had Shannon groaning wantonly with but a few thrusts.

She clutched wildly at his back, startled by the sheer swiftness of her own response. Her eyes fluttered shut and she leaned her head back, allowing Rick total possession of her body. And in just a few more moments, she abandoned herself to a powerful climax.

For the first time she could ever remember, she lost total control of herself, even to the point of crying out loudly, something else she had never done before. It was such a pure, liberating experience that she was left weak and limp in Rick's arms.

Her eyes fluttered open again, and she saw the onset of his own crescendo. It, too, rapidly progressed to a peak and exploded while Shannon wrapped her legs around his back and held on for dear life. She was entirely his, to do with as he pleased, for she lacked the strength for anything else.

At last, Rick's own prodigious strength gave out and he slipped from her. They stood beneath the restoring spray, holding each other up until they could recover.

When they did, Shannon washed him, luxuriating in the slick feel of his skin beneath her hands. Rick then returned the favor. Finally, they turned off the water and stepped out, and again took turns drying each other off.

Shannon kissed him. "Now, that is what I call fantastic morning coffee," she exclaimed.

"Why, thank you, ma'am." Rick winked at her. "We'll have to try it in a pool sometime."

"Yes, I'll bet you're an expert in pools," she teased.

Though tempted to fall back into bed, they knew it was time to get moving. As it turned out, they were both morning people, which was good since this would be a busy day. After they dressed, they had a light breakfast of fruit and more coffee and then headed downtown.

Shannon had to check in with her department, and probably sort through a small mountain of paperwork. Rick, meanwhile, would use the time to make sure everything was okay at the warehouse and grab a change of clothes. As they parted company in the Lyon's employee parking lot, their passionate kiss did not go unnoticed.

"Have a nice night?" Pop's secretary asked, winking at Shannon suggestively as she walked by.

"Yes, thank you," Shannon replied. She knew the smile on her glowing face said it all, and didn't care who saw it. "Is Pop going to be in this morning, Carla?"

She paused and nodded. "I imagine he's already here, watching the waves on TV. They're all up and down both coasts now and moving inward."

"The Arnies, you mean?" Rick asked.

"What else? It is sort of exciting, even if we have to give ours up. Either way, we'd better get them soon, or Pop will bust a gusset," Carla said. "Any leads on Leo yet?"

"One," Shannon replied. "We're going to check it out later today."

"Good. Oh, Pop wants a full report, by the way," Carla said, then turned and continued walking toward the building.

"That was going to be my first stop, anyway," Shannon told Rick. "I think Pop is in closer contact with those two kidnappers than he's letting on."

"Oh? What kind of contact?"

"I'm not sure. All I know is that's the same thing Leo said on the phone last night. The kidnapper he calls Joey told him he knew about the waves. Pop and I are the only ones you told about that strategy, right?" Shannon asked.

"Yes. But like I said then, I could only tell you because it was about to become public knowledge, anyway," Rick replied. "It's all over the news. The kidnappers might have picked up the expression from somebody on television."

"Maybe. But if Pop has talked to them again, it wouldn't hurt to compare notes."

He shrugged. "I suppose not."

Shannon looked at him, a slight frown wrinkling her forehead. She had become so caught up in her own feelings that she had nearly forgotten about Rick's connection to all this. He had even admitted last night that there were still things he was keeping from her. That bothered her, but there wasn't much she could do about it.

"*Are* we going to be getting our Arnies soon?" she asked.

Rick grinned. "I'm not at liberty to discuss that."

"Not even after all we've shared?" she coaxed.

Rick's grin melted and he took her into his arms again, gazing seriously into her eyes. "It's not that I don't trust you, Shannon," he assured her. "It's more a matter of my not trusting myself, now more than ever, in fact. I have to do what I came here to do, no matter what."

Unfortunately, Shannon thought she knew exactly what he meant. "What if we don't find Leo by the time the Arnies arrive, Rick?"

He gave her a reassuring hug, then released her. "We'll find him," he said, then turned to go. "But only if we get a move on. See you in a few."

Shannon scowled at his departing back. "You don't have any intention of just turning those toys over to the Bayers, do you?" she shouted after him.

"Let's cross that bridge when we come to it, Shannon," he called back without breaking stride.

She stamped her foot in frustration, then headed into the building. When she was gone, a man emerged from behind the Dumpster he had been hiding behind for the better part of the morning and started following Rick. It wasn't easy, because his old legs with their alcohol-impaired circulation were no match for the purposeful stride of the younger man, especially in the chill morning air. But he managed. The promise of good pay helped move him along.

Rick continued toward his destination, his mind full of all the things vying for his attention. For someone who had had next to nothing in his life just a few days ago, there was certainly a lot going on. It was impossible to concentrate on them individually, because they were so interdependent. Find Leo. Save the Arnies. Get back into Chelsea's life. Destroy the Bayers, or, at the very least, Angela.

And then there was Shannon. Sweet, sexy, problematic Shannon. Just the thought of her gave him something he had feared he would never have again. Hope.

He had never really felt about a woman the way he did about Shannon. With Angela, it had been lust, which had quickly dissipated into apathy and, later, outright hatred. While Shannon certainly evoked his lust, it was in a different way. Just as strong, but softer, somehow. And there was more. Her needs and wants were becoming more important to him than his own. That, supposedly, was one element of love. Up until now, the only other human being he had cared about that much was Chelsea. Now it seemed there was room in his heart for two.

Therein lay the problem. Soon, whether they found Leo or not, Shannon was likely to become very unhappy with him. She would ask him to choose. But that choice was so unfair.

Rick wanted to do the right thing. That he was holding out on Shannon was already eating him up inside; getting closer to her had only made things worse. But this was his one best chance to regain some control over his daughter's life. It was imperative that he hold on to every possible edge until the last moment, or the Bayers might squash him again. And he didn't think he had it in him to rise above that one more time. This was it, and he had to make it work.

All he could do was continue to weave in and around the truth, and hope that when the time came, Shannon would know him well enough to understand the decisions he had made.

With some surprise, Rick looked up and realized he was standing in front of the warehouse. He cursed under his breath. His thoughts had so carried him away that he hadn't taken his usual circuitous route, nor been on the alert for anyone following him, now more a threat than ever before.

Rather than do something totally suspicious, though, he decided to simply take one trip around the block and try to make amends for his negligence. Since the area comprised mainly warehouses, it was a long block, probably a mile at least. Even though the sun was out and shining brightly today, his suit jacket wasn't much of a barrier against the wind. He gritted his teeth and walked on, considering it his punishment.

The zone was quiet this morning, with few people braving the cold, and not even much traffic. Finally, near-frozen but satisfied, he slipped around the back of the warehouse and used his customary entrance, reveling in the relative warmth the building's cavernous interior provided. As usual, it was quiet.

First, Rick went to his apartment, where he changed into more serviceable, if less elegant, attire, layering for warmth.

"She's spoiling you already," he told himself as he slipped into jeans.

Nothing with a patch would do now; he had chosen his newest pair, still dark blue, and a soft, tan-colored chamois-cloth shirt he usually reserved for special occasions. But in a way, he supposed, this was a special occasion. His hiking boots looked fine. Besides, he wasn't going into the mountains wearing slick-soled loafers.

Next, Rick headed for the office to call Charlie. There were some instant coffee packets left, he noticed, but he decided he'd rather not, thinking of how he'd recently put his friend down for doing the same. This life hadn't been so pure, after all.

He dialed the number. "Martin, Brindle and Prine," the secretary answered. "How may I help you?"

"Charles Prine, please."

"Who may I say is calling?"

"This is Mr. Bonner."

Her tone turned immediately from brusque to dulcet. "Just one moment, Mr. Bonner. I'll put you right through."

"Hello, Mr. Bonner, sir," Charlie said when he came on the line. "At your service, sir."

"You play the perfect toady, Charlie," Rick told him.

"That's how one becomes a full partner, my friend."

"Uh-huh. Well, can it. I'd like an update, please."

There was the sound of a computer keyboard being poked into submission. "Okay. Detailed or general?"

"General will do."

"Let's see . . ." More tapping of keys. "West, I'm looking at a line roughly defined by Boise, Salt Lake City and your old hometown of Phoenix."

"How are we doing there?" Rick asked curiously.

Charlie laughed. "That's a joke, right?"

"I've been a little too busy to watch TV, Charlie."

"Oh? Santa duty?" His interest was clearly piqued.

"If you've been a very good boy, perhaps I'll explain in a moment. Now, just how well are things going?"

"All units thus far," Charlie replied simply.

Rick arched his eyebrows. "All?"

"All. Our stockings are going to be *very* full this year."

Rick sat down in the desk chair, suddenly feeling a bit light-headed. Until right this minute, he still hadn't been able to make himself believe something this good could happen to him. And to think, he owed it all to being in the right place at the right time, a silly job on a toy company loading dock. A job he'd almost been too dejected to even apply for.

"Hello?" Charlie asked. "You still there?"

"Yeah. I just got a bit dizzy. Must be the altitude."

Charlie hummed in agreement. "You should see the figures."

"That'll wait," Rick said, glancing at his watch to help himself get a grip on reality. "Where are we in the East?"

"Oh, roughly Detroit, Louisville, Atlanta. Slower going, of course. More densely populated. But plenty of saturation. Speaking of which, I suppose you've started?"

"No."

"Shouldn't you? They'll be north and south of Denver by tomorrow morning, buddy."

"I know."

"And all over the United States by that afternoon."

"I know!" Rick exclaimed. That was the trouble with waves. Once started, they were difficult, if not impossible, to stop. "I've run into some problems here."

"You don't mean that Lyon kid? I thought that was some kind of publicity stunt. Morning news said the paper that ran the story printed a full retraction."

Rick took a deep breath, then blew it out in a sigh. "I didn't see it. But it's an indication of how difficult this situation has become. There's a lot of strange stuff going on here, Charlie, and until I can sort some of it out, I don't want to risk ruining my own plans."

"Whatever you say. You're the man with the mission," Charlie said. "Just don't let it run you over while you're busy looking at something else."

"I won't."

Charlie cleared his throat. "That was a hint, pal."

"Excuse me?"

"I have been a very good boy this year, Santa. So tell me a story about why you're so distracted."

"Oh." Rick laughed, glad to ease the tension. "Let me just say that I'm wearing my best jeans, and seem to have lost my taste for coffee made with rusty tap water."

"I thought I detected just a hint of your former, less austere manner coming through," Charlie noted. "Since you haven't blindsided the Bayers yet, I guess that can only mean one thing. So tell me. Is she pretty?"

Rick leaned back and put his feet up on the desk. "If you could see the smile on my face right now, Charlie, you wouldn't have to ask. She's gorgeous. Red hair, green eyes, a curve for every occasion." He chuckled. "Absolutely adores Christmas."

"Ho, ho, ho! And Father Christmas?"

"Well, she took me home to meet her cats."

"Wow." Charlie whistled. "Serious stuff."

Rick was nodding his head thoughtfully. "I never thought I'd say it again, but yeah. It could get that way."

"I sense some unease in that statement," his friend said. "Am I to assume you haven't, shall we say, been entirely honest with this goddess yet?"

"She knows most of it, but not all," Rick admitted. "You see, she's very attached to Leo Lyon, and his ransom is a shipment of Arnies, so if she knew everything..." He trailed off, knowing Charlie would figure it out for himself.

He did. "My. That's an interesting tightrope you're about to fall off," Charlie told him candidly.

Rick could hardly deny it. "It's swaying. But I'm on my way now to check out a lead on the Lyon boy. Finding him will calm things down a lot."

"Maybe. You of all people should know that deception has a long half-life." He sighed, and his voice filled with worry. "Listen, my friend. You do what you think you have to. But I advise you to wise up. I don't even know this woman and I like her, because I can tell that in just a couple of days, she's started to undo all the damage you did to yourself in three years of wandering down blind alleys. In other words, don't screw it up."

"Believe me, I'm trying not to." Rick sighed. "Charlie, I need a favor." He quickly explained about Chelsea's name change. "Find out what happened if you can."

"Will do."

He glanced at his watch again. "I have to go now, Charlie. Thanks for everything."

"Take care."

Rick hung up, then left the office and went back to his apartment. It had occurred to him that he didn't know where he might end up tonight, so he packed a change of clothes into a blue duffel bag to take with him. He was halfway to the exit door, when he noticed it was slightly ajar. At first he felt a surge of adrenaline. But then he saw that the inner padlock was hanging on the hasp, unlocked. He'd made yet another stupid mistake.

"Three strikes and you're out," he muttered to himself.

As a precaution, he checked around the warehouse, taking particular care to make sure one large crate and its smaller companion were still in the dark, dusty corner where they'd been put several weeks ago. They were undisturbed, just as he had found them upon his arrival in Denver. Or almost.

This time he made no mistake. Grabbing a coffee can that he'd filled with floor sweepings for just this purpose, he carefully sprinkled a fine layer of dust over his footprints, obliterating them. Again, that corner of the warehouse looked as if it hadn't been used in years.

Rick then retrieved his bag from where he'd dropped it near the door and slipped out, locking the door behind him. As he rounded the corner of the warehouse, he nearly fell over the old man stretched out on the cracked and broken sidewalk.

"Hey, old-timer," Rick said, bending down and gently shaking the man's shoulder. "You can't crash here. You'll freeze."

The man stirred and looked up at Rick. Rick didn't know him, but he had seen those eyes before, in a dozen other cities in surroundings just like these. The man's voice and the words he spoke communicated the same chilling message, as well.

"So I freeze. Who cares?"

"I care," Rick replied, hauling him to his feet.

"Who do you think you are?" the old man asked with heavy, liquor-soaked sarcasm. "Santa Claus?"

Rick smiled. "As a matter of fact, I do. Now come on," he told him, all but pulling him along. "There's a mission down there around the corner."

"They don't let you in if you're soused."

"No, but they'll give you a blanket and let you sleep it off in the lobby." He kept tugging the old guy along. "If you wander back out, that's your business. But I'm not leaving you out here on the street."

"It doesn't pay to be nice to bums, sonny boy. Most of us would stab you in the back for a couple of bucks."

Rick looked at him. "I know. I've even got the scars to prove it. But for some reason, I keep doing it, anyway."

Chapter Sixteen

Shannon had everything pretty much under control by the time Rick came to get her. Ironically, he found her in about the same spot as he had the day before yesterday, in the narrow passageway that led to the storeroom. But this time, when she saw him, she stepped into his arms and gave him a kiss.

"Mmm," Rick hummed appreciatively. "You taste like chocolate."

"I keep my stash back here," she explained. "Want some?"

"Just another taste." He kissed her again. "About ready to go?" he asked.

"About."

She would always like the way he looked in a suit, but approved of his clothing change for today's journey into the mountains. Her own attire was more casual, as well, consisting of a pair of taupe wool trousers, a heavy cable-knit turtleneck sweater the color of roasted chestnuts and black suede boots to match her usual long black winter coat.

However, even though he'd left his duffel bag in her car, that old peacoat of his still gave him something of a vaga-bond air. She approached the matter tactfully.

"It's going to be cold up there today," she said.

Rick grinned. "Don't like the coat, huh?"

"It's a good look," she replied. "For a lumberjack. Or maybe a gonzo snowboarder."

"Ah." He took it off and hung it in the locker he'd been assigned in which to keep his Santa suit. "Lead me to Carl. I have only one request. Nothing in a color that has to have a cutesy name. Plain blue, maybe. Or even forest green. But absolutely no watercress."

Shannon laughed. "Forest green it shall be. And don't worry. Carl doesn't dabble in sportswear. That's Mike Alard's department."

"Mike." Rick nodded his approval as he followed her out of the passageway. "Now there's a trustworthy-sounding name."

He was, and Rick ended up with a very nice coat in deep forest green, with lots of pockets and a serviceable mid-thigh length. He hadn't been too sure about the zip-in lining, with its southwestern saddle-blanket look, but the coat was so warm, he decided he could stand being a little fashionable.

The task did take a while, though. The store was crowded to capacity. As they made their way to the nearest exit, Rick was glad to see that Hans was being relieved at Santa duty on a regular basis. Shannon informed him that a group of other employees had gotten together to share the task. It was extra pay, but they seemed to actually enjoy the change of pace.

Finally, they emerged into the fresh, cold, late-morning air, made a beeline for Shannon's car and then set their sights on the not-too-distant mountains. Traffic wasn't bad, especially once they got into the flow on the Interstate 70 bound for the ski area. Shannon kept pace with the other cars and didn't pay too much attention to the speedomeer. If she went much slower, they'd run right over her, even n the far right lane.

"Did you corner Pop?" Rick asked.

"You can get his attention if you stand right in front of he TV in his office. I swear, the way the media is behaving, it's as if somebody started an all-Arnie channel."

"That was the general idea," Rick informed her. "I don't know if you noticed, but the ads stopped yesterday when he first units hit the stores. We're counting on the media o do that job for us from now on."

Shannon nodded appreciatively. "Pretty cagey. Which, by the way, sums up Pop's behavior when I asked him about talking to the kidnappers. He said they called and were worried, so he had to tell them something."

"Sounds straightforward to me."

"It was the way he said it." She shook her head. "I don't know. You had to be there, I guess. I just get the sneaking suspicion he's got something up his sleeve."

"At his age and level of experience, I'd be amazed if he *didn't* have something up his sleeve," Rick observed. "And 'd be willing to bet he'll accomplish whatever it is, too, with or without us. So there's no use stewing over it."

"I suppose not. Anything new at the warehouse?" she asked, taking a quick glance at him to gauge his reaction. There was none, or at least nothing she could decipher.

"Some old guy had passed out on my doorstep. I took him to a shelter. Other than that, it was remarkably quiet down there," Rick replied.

Shannon winced as a brand-new Porsche went by her as if she were standing still. It zipped in and out of the traffic ahead of her and was quickly gone from view.

"Yipes! Did you see that?"

"Barely. More money than brains," Rick said in disgust.

She nodded. "These mountains are full of people like that. It's a playground for the rich and famous." They drove on in silence for a moment. "What would you do if you had a lot of money?" Shannon asked.

Rick shrugged his shoulders. "'A lot' is such a relative term. But I don't think I could in good conscience see myself spending it on a two-hundred-and-fifty-thousand-dollar automobile, in any case. I suppose it all depends on one's tastes. Like those kids I told Leo about, I'm pretty thrilled with this new coat."

"Come on," Shannon urged. "Don't be such a Scrooge. It's Christmas. Make a wish."

"Oh, all right," Rick returned, laughing at her childlike attitude. "I guess it would be nice to have a house again. I miss puttering. I was a world-class putterer."

Shannon laughed now, too. "Somehow, I do see you in that role," she told him. "Mowing the lawn, fixing the gutters. Maybe even trimming trees into topiary shapes."

"Actually, I did that," Rick admitted sheepishly.

"Cute! What animals?"

"Just one. A horse. Chelsea is wild about horses."

Shannon could sense him going into a funk, and so she quickly told him her own secret desire. "I want a house, too. A big one." She glanced at him and arched her eyebrows. "So I could have more cats."

Rick smiled, then laughed again, well aware of what she was up to. "Oh, yes. That's just what you need."

"I do! Two is just barely enough."

"It is for a queen-size bed."

"That's why I need the big house. I don't believe in letting them outside, so I'd have to bring the outside in." She pursed her lips, thinking, because this was, in fact, a dream of hers. "I'd build it with an atrium, the way Lyon's has, with a big garden, with trees and green plants and topiary hedges.''

Rick was looking at her curiously now, studying the way her expression had gone soft and introspective. "And cats, of course.''

"Naturally.''

"Any room for children in there?'' he asked.

To his utter confusion, her dreamy look disappeared as if yanked behind a blank curtain. "Sure.'' She fished around in the pocket of her coat and handed him a piece of paper. "Help me look for this cutoff, will you? I don't get up this way very often.''

Rick frowned. Diversionary tactic? Or was she really concerned about missing her turn? Either way, her mood had clearly shifted and he didn't think she would be as easily turned around as he had been.

"Shannon—''

"It's so beautiful up here in the winter,'' she exclaimed, interrupting him. "I love the way the snow sits on the pines, like a layer of white frosting. And in the shadows, everything looks so cold and forbidding. It makes you want to curl up in front of a roaring fire.''

Rick knew when to quit. And she was smiling again. "Just the two of us. Maybe a storm whipping up outside. Mmm, snowed in.''

Shannon reached out and touched his thigh briefly, before returning her hand to the wheel. "That does sound nice, but don't tempt fate.'' She nodded at a bank of rather ominous-looking clouds that was moving in from the south. "We need to find Leo first.''

They drove on toward that goal, ever deeper into the rocky, snow-covered mountains. Finding the cutoff was the easy part, as it turned out. From there, they wound their way along a series of narrow, snow-packed dirt roads, some

without names or markers, and with drifts along both sides
that were higher than the car in some points. But her informant had done a good job with his directions.

"This is supposed to be a cul-de-sac," Rick told her. "I
propose we find a wide spot in the road and park, then
continue on foot. If this is where they're keeping Leo, it
doesn't seem wise to drive right up on them, no matter how
nice the kid says they are. They might not be so nice to us."

"Good point."

Shannon looked for and found just such a spot, nosing
her car out of the way of whatever traffic might come
along. For the last fifteen minutes or so, however, they
hadn't seen anyone at all. When they stepped out of the car,
that feeling of total isolation increased. Except for the slight
whisper of the wind in the pine trees, it was silent.

They started walking, hand in gloved hand, keeping to
the cleared roadway. There wasn't much choice. Everything else was covered by several feet of snow. In the low
area where they'd parked, it was mounded over their heads,
but as they climbed the slight rise that lay ahead of them,
the wind had swept the snow away, and they could see a
fantastic mountain vista stretching before them.

There was more than one house down this lane, as evidenced by the way the snow beneath their feet had been
packed down by vehicular traffic. Then, too, they caught
an occasional whiff of wood smoke on the air. But the
dwellings themselves had been built to take advantage of
the trees and other natural cover, to ensure the occupants'
privacy. It was hard to get a clear view of the house.

At the top of the rise, however, if they stood in just the
right spot, they could see a couple of the homes through the
trees.

"That's it," Shannon said, pointing with her gloved hand. "The one on the left down there in the middle of that swale."

"How can you tell?"

"He said it had a lot of south-facing windows, and a great big stone chimney." She shrugged. "Anyway, let's go check it out."

Rick nodded and started walking. "Better than standing here looking conspicuous."

With that in mind, they sought the cover of the trees themselves by staying in the shadows toward the side of the road, especially as they neared the house. And the closer they got, the more it seemed to fit Shannon's description. Of course, the real clincher was the white Mercedes limo parked in front with the personalized plates.

"Bayer's," Shannon read. "Cute."

Rick just scowled. They were standing behind a very thick ponderosa pine that marked one corner of the driveway leading down to the redwood-and-stone structure. There was no movement outside, and they were in the wrong position to look into any of the large windows.

Shannon was getting impatient, and cold, now that they had stopped moving. "What should we do?" she asked.

"This is your plan," Rick said. "Not mine."

"Your assistance would be greatly appreciated."

He smiled at her. "I'm no spy. But it seems logical that we get closer. Let's head for the pile of firewood near that shed."

They did so, moving quickly but carefully from tree to tree at the edge of the driveway. Finally, they came to a large open section that stood between them and the woodpile, where they could take cover.

"You go first," Rick said, keeping his voice low. He held out his gloved hand, thumb up and one finger pointing like the barrel of a gun. "I'll cover you."

"That's not funny." Shannon whispered back. But she was grinning. This all did seem like one of Leo's fantasies. She just hoped he was in there to participate. "Won't they see?"

"Only if they're looking."

"That really *isn't* funny."

Rick indicated the house with a nod of his head. "I mean, looking right at us. There's only one window on this side, and I don't see anybody at it." He frowned. "In fact, it's awfully quiet around here, period. Not even any smoke from the chimney."

"I noticed that, too." They would have to get closer, maybe right up to that window. She didn't like the prospect, but it was better than standing there freezing. At least the woodpile was partially in the sunlight. "Okay, here goes."

Shannon skittered across the driveway. When she got to the portion of it that was in the sun, however, she discovered it was icy and very slick. She skidded and nearly fell, but caught herself just in time. From there on, she took careful, deliberate steps.

Until the front door opened. Shannon's eyes went wide, and she looked back at Rick, who was about ten feet behind her and motioning her forward. She turned back around just in time to see a raven-haired man in a dark suit emerge from the house. Throwing caution to the wind, she scrambled for the woodpile and ducked behind it. In passing, she bumped one corner. Snow cascaded down the back of her neck. A yelp of surprise escaped her, but Rick muffled it by clamping his gloved hand over her mouth.

Still, the man paused on the wooden steps leading down to the driveway and looked in their direction. Apparently seeing nothing, he continued toward the Mercedes. He opened the trunk, tossed the two overnight bags he was carrying into it and then slammed it shut. Judging by his quick, economical movements, he was in a hurry. After starting the engine, he returned to the house, where a woman met him on the steps.

It didn't surprise Shannon or Rick all that much to see Angela there. After Shannon had confronted her yesterday, Angela was bound to come check on things. But what happened next certainly surprised them both. The pair on the steps embraced and exchanged a deep, passionate kiss. When they came up for air, they spoke to each other softly. Shannon and Rick could just make out what they were saying.

"That old sot better have found something," Angela told him. "I'd prefer to stay in our nice warm bed."

"He was supposed to call." The raven-haired man pressed himself against her. "We must check. There will be other beds."

They kissed again, briefly, then he released her. Angela turned and locked the door. "Lord! How I hate the thought of going back to the city and all that whining and crying," she said as they walked toward the softly purring automobile.

"I will enjoy seeing Nathan cry when he realizes we have taken the profits for ourselves."

He held the rear passenger door open for her. "So will I," Angela said, touching his cheek. Then she lowered her hand, and her manner changed. "We should hurry, Emilio."

"Yes, Mrs. Bayer," the man said, his own manner changed.

He helped her into the car, closed the door, then walked around to the driver's side and got in. The pair hiding behind the woodpile were just close enough to see him put on a black chauffeur's cap before he backed the car out of the driveway. Once onto the road, the Mercedes reversed directions and sped away. It was quickly out of sight.

Shannon and Rick waited a moment to make sure the car didn't come back, then turned and looked at each other.

"That was interesting," Shannon remarked softly, aware of the continuing need to be quiet.

"Very," Rick returned, his voice also low.

"What now?"

He pointed to the lone window on this side of the building. "I'm going over to take a look. Stay here."

"I don't have a problem with that."

The snow had drifted against the side of the house, and was quite deep in some spots. Shannon was more than willing to let Rick wade through it. He did so, and carefully took a peek through the window. Apparently satisfied he hadn't been spotted, he cupped his hands to block the glare and had a good look. Then he retraced the path he'd made for himself and squatted next to Shannon.

"Well?" she prompted, seeing his puzzled frown.

"Open floor plan," he said, a bit out of breath. The air was thin and cold at this elevation, and wading through the crusted snow had been more work than he'd thought. "I could see most of the house. Nobody in there."

"Nobody?"

Rick shook his head. As he spoke, little puffs of vapor marked his words. "Not that I could see. No lights. And no fire in the fireplace, either."

Shannon cursed under her breath. "I don't understand."

"Just telling you what I saw."

"I want to look for myself."

"Knock yourself out," he told her, wiping the snow off his pants and boots before it could melt and freeze him. His breathing was still a bit labored. "I know I nearly did."

Shannon appreciated it, too. By using his footsteps to guide her through the snow, she didn't have to work as hard. But when she returned she was still a little winded. Like Rick, she dusted herself off before the melting snow could soak her pants.

"And?" Rick asked.

"Same thing." She looked at him, a determined set to her jaw. "I want to get in there. Will you help me?"

Rick's shoulders sagged and he groaned softly. "I was afraid you were going to ask that."

"I'll do it alone if I have to."

"I know you will," he said, resigned to his fate. "Okay, why not? I've already been in jail once this week. But let's try the easy way first, all right?"

"What's that?"

"Check around the front and back doors for a key."

"Oh." Shannon grinned. "I knew that."

Unfortunately, even that wasn't going to be easy. Getting to the front door was a snap, but they could find no key there. And since no one had bothered to clear a path for them to the back door, they had to make their own. Luckily, they did find a shovel. Rick winded himself again using it, though.

"Man! And I thought I was in pretty good shape."

Shannon patted him on the back. "You are in good shape." She smiled and arched her eyebrows. "In fact, I'd even call it great. But you are at nearly ten thousand feet. That takes some getting used to, especially for a flatlander like you."

"Guilty as charged." He waved her on. "You look for the key. I'll watch."

The back of the house was dominated by a huge redwood deck. She looked all over, but had no luck. "Any ideas?"

Rick nodded, and stepped up to the back door. "This place belongs to the Bayers, right?"

"It's a time-share. Since they can obviously use it as they see fit, even over the Christmas holiday, I'd say they probably don't share it very much," Shannon replied. "Why?"

"Just securing the proper motivation," Rick said.

He nudged the door experimentally with his shoulder. Then he nodded, stepped back a pace and gave it a good kick with his hiking boot at door-handle level near the lock. The jamb splintered and the door swung open.

"Enjoy that?" Shannon asked.

"Yes, I did, actually."

She smiled and led the way into the house. "Me, too."

The place smelled of wood smoke, Angela's expensive perfume and another, citrus scent they assumed belonged to the raven-haired chauffeur, Emilio. Other than an unmade bed, a couple of empty champagne bottles and the remains of a few microwave meals, however, those were the only lingering signs of anyone's presence. Leo wasn't there. What's more, it didn't seem as if he had ever been there.

"This isn't the place he described to me," Shannon said.

"No," Rick agreed. "We should have known that right away, really. There isn't a satellite dish outside."

Shannon cursed quietly. "Now what? He's up in these mountains somewhere, I just know it. But we can't very well go door to door asking for him."

"Not even those houses with a dish." Rick paused, a thoughtful look on his face. "But it would be a start."

"Have you lost your mind? That's still thousands!" she exclaimed. "Probably more."

Rick crossed the huge living room to where she stood looking out the windows. The threatening clouds of earlier still hovered to the south. Though the view was breathtaking, however, she obviously saw no beauty in it at the moment.

"Embrace the theory if not the specific application, Shannon," he told her.

"Huh?"

"The place we're looking for has a satellite dish. That's one descriptor," Rick explained. "There have to be more."

"Yes, of course." For a moment, hope shone in her eyes. But it quickly flickered. "The other things he told me about the place are inside the house, though."

"Still, you never know." Rick headed for the kitchen, where he remembered seeing some paper and a pen. "We'll go through your conversations with him and make a list, see what we can come up with. But first, I want you to call Pop."

"Pop?" she asked. "Why? I'd hardly call this progress."

"No, but he can help us make some. Didn't you say Leo called you on his cellular, the one Pop gave him?"

Shannon nodded. "Yes. At least the first time. I'm not sure about the second. But come to think of it, he did say something last time about Joey's wanting him to hang up so the spies wouldn't trace it. I don't think you can trace cellular calls, can you?"

"I'm not that up on the technology myself, but I'm sure it's possible with the right equipment," Rick replied. "Sort of like triangulating a radio signal. It probably takes a while, though, and I doubt they'd let Leo talk that long."

"I'm sure of it."

He shrugged. "But that's a little out of our reach at the moment, in any case."

"Then what can Pop do?"

"As the cellular's owner, he can request a list of calls made from that phone."

"He called me, Rick," she said, thinking that perhaps the altitude was getting to him again. "I don't think my number is going to do us any good, do you?"

Rick chuckled. "Don't worry, I'm not addled. You see, a cellular works by passing a signal from the phone to different repeater stations, or cells, hence the name. As it does so, it leaves its signature, so to speak. That's how they know who to bill and how much."

"Are you saying there's a record of what cell Leo was using when he called me?"

"If I'm not mistaken, yes. But don't get your hopes up too high," Rick cautioned. "A cell can cover a pretty large area. It's just another descriptor we can use to narrow down our search to a reasonable size."

Shannon was barely listening. She was already headed for the phone by the fireplace. Angela must have used it, because her scent was all over the receiver—which had been unplugged. Obviously, she hadn't wanted to be disturbed in her tryst.

"What if Angela called the place where they're really holding Leo from this phone?" she asked while dialing Lyon's number. "Wouldn't that help?"

"Yes, but I don't think we could get access to those records. We can make note of this number, though, and see if it shows up on Leo's list. It won't help us find him, but it could establish a paper trail to help us nail the Bayers later."

Shannon finally got through to Pop, who promised to get back to them with the requested information as soon as he could. They gave him the number to the lodge, figuring it was safe enough to stay there for an hour or so. She had scarcely hung up the phone, when it rang. Thinking it was Pop calling back to make sure of something, Shannon picked it up.

"Pop?" she asked.

There was a pause. "Angela?"

Rick could tell something was wrong by the startled look on Shannon's face. He stepped over to her and put his ear next to the receiver, as well.

"Angela?" the man on the other end of the line repeated. "Angela, baby? Is that you?"

"It's Nathan Bayer," Rick whispered. "Just hang up."

Shannon held up her hand, indicating that she had an idea. She couldn't fool him long, but maybe long enough to learn something interesting. Maybe even Leo's whereabouts.

"Angela?"

"Hmm?" she hummed.

"What the heck is going on up there?" Nathan bellowed. "I've been calling steady since six this morning!"

"Ooo," Shannon cooed sympathetically.

"What? Were the phones out again?"

Shannon hummed another affirmative. So far, so good. Still, sooner or later, he was bound to ask something she couldn't hum an answer to.

"Yeah, I thought that might be it. I tell you, I am going to raise some kind of stink with that stupid time-share association," Nathan groused. "I don't suppose you've seen hide nor hair of those two idiots, either, huh?"

Shannon raised her eyebrows and looked at Rick, who was still listening in. He shrugged. Since it seemed almost a rhetorical question, Shannon just waited to see if he would go on without her risking any more vocalizations.

It worked. No wonder Angela felt the need to go outside her marriage for interaction with another man.

"Me, neither," Nathan continued. "I called all their old haunts, talked to all their cronies. They have just freaking disappeared, and taken the kid with them. But I'll find 'em. And when I do, I'm going to fry their livers for breakfast."

Shannon covered the receiver with her hand. "They don't even know where Leo is. Oh, Rick. I'm really worried now."

He put his arm around her. "The same guys have him, Shannon. Remember that. And I'm not so sure it's a bad thing that Nathan doesn't know where they've taken him."

"But Angela might," Shannon said. "The chauffeur said something about taking the profits for themselves."

Rick frowned. He couldn't argue with that. "You're right."

"What are we going to do?"

"The only thing we can do. Make that list and wait for Pop to call," Rick replied. "Which means getting that turkey off the phone."

They both listened again. Nathan was still whining and complaining, apparently not needing any sort of response at all anymore. Shannon shook her head in disbelief.

"This guy deserves a wife like Angela."

Rick grinned. "What was that chauffeur's name?"

"Um, Emilio, I think."

"That's it. Think you can say it with more feeling?"

Shannon was grinning now, too. "Definitely. I've had a lot of practice of late."

She cleared her throat and then uncovered the receiver, lifting it to her mouth. When Nathan paused to take a breath, she let out a deep sigh. Then she moaned.

"Angela?" Nathan asked. "You okay?"

"Oh, yes!"

"What's going on? Angela! Have you got a real man up there with you?"

"Oh, Emilio!" Shannon moaned again, as if on the verge of ecstasy. "Yes! Oh, yes! Oh, yes!" she exclaimed breathlessly. And then, with a wicked grin, she hung up on him.

Chapter Seventeen

"Persistent, isn't he?" Rick observed.

The phone had been ringing since Shannon had hung up the receiver. There was little doubt about who it was, and it had been funny for a minute or two. But now, it was about to drive her crazy.

"I think I'd better call Pop and tell him we'll check in with him every fifteen minutes or so," she said. "And then unplug this thing so we can work on our list in peace."

"Excellent idea," Rick agreed.

When that was accomplished, Shannon sat down to think of those clues Leo had inadvertently dropped during their two conversations. Unfortunately, there were very few, and the process only depressed her.

"Keep thinking," Rick prompted.

Shannon scowled at him. "Of what possible use is it to know that the house we're looking for has a white rug with blueberry syrup stains on it?" she asked irritably.

"None," Rick admitted. "Unless we can narrow it down in some other way. Then it might come in very handy." He sprang to his feet from the couch and pretended to be peeking in a window. "Yes, this is it! There are the stains!"

She had to chuckle at his antics, which was exactly the effect he had had in mind, she knew. "You're quite a guy, you know that?"

He shrugged and sat down beside her again. "If you say so. In fact, you can say it again if you like. My ego still has a couple of years of being kicked around to recover from."

"How about if I show you, instead?" Shannon leaned over and kissed him soundly on the lips. "Thanks for trying to cheer me up. This list certainly isn't doing that."

"What else have you got?"

She made a face. "Not much. The first time he called, on the cellular, he said the real phones were out."

"That's right. We had that storm. It wasn't too bad in Denver, but they must have gotten hit pretty hard up here, judging by the new snow out there." Rick patted her on the leg. "See? That pretty much confirms your intuition that he's up in these mountains somewhere."

"Yeah," Shannon groused. "That's just great."

"We might also be able to ask the phone company what areas were affected by the outage."

Her mood lifted a bit. "You're right."

"What else?"

"That's it, except for the stuff I already told you about, like the names Joey and Irv that may or may not be aliases," Shannon replied. "Oh, and lots of electronic gear, evidently. The latest in video games and equipment. And Leo did say the rug with the stains was in the entertainment room."

"Well, that sounds to me as if we can rule out run-down shacks and cabins. Nice things usually have a nice package, if you know what I mean."

"Some of the ritziest ski areas in the nation are within two hundred miles of here, Rick," Shannon said. "There are a lot of nice packages around."

Rick leaned over to look at her list, in case she was overlooking something. "There's a pool?" he asked, pointing to the last item on her short list.

"In the basement."

"Really?" Rick arched his eyebrows. "Now we might be getting somewhere."

"Oh, I don't think so," Shannon said doubtfully. "What with the fitness craze, a swimming pool probably isn't all that uncommon. Not around these parts, anyway. More money than brains, remember."

Rick seemed almost affronted. "Actually, pools are a very wise investment," he informed her.

"Sorry. I forgot you used to make your living selling them. But that means you should know. They're pretty common, aren't they?" she asked.

"Pools in general are, yes. I'm not that familiar with the trends in this area," he replied. "But a pool in a basement? That sounds specialized. Did he describe it?"

Shannon thought for a moment. "He said it was a lap pool, I think."

"Oh." That dampened Rick's enthusiasm a little. "That could mean almost anything, but a real common type is an aboveground model with a heavy vinyl liner. Any reasonably adept person can order one of those and install it himself."

"Sorry," Shannon said, her own mood faltering again. "But I'm pretty sure that's what he said. I was a bit distracted when he called, remember?"

Rick had to grin. "I was, too."

"I'll see if I can remember anything else while I help us to some coffee, courtesy of the Bayers."

"They owe us that and then some, I'd say," Rick agreed. "While you do that, I think I'll go get the car and bring it back here. From the look of that sky, if I don't do it now, we'll be doing it in the snow."

"Then by all means, do it now," Shannon agreed.

She had the coffee ready when he got back. Rick needed it, too. Although it wasn't snowing yet, it probably would be soon, and the wind had picked up considerably.

Shannon also had more information for him. "I called Pop while you were gone," she said, handing him a slip of paper along with the steaming mug of coffee. "You were right. The record on Leo's phone shows he called from a cell in this area, which is big. But it does narrow things down some, I suppose."

Rick studied the paper, on which she had written the rough boundaries Pop had gotten from the cellular phone company, in the form of street names and county lines. Except for the major highways, none of it made much sense to either of them. A few minutes with a map would take care of that, though, and they had one in the car.

Rick went to get it, and they spread it out on the kitchen table. Shannon started outlining the area with a marker she'd found in a drawer.

"Remember anything else about the pool?" Rick asked.

Shannon nodded. "As much as I'm ever going to, I think. Leo said there was a special kind of pool in the basement made for swimming laps while you stay in one place." She finished marking the map and looked up at him. "Help any?"

Rick's eyes were open wide. "For swimming while you stay in one place?" he asked.

"Uh-huh."

"You're sure he said that?"

"Positive. Why? Is it really that special?"

"Very," Rick informed her. "Flumes they call them, with water jets that form a moving stream of water you can actually swim in, as if you were swimming against a current. Olympic training centers have them. There are a couple of home models available, though.'' He raised his eyebrows. "And let me tell you, they are not cheap. I think we've found our key descriptor."

Shannon wasn't so sure, but his excitement was infectious. "But how are you going to find out who has one?"

"I'm going to ask," Rick replied, already heading for the living room. "Grab those Denver Yellow Pages for me, please."

She handed him the volume he needed. He opened it to swimming pool suppliers, looked for the largest one and made a call. They referred him to someone else, who passed him on to yet another person. Seeing that it might take a while, Shannon went to raid the Bayers' larder.

Microwave meals were the catch of the day. Shannon found hers quite tasty, perhaps because it was nearly three in the afternoon and she was famished. Rick ate his while still on the phone, and might not have even tasted it. But his hard work paid off at last.

"I have good news and bad news," he announced.

"I always prefer bad first," Shannon told him. "Makes the good seem even better."

"Okay. The bad news is, you were right. There really are a lot of rich people around here. Then, too, the price on these pools has come down a bit since I was in the business. I thought we'd be looking at one or two of them, tops. But the distributor for one major brand claims sales of over a hundred statewide."

"Oh, no!" Shannon exclaimed. "You'd better tell me the good news quick."

"Let's take a look at the map again."

They went back into the kitchen and sat at the table. Rick picked up the marker and checked his notes.

"There are a lot of installers in the state," Rick began. "But naturally, a lot of them operate out of Denver, since it's the biggest city. I asked around and found the ones who do these kinds of pools, and then narrowed those down to the ones who do a lot of work in the mountains. That reduced it from one hundred to twenty."

"Wow."

Rick nodded in agreement. "A lot of well-to-do indoor swimmers up here. Anyway, I then narrowed down the possibles even further by asking specifically about this area." Rick indicated the zone Shannon had marked earlier. "Considering that Vail is in this cell, I suppose it's not surprising that we're still left with ten out of that twenty."

Shannon was starting to feel much better. "Ten houses," she said. "That's not so bad."

"It gets even better. While you were slaving over a hot microwave, I saw what direction this was headed and decided to try chasing down the other clue you remembered. About the phones being out during that storm?"

"And?"

Rick drew two parallel lines down the middle of the cell. "This area in the middle, more or less along the interstate, was the one affected."

"How many pools?" Shannon asked excitedly.

"Three." He held up that many fingers. "They probably all have satellite dishes, and they might even have white rugs with purple stains in their entertainment rooms. But it's a pretty good bet that only one of them has a Lyon."

Shannon was on her feet, gathering their things. "Then let's go find that one!"

"I did save a small piece of bad news for the end, I'm afraid," Rick admitted. "But only because I just noticed it."

"What's that?"

Rick pointed out the window. "We'll have to find that one house in what could become a full-blown blizzard."

Chapter Eighteen

As Shannon and Rick pulled away from the Bayer lodge, they could see that the clouds were moving in from the south with a vengeance now, boiling over the nearby peaks in a dark gray sheet. They had only gone about a mile, when the snow started coming down in big, fat flakes.

Shannon was at the wheel, and Rick wasn't making any macho noises about wanting to take over, either. Although he had been in some dandy snowstorms during his wanderings, especially back East, it had been years since he'd driven a car in one. Still, he couldn't help fretting a bit.

"Is this car pretty good in the snow?" Rick asked.

"Decent. It's a front-wheel drive." She glanced at him and smiled. "I've never gotten stuck, if that's what you're worrying about."

"I'm not worried," Rick objected.

"Yes, you are. But you can stop. It's going to take a lot more than a few snowflakes to keep me from finding Leo."

"That's sort of what has me worried," Rick muttered.

Nevertheless, Shannon decided to start at the westernmost end of the corridor Rick had marked on the map, since the one house they needed to check there was also the one deepest into the mountains. She wanted to get there and back as soon as possible, because of a pass they had to go through that the State Patrol might close, should the storm become severe.

Once back on the interstate, they both relaxed. Snow was falling, but the roads were still clear. It only took about half an hour to reach their destination. Shannon's map didn't give a street-by-street breakdown for the little ski-resort towns, so they had to stop at a gas station and ask directions. At the same time, they bought a better map. Like the gas they didn't buy, it was enormously overpriced, but necessary.

The house at the address Rick had tracked down wasn't at all what they expected. Small and unassuming, even a bit tacky-looking among its ultramodern stone and glass neighbors, it was a simple frame home with weathered cedar siding and a single-car detached garage.

There was a lot of traffic moving up and down the road in front of it, mostly pricey four-wheel drives with fully loaded ski racks on top. They had no skis, but the pair of amateur sleuths didn't think they'd look too suspicious if they stopped and pretended to check their map, while covertly scanning the area for signs of kidnappers.

"Satellite dish," Rick said, looking at the side of the structure. "And I guess there's enough space for an entertainment room in there somewhere."

"Hard to imagine any white carpeting inside, though," Shannon said doubtfully.

"True."

"What do you think we should do?"

Rick sighed, then reached for the door handle. "I'm going to go ask to see their pool."

"You're kidding, right?"

"Nope."

With that, Rick climbed out of the car and dashed through the steadily falling snow right up to the front door of the house. Shannon watched, incredulous, as the man who came to the door ushered Rick in almost immediately.

Ten minutes went by. Shannon was starting to have a horrible vision of Rick floating facedown in the pool he had so blithely gone to see. But he suddenly emerged from the house, waved to his host and dashed back across the street to Shannon. Though he did the best he could to brush himself off, his shoulders were still covered in a mantle of white.

"Whew!" he exclaimed. "Really coming down out there."

Shannon sniffed. "Surely that's not beer I smell on your breath? Not when I was out here worrying about your having fallen prey to murderous kidnappers."

"Sorry," Rick apologized sheepishly. "But Bill brews his own, and refused to let me go unless I tasted some."

"Bill?"

"The guy in the house. Bill Enright. He's a retired heating contractor. A real nice guy," Rick informed her. "But he does like his beer. Got the pool so he could swim off the excess calories year-round." He leaned closer with a conspiratorial air. "Bill's pension fund has done very well."

Shannon chuckled. "You're doing very well, that's for sure. Must have been one incredible beer."

"He did tell me the combination of it and the altitude might have a considerable kick," Rick said.

"Uh-huh." Shannon pulled away from the house. "I think I'd better find you some coffee. I need you clear-headed."

"I'm fine," he insisted.

"You did remember what you went in there to do, right?"

Rick scowled at her. "I know you, Ms. O'Shaughnessy. You're just sore because I didn't bring you one. And yes, I checked. No white carpeting, no kidnappers and no Leo. He did have a parakeet, though."

"Do tell."

"Its name was Ouch."

Shannon sighed. "I know I'm going to hate myself for asking this, but why did he name his parakeet Ouch?"

"I asked the same thing. Bill told me to put my finger in its cage and I'd find out." He chuckled. "Bill's a riot."

Shannon got them both some coffee at a convenience store and then headed back east on the interstate. The snowfall was increasing, and it took them twice as long to get back to the pass. By then, Rick had sobered considerably. "My finger hurts," he told her.

"What did you expect from a bird named Ouch?"

"My head hurts a little, too. I suppose I should have known better than to imbibe a beer called Malted Mayhem, as well, shouldn't I?"

"It was probably unwise," Shannon agreed. "But then, so is driving in this weather."

"We could go back and stay with Bill. He did offer."

"Hah! I'll take my chances."

She studied the winding road of the mountain pass up ahead of her. Snow had long since started sticking to the pavement at this altitude, and the conditions were far from ideal. If a sand truck hadn't been about four vehicles ahead of her, her car wouldn't have made it. As it was, they skewed sideways a couple of times on the long uphill climb, giving both of them a thrill they could have lived without.

At last they reached the crest of the pass and started downward. Now, the biggest problem wasn't getting stuck, it was sliding off into the deep ravines on either side of the snowpacked road. By taking it nice and easy, Shannon managed just fine. But caution did have a price. When they again passed the cutoff for the Bayers' lodge, Shannon glanced at the dashboard clock. The return trip had taken them three times as long, and it was now full dark.

"Where's the next house?" she asked.

"Well, the crossroad is about ten miles ahead. And I'd say it's about another five from there." Rick peered out the windshield at the snow. It was falling so heavily now that it was a virtual wall of white in front of them, reflecting the headlights back and creating an annoying glare. "I don't think we're going to make it."

"I'm doing fine," Shannon objected.

"Sure you are. Now. But you have a string of cars ahead of you blazing the trail," Rick said. It amazed him how heavy the traffic was, considering the strength of the storm. "It looks like those who have to are getting out of the mountains while the getting is good. We should join them."

"No!" Shannon was adamant. "I don't know what Angela and her paramour are up to, but if it involves Leo, I want him safely away from it."

Rick touched her shoulder. "We won't do him much good stuck in a ditch and buried under three feet of snow, either."

"That won't happen."

It was already two inches thick on the hood of the car, and they were moving. He could only imagine what the actual accumulation was. But Rick could tell by the look on her face that arguing with her was useless. And he wasn't accustomed to weather like this. Maybe Shannon did know what she was doing.

When they reached their turnoff and plunged into the blackness on their own, however, it became apparent just how much of an aid to navigation the headlights of other cars and an occasional streetlamp had been. Though it seemed impossible, the snow started falling even harder.

Shannon had the wipers on high, and still couldn't keep the windshield clear.

They slowed down to a crawl, scarcely able to see one car length in front of them. The blowing, drifting snow made the road ahead seem little more than a footpath through the dense pine trees. It also had a hypnotizing effect as it danced in the glare of the headlights. Shannon felt as if the entire car was moving from side to side.

"Uh, Rick?" she said at last.

He was sitting in the passenger seat, arms crossed over his chest, a dour expression on his face. "Yes, Shannon?"

"I think we're in trouble."

"Really? But you said that wouldn't happen."

She sighed. He had every reason to be mad, and he clearly was. "I was mistaken."

"Thank you for sharing that with me."

"Any suggestions?"

"I assume you mean one other than the obvious, considering the approaching religious holiday."

"Yes. I started doing that a few minutes ago," she said.

"Me, too."

Rick glanced at the speedometer. They were barely going five miles an hour, and that was pushing the envelope. Except for the pitiful, snow-clogged glow from their headlights, they were immersed in inky darkness. As a final insult, it seemed the heater was having trouble keeping the windows from fogging up. He reached over and, using his glove, cleared a spot for Shannon to see out of.

"Thank you," Shannon said. "But I'm driving mostly by instinct, anyway."

"I thought as much. You'd better just stop right here. I'll get out and scout ahead to see if I can find a place to pull off, and we'll just wait for a snowplow to come along."

Shannon did as he asked. It was a relief to be able to stop concentrating on the road. There was a spot in the middle of her shoulder blades that felt as if someone had stuck a red-hot poker in her and left it there.

Rick disappeared the instant he passed the front fender. An occasional gust of wind shook the car, as a reminder of what he must be going through outside. Shannon nearly jumped out of her skin when he knocked on her window.

She rolled it down. Rick was a mass of white from head to toe. "I'm going to walk in front of you. Just follow slowly and try not to run me down, okay?"

"Okay."

Shannon rolled her window up again as quickly as she could, and even then the side of her head was plastered with blowing snow. Rick stood in front of the car and motioned for her to start moving. She eased forward. They crept along that way for what seemed like forever, but was actually only a few minutes and probably less than a hundred yards. At last, Rick stopped and held up his hands. Shannon stopped, too.

He didn't even bother trying to shake himself off until he got back into the car. It was a lucky thing that the coat he'd chosen had a hood, or his whole head would be a frozen snowball. As it was, his nose and cheeks were pink from being scoured by the blowing snow.

"Go ahead and turn your headlights off," Rick told her.

"But how will anyone see us?"

"We don't want them to."

Shannon helped brush the snow off him, and then held her warm hands against his face. He moaned and nodded.

"That feels good."

"We need to thaw you out." She chuckled. "It sounded like you said we don't want anyone to see us."

"That *is* what I said," Rick said.

He held his hands over his ears for a moment to warm them, too. Before, the car heater hadn't felt very warm. Now it was heaven. But the windows were fogging up worse than ever, thanks to the snow melting off his clothes.

Shannon frowned at him. "What did you do? Meet up with home-brew Bill out there?"

"Better. Santa Claus."

"Excuse me?"

"Well, somebody gave us a Christmas present," Rick told her. "I didn't go ten feet, before I ran smack into a mailbox. We'd come farther than we thought. We're there."

"The house with the pool?" Shannon asked, mouth agape.

"Yup. We're sitting about a hundred feet or so down their driveway, parked behind a copse of juniper bushes," he informed her. "The satellite dish is off to our right. It seems to be the sort of house to have a white rug, too. Give me a minute or so more to warm up, and I'll go back out to take a closer look."

Shannon started pulling her gloves on. "No, you've played Arctic explorer enough for one night. I'll go."

"It's nasty out there," Rick warned her.

She wrapped her wool scarf over her head and down around her ears, then tucked it into the collar of her coat, which she buttoned all the way up. Her boots, though suede, had good soles and a dose of waterproofing on them.

"I'm not made of cotton candy," she said. "I won't melt. Besides, it's my fault we're out here in this storm, so it's only fair I do my share."

"Suit yourself, but be careful." Rick held out his hands to warm them on the flow of air coming from the heater vents. "I'll keep the home fires burning, so to speak."

"You do that."

Shannon got out of the car. She took about two steps and realized Rick had lied. It wasn't nasty out; it was horrible! The wind howled through the trees, and made the snow hitting her face feel like stinging grains of sand. That wouldn't have been too bad if she could move quickly, but every step was a struggle, the fallen snow already up to her knees.

By chance, she found the remnants of some recent tracks. Evidently, a vehicle had pulled in or out of the driveway not long ago. This made the going much easier, though walking in one wheel track was still a little awkward. She followed it all the way up to the house, where the tracks disappeared into an attached garage. The snow was still falling so heavily that she didn't worry much about being seen. Then, too, there were no lights on at all, not even on the front porch.

It was deathly quiet, except for the wind, which even blew away the sound of her running car engine not more than a couple of hundred feet away. She moved toward the porch. As she did so, her boot caught on some sort of obstruction buried under the snow.

Shannon fell flat on her face. *"Oof!"*

She struggled to her knees, covered in snow, and grabbed for the bottom part of the porch railing to help herself up. But the railing was loose, and wiggling it dislodged a shovel that had been propped against the railing at the top of the steps. It came clattering down, just missing her head. She jerked back, which caused her to slip again and clutch the flimsy railing for support. The piece she was holding broke with a loud crack. Shannon went down again, on her rear end this time, thankful for the cushion of her coat and several feet of snow.

"For heaven's sake!" she muttered, getting carefully to her feet again. "Some spy I am."

But she had determined one thing, at least. Either there was nobody home, or they were deaf, because she'd made enough noise to wake the dead. She decided to go report this fact to Rick. Since snow now covered her from head to toe, she figured they were even.

Rick thought so, too. "I feel much better now," he said, laughing as she got into the car. "What on earth did you do? Roll in the stuff?"

"In a manner of speaking," Shannon groused. "Suffice it to say, I have determined the place is unoccupied at the moment. Or the occupants are wearing earplugs. Either way, this is a dead end, too." She looked at him plaintively. "Well? Aren't you going to help me brush off? I helped you."

"Why bother? You're just going right back out in it."

"Not me!" Shannon objected. "If you want to reconnoiter, do it yourself. It's cold out there."

"It'll be cold in here, too, as soon as the gas runs out."

Shannon crossed her arms. "I'm a Colorado girl, remember? I know what to do in emergencies like this. You only run the car for a few minutes every half hour or so. And get out and exercise every now and then, to keep from falling asleep."

Rick shrugged. "Suit yourself. I'm going to go see if I can get into that house."

"You can't do that!"

"Why not? We did it just a few hours ago, and that wasn't an emergency. In fact, it was even your idea," he said pointedly.

"That was different. We knew who the place belonged to."

"We know that here, too." He reached up and turned on the dome light so he could read the piece of paper with the addresses on it. "Ralph and Kim Jeffries."

"But we don't know them."

"We aren't exactly pals with the Bayers, now, are we?" Rick said. "And I for one, am willing to bet the Jeffrieses are a lot nicer folks." He reached out and brushed some melting snow off her hair. "We really don't have much choice, Shannon. The temperature is dropping and we're both soaked. There's no telling when someone might come, but by the look of this storm, it could be quite a while, maybe not until tomorrow morning. And the next nearest house is miles away. It's crazy to risk freezing, when we're so close to this one."

Shannon knew he was right. There was also a part of her that realized their shared fantasy of earlier had a chance of coming true. They were going to be snowed in, and with any luck, would soon be sitting in front of a roaring fire.

"All right," she said. "But this time, let's try not to break the door down if we don't have to, okay?"

Rick made a crossing motion over his chest with one finger. "I promise. Last resort. And who knows? The phones don't seem very reliable around here, but if they are still working, we might even be able to call for help."

That didn't sound nearly as romantic to Shannon, but it was the more responsible approach, she supposed. Still, she found herself half hoping that the phones were out again.

As long as they might have to help themselves to the place for the night, they decided they might as well park right in front. Though it slipped and slid all the way, her car made it down the rest of the driveway. Shannon parked it right in front of the garage. When she turned the engine off at last, it seemed to breathe a sigh of relief. She gave it an affectionate pat on the wheel, then got out to join Rick in his search for a means of entry.

"What on earth did you do?" he asked her, upon seeing all the marks in the snow near the front porch. "Meet up with a bear, or something?"

"I fell, okay? Now come on. It's freezing out here."

Rick was still studying the prints. "I recognize that one. Must have hurt." He patted her lightly on the rear end. "Are you okay?"

"Rick! Would you come on?"

"I'm working on it," he said.

Except for Shannon's footprints and the places where she had fallen, the only other tracks were those of the vehicle that had obviously left the house—and not long before they'd arrived, judging by the rate at which the tracks were disappearing. The porch was covered with snow, as were the steps. No walkways had been shoveled for quite some time, if the drifts were any indication.

"Must be an entrance in the garage," he told her.

"So?"

"So I installed garage doors for a living at one time, as well," Rick replied. "I know a few tricks of the trade."

Shannon was stomping her feet to keep warm. "Then might I suggest you perform a couple before we turn into snowmen?"

Rick looked it over. As he thought, it had an automatic opener. Remembering that Shannon had one, too, he tried her remote to see if, by chance, the frequencies matched. No luck.

Shannon, meanwhile, was beginning to rethink her moral position on breaking and entering, and went looking for a suitable door for him to kick down. Using the shovel she had found earlier, she dug a little path around the house. It gave her something to do and helped keep her warm. By the time she got back to the garage, however, Rick had the door open.

"How did you do that?" she asked.

He put his finger to his lips. "Trade secret. If I told you, you'd go around breaking into houses higgledy-piggledy."

Though tempted to whack him with the shovel, she tossed it aside and followed him into the garage. As he said, there was an entrance to the house. He pushed a button near it, and the automatic door rattled down. A light came on as it did so.

"Oops!" Rick said. "Trouble."

Shannon joined him. "What?" Then she saw the fancy lock on the back door. "Oops is right. I guess we kick it in, huh?"

"I'm worried about you, Shannon. You seem to be developing a penchant for destruction."

"Me? It's your footprint they'll find on the Bayers' door."

"True. So help me stop this senseless crime spree and look for a key to this lock. I know I used to keep one hidden in my garage, just in case."

"Me, too," Shannon agreed. "I guess cats are right. We humans are hopelessly predictable. What sort of key?"

"A plastic one. It'll look like a credit card."

Shannon made a face. "Fancy."

"Nothing is too good for the Jeffrieses, apparently."

"I just hope they have a good heater."

It was Shannon who found the card, stuck in between the pages of a dog-eared workshop manual on a shelf above a tool bench at the back of the garage. The manual, she noted, was for a classic model Jaguar.

"If they really own this car," Rick said, "I'd say good old Ralph and Kim are probably bloody rich."

Shannon swiped the card through the groove in the lock. There was a click, and the door popped open. "Let's go inside and find out, shall we?"

If they weren't rich, the Jeffrieses were on very good terms with several credit card companies. The house had one of everything. Two, if they could be made to fit. There was even a color television in the kitchen.

Unfortunately, the place was also a pigsty. Especially the entertainment room, where dirty dishes littered almost every horizontal surface.

Shannon grabbed Rick's arm and pointed to the floor, where a once-beautiful white Berber rug had recently taken a beating from which it might never recover. "Sure look like blueberry syrup stains to me," she said.

Rick nodded. He had a puzzled look on his face. "Do you hear something strange?"

"What?" She was quiet for a moment, then nodded. "Yes. A sort of knocking sound. You don't suppose..."

With Rick in the lead, they followed the sound toward the back of the house, where they found some steps leading to the basement. Rick flipped a switch and some lights came on to guide them. As they descended, an unusual smell reached them, one Shannon could only describe as that of fresh running water.

They had found the pool they'd been looking for. And there was something floating in it.

Chapter Nineteen

Whoever had used the pool last had forgotten to turn the water jet off. There was something caught in its artificial current, causing it to knock on the fiberglass side.

"What is that?" Shannon asked uneasily.

"Relax," Rick told her. He stepped over to the side of the pool and fished out the floating object. "It's just the hard plastic head off a Santa Claus lawn ornament."

"That's twisted!" Shannon removed her sodden coat and sat down on the redwood bench near the pool. "And just like Leo. He was here. But we're too late."

"From the looks of things, they took off pretty fast, too," Rick said. He removed his coat as well, hanging it on the bench beside hers. "I wonder why."

"Uh-oh." Shannon looked at him, her eyes going wide. "You don't suppose the Arnies arrived?"

"No, that's impossible. They're—" He stopped himself in the nick of time. "They're not due until tomorrow."

She was studying his face suspiciously. "I thought you didn't know when they were going to get here."

"I, uh, checked with Arnie central this morning."

"Maybe they came in early. It would also explain why Angela and Emilio were in such a hurry before."

In a way, she was right. Rick's forehead furrowed with worry. "What was it Angela had said? Something about an old sot?" He turned and started back up the stairs. "I'm going to see if the phones work."

"I have to call Lyon's," Shannon agreed, hot on his heels. "And my next-door neighbor. My cats will worry."

The house had plenty of phones. Rick tried the one in the kitchen and another in the entertainment room before admitting defeat. He slammed the receiver down with a bang.

"This stupid weather!" He glanced at Shannon. "I can't believe I let you pull off the interstate. We'd be safe and sound in Denver by now."

"Maybe. Or maybe we'd be in a ditch waiting for a tow truck," Shannon countered. "At least we really are safe here."

"Yeah, right." Rick kicked a pillow that was on the floor and sent it flying across the room. "Safe and stuck."

Shannon's hopes for a romantic evening were melting like the snow that still clung to her hair. "Earlier, you seemed to think that wouldn't be so bad," she reminded him.

"That was before I realized Angela and her pet stud might have gotten the jump on me," Rick grumbled.

He was searching around for the television remote. When he found it, he turned the set on, muting the sound and clicking through the channels. At last he found one that was showing the latest Arnie the Arachnid news.

"Nothing so far," Rick said after a moment, and plopped down on the couch with a sigh of relief. "I can't imagine that they'd be sitting on their thumbs. Maybe he hasn't sobered up enough to tell them anything."

"Who?" Shannon asked, confused.

"That old sot, as Angela called him," Rick explained. "I told you about him, remember? Well, I don't think he just happened to fall down in front of the warehouse. He followed me there. I suppose it's possible he decided not to tell them anything because I was nice and helped him. But then, he did warn me he'd stab me in the back for a couple of bucks. He's probably just too hung over to remember what he saw."

"And what did he see, Rick?"

He sighed again. It was time to face the music, or at least the overture. "There's been a load of spiders at the warehouse all along."

"You lied to me?" Shannon asked through clenched teeth.

"No. Or at least, not really," Rick added quickly. "You see, they're not actually Arnies."

She frowned. "Then what are they?"

"Fakes," he replied. She was too close to the edge for him to quibble over the fine points of toy spiders just now. "I had originally intended to let the Bayers steal them. That way, when they tried to sell them as the real thing, it would put them right in the cross hairs of a legal suit."

"But then Leo was kidnapped," Shannon said.

Rick had his feet up on the coffee table now, and was too wrapped up in his own thoughts to see how mad Shannon was really getting.

"Even then, I thought that if I foisted the fakes off on them as a ransom, the end result would be the same," he went on. "But I decided it would be best to see if we could find Leo first." He frowned. "Everything might still work out, I suppose. I just wish I could get to the warehouse and find out if Angela has the spiders."

Shannon was in no mood to reassure him. She had her own problems, and it now looked as if he was partly responsible for the largest of the lot. She stood beside the couch now, looking down at him.

"Aren't you forgetting something?" she asked.

"Probably," Rick replied. He started to chuckle, but then caught sight of her face. It was a mask of fury. "Oh."

"That's right. Oh. As in Leo. You remember him, don't you?" she asked in a soft tone that belied the anger she felt inside. "The little boy we came up here to find? Instead of wondering where your precious fake Arnies are, don't you think you should worry about who has Leo and what they're planning on doing with him, especially if you've lost those spiders?"

Rick patted the couch, indicating that she should sit down beside him. "Take it easy, Shannon. I'm sure he's fine."

Shannon had no intention of sitting down. In fact, she gave the coffee table a push with her foot, causing Rick's feet to slip off. It jerked him upright on the couch, and Shannon bent down to meet him, her nose almost touching his.

"That's probably true," she agreed. "*You're* the one who's in trouble! Didn't you think Pop and I should have been in on the decision on whether to use the fakes as a ransom?"

"I—"

"Didn't you think it might have been better for all of us if you had simply handed them over right away?" she interrupted. "Instead of letting Leo go through all this?"

Rick wasn't accustomed to being harangued by anyone, and didn't intend to take it sitting down. He got to his feet, making Shannon back up quickly.

"All this?" Rick asked, looking around the entertainment room. "It appears to me that all Leo has been going through is two days of juvenile bliss."

"That's not the point!" Shannon exclaimed. They weren't quite shouting at each other yet, but it wouldn't be long.

"Then what is? Your concept of right and wrong?"

"My concept! What about yours?" she demanded. "You just unilaterally decided that you knew what was best for everyone, didn't you?"

Rick scowled at her. "Stop playing the injured party. I told you from the very beginning that my major concern was getting something on the Bayers so I could work my way back into my daughter's life. And it still is!"

Shannon nodded once, curtly. "Fine! From the very beginning, I told you that *Leo* was my main concern. And that hasn't changed, either." She put her hands on her hips. "But so help me, Rick Hastings, if it turns out that I need those spiders to get him back, you'd better find some but quick."

With that, she stalked off and started searching the house. Rick watched her, the sway of her full hips taunting him, making him realize that what might have become a night of fantastic passion had just disintegrated into a foolish tiff.

Foolish because she was right. It was all his fault. He could almost hear Charlie telling him I told you so. In fact, he was saying it to himself. And worse.

"You idiot," he admonished himself under his breath.

Shannon was the best thing that had ever happened to him, and he had just ridden roughshod over the one thing that concerned her the most. She was right about that, too. No matter who had Leo or how well they were treating him, it still hadn't been right for him to hold the ransom for ransom, so to speak. If he had turned it over the night Leo had disappeared, they probably wouldn't be going through this right now.

Of course, that would mean he might not have gotten as close to Shannon as he had, either. Had that been in the back of his mind all along?

Yes, it had. And it was high time he admitted that much at the very least. He followed her to the den, where he found her going through some papers on an antique roll-top desk.

"Shannon?"

She didn't look up. "What?"

"I'm sorry."

Shannon hesitantly met his gaze. "That's a start."

"I should have told you. I have plenty of excuses why I didn't. For what it's worth, the most important ones did have to do with people, not revenge. My daughter means a lot to me."

"I know."

"So do you," he told her softly. "I think I sensed that would be the case right away. And I thought that if I helped you look for Leo, rather than turn over the spiders, maybe we could get to know each other better. Leo was fine, and he apparently wasn't in any real danger. It seemed like a lark, almost. I guess I just didn't realize how important the little guy really is to you."

Shannon turned away, and he could see by the dim light of a banker's lamp on the desk that there were tears glistening in her eyes. "Then you don't know me very well at all, do you?"

"Be honest, Shannon. That's your fault, not mine. You've let me close to you in every way but one. I don't know you very well because you haven't allowed me to."

Shannon knew he was right. She also knew it was senseless to keep pushing him away when he neared the sore spot in her life. Rick was offering his help, and she needed it. It was plain to see how much she had helped him, simply by being there to listen. And he had been there for her all along.

"You're right," she admitted softly, tears streaming down her cheeks now. "I haven't let you in. I don't know why. It's silly, really. I just..." She trailed off, sobbing.

Rick crossed the room and knelt beside the desk chair so that he could put his arm around her shoulder as she cried. He knew he was to blame for causing this sudden break-down. But the roots of her sorrow clearly went much deeper.

When her sobs had lessened somewhat, he tried to get her to look at him. "I don't know what's troubling you," Rick said softly. "But whatever it is, it doesn't seem as if you've let it go. Talking will help." He rubbed her back in gentle, soothing strokes. "Believe me, I know. You taught me that."

Shannon lifted her head, nodding, and took the tissue he offered her. Her tears dried up quickly, which wasn't un-usual for her. She had cried too many of them in years past to allow them to linger for long.

But the pain was still there. And it was time to share it with someone who knew what such pain was like. "This thing with Leo has me so on edge because I couldn't bear to lose him," she began. "My head knows that he's okay. But my heart isn't so easily persuaded."

Rick held her tightly. "Tell me why," he urged.

"Greg and I...had a child together. A beautiful girl. She died in an automobile accident when she was just a baby." Shannon started crying again, but softly this time. "Her name was Melissa. She was such a good baby, so quiet and always happy. We were on our way home from the market. I was driving and I...I never saw the other car. It ran a red light and hit us broadside. There was nothing I could do. She was killed instantly."

"Oh, my Lord," Rick said, his voice scarcely above a whisper. "Shannon, I'm so sorry."

"I was knocked unconscious. To this day, I don't really remember what happened. I do remember being in the hospital, on medication, for a long time. When I came out of the fog, I was just plain numb."

"And your husband?" Rick prompted.

Shannon sighed. "Coped with things differently, I guess you'd say. I don't remember seeing much of him while I was in the hospital. But when I came home, I was desperate for his love and support. What I got were accusations," she said, the bitterness clear in her voice.

Rick was stunned. "Accusations. About what?"

"Greg believed it was all my fault," she replied. "At first, I didn't blame him for that. After all, it was such a horrible, senseless thing. But he just got worse. To him, Melissa's death was a failure on both our parts, somehow. He wanted me to wallow in guilt with him. As he sank deeper into despair, I realized that what I wanted was to heal, go on with life. I couldn't help him and he wouldn't get help for himself."

"So you divorced?"

"It took a while. A couple of years, holding on by a thread and watching him try to kill himself. I should be thankful his weapon of choice was food, I suppose." She shrugged her shoulders, her tears once again fading away. "But then, if it had been alcohol or drugs, I would have left sooner, or perhaps someone would have been forced to intervene. But, yes. I finally divorced him."

Rick nodded. "For which he never forgave you."

She uttered a short, curt laugh. "And then some. He still calls me every year around her birthday, never the same day or time. He likes to catch me off guard. And always at work, pretending to be a customer, so I have to take the call."

"That's awful!"

"In a way, I've come to accept it as a form of therapy for both of us. It's hardened me to the memory, and Greg has gone on to lead a more or less normal life otherwise. I'm okay with it most of the time myself, but this thing with Leo just seems to bring it rushing back."

"I'm sorry if what I did caused you worry and pain," Rick said. "But you of all people, who lost a daughter irretrievably, should understand why I'm willing to do anything to get mine back into my life."

She nodded solemnly. "I do understand. But we're both on a mission, Rick. Let's try to remember that."

"I promise." He got to his feet. "Right now, however, I need a swim," he announced, thinking it would be just the thing to raise both their spirits. "Join me?"

"Not right now, thanks," Shannon told him. "I want to go through these papers, see if I can find any clues."

"You'll think better when you're relaxed," he coaxed.

"Not right now."

Rick glowered at her with mock severity. "Now who's spoiling a perfectly good snowbound evening?"

"Shoo!"

He sighed, then did as she asked. He had so much pent-up frustration and energy that he felt as if he could bounce off the walls. But the house had suffered enough indignities, as it was, he supposed, and there was a better means at hand for giving vent to his emotions.

The pool beckoned to him. He had no suit, nor did he care to go looking for one. Nudity suited him just fine. The water was brisk, almost cold, in fact, the temperature set for exercising, not soaking. He adjusted the current for a fairly rapid flow and leaned into it, then started to swim, the movements of the stroke a balm to his tense muscles. Soon he lost himself in the steady, rhythmic repetition.

Shannon heard the splashing. At first, she hesitated, having found something very disturbing among the papers in the den and wanting to examine them further. Finally, however, her curiosity got the better of her and she went to investigate.

The current in the pool was running at a faster speed than before, and for a moment she was mesmerized by the flowing water more than by anything else. But as she watched Rick swim in its frothy currents, Shannon became aware of another sort of flow, that of her own surging desire.

The sleek muscles of his back and arms working in concert, the pumping of his powerful legs and especially the rhythmic clenching of his solid buttocks, all combined to give him the look of something other than what he was. An aquatic mammal, perhaps, at one with the water. It was very erotic, and much too arousing for her to ignore.

So far, he was unaware of her presence. She slipped out of her clothing and into the pool, careful to stay near the back and out of the ebb and flow of his movements. The water was cold, making her nipples harden instantly. But it felt good to her. There wasn't enough room for her to swim with him, and she wasn't quite sure how to work it, anyway, so she watched. From this position, it was even more thrilling than before, and she felt a sweet ache in the pit of her stomach.

Finally, Rick tired, and he let the current push his legs down and into a standing position. It pushed him backward, as well, and into the soft, waiting flesh of Shannon's body.

He turned to face her, and she immediately kissed him, communicating a need so strong that it swept him away.

But his breathing was still labored, and he paused, holding her in his arms, reveling in the slick feel of her skin against his.

"I'm sorry," she told him softly.

"For what?"

"Pushing you away again. But I did find something."

"Do tell."

Shannon leaned back against the pool's rim and let her legs float up and around his hips. "Not right now. I think I have my priorities straight this time."

Rick groaned, his hands running over her water-slick skin, gliding under her buttocks and then up over the soft swell of her stomach to her full, waiting breasts. Their tips were hard as diamonds, and he bent to soften them with his tongue.

Impatient, Shannon pulled him closer still. She wanted him inside her, and he found her ready, waiting for his every thrust. His tongue thrust into her mouth at the same time, searching deep for the honey-sweet touch of hers. All the while, the current of the pool pushed steadily at his back, a silent partner in their lovemaking.

Shannon's climax was so fierce that Rick had to use all his strength to hold her and prevent her from sinking beneath the water. His own followed closely, an explosion of feeling that left him even more breathless than had his vigorous exercise of before.

Afterward, they both clung to the rim of the pool with one arm, and embraced tightly with the other, letting the currents buffet them about. They looked into each other's eyes, and knew they had shared something special, something more meaningful because of the unspoken emotion between them.

"I want to try," she said, pulling away from him at last and taking a few experimental strokes.

When she couldn't quite get the hang of it, Rick moved to the middle of the pool and held her up by putting his hands under her stomach. It tickled at first, making her laugh and float to the back of the pool. But she tried again and this time managed to get into the flow. Rick released her, and moved away, letting her work out the rest of her tensions as he had done.

When she was spent, he took her into his arms and carried her to a discovery of his own, one Leo hadn't mentioned. By modern standards, it was a small hot tub, and much less high-tech than the pool, but there was something comforting about its rustic redwood and old-fashioned barrel shape.

Shannon sank into the water with a sigh, welcoming its soothing heat. She closed her eyes. When Rick didn't join her right away, however, she opened them again and realized he had left the pool area entirely.

"Rick!"

"I'm upstairs," he hollered back. "Be down in a jiffy."

Though wondering what he was up to now, she felt the hot water call to her, and sank into it again. True to his word, Rick returned a minute or so later. He was carrying a tray laden with dark rye bread, assorted hunks of cheese and fruit and a bottle of white wine with two glasses.

"That looks good," Shannon exclaimed. "And so do you. Any place with a naked waiter running around is definitely my sort of establishment."

Rick placed the tray within easy reach and slipped into the hot water beside her. "An establishment that also has a well-stocked larder," he said. "They prepared for this situation nicely, whatever it is. I'm hesitant to call it a kidnapping any longer."

"I agree. And there's something else interesting about this place." Shannon took the glass of wine he offered and ipped at it before continuing. "It's not a rental. The Jeffrieses own it. What's more, they left bills and all sorts of personal stuff lying around. Obviously, they had some kind of a previous arrangement with the kidnappers." She frowned. "I guess I'll just call them Joey and Irv now."

Rick passed her the tray. Shannon took a piece of cheese and nibbled it, feeling like a large, very contented mouse. But there was something nibbling at the back of her mind, as well. And she wasn't alone in her suspicions.

"I have a theory," Rick said. "If I mention it, will you promise not to get mad?"

"Yes. I have a theory, too, because of a name that kept cropping up in the Jeffrieses' personal papers."

Rick had the feeling they were talking about the same thing. But he was hesitant to say it. One fight a night was plenty. "Does your theory help to explain why Joey and Irv just happened to take off with Leo not long before we arrived?"

Shannon was having trouble saying it outright herself. "It does. And it isn't dependent upon anyone's having found the fake Arnies, either."

They looked at each other and nodded. "It's Pop."

"I was looking for Nathan Bayer's name, but found Pop's, instead," Shannon said. "Evidently, the Jeffrieses are old and very dear friends of his."

"When they find the mess his other friends and Leo made upstairs, that might change," Rick noted wryly. "It does explain how Joey and Irv knew to take off, though, doesn't it? We call Pop about the cellular, he realizes we're closer than he thought, so he calls them up and warns them."

Shannon nodded. "And no wonder Pop managed to convince the police this was all a publicity gimmick. It is!"

"But is that all it is?" Rick wondered aloud. "And what about Joey and Irv? It's hard to believe they really are friends of Pop's, too, especially if the Bayers trusted them."

"Clearly, this really did start out as a kidnapping, or at least an attempt to take control of the Arnie shipment," Shannon agreed. "And at some point, Joey and Irv made a deal with Pop. But what sort of deal? And why?"

"I think these are all questions only Pop can answer."

"And you better believe he will," Shannon exclaimed. But then she stretched, put her glass of wine down on the tray and moved closer to him on the submerged redwood bench. "As soon as the roads are plowed, that is. Right now, we're safe, I remembered that I gave the boys plenty of food this morning just in case, and I don't know about you, but I've had more than enough sleuthing for one day."

Chapter Twenty

Paul Sanchez was standing just outside Lyon's service entrance, breathing in the cold night air and taking a much-needed break from the crowds inside. Watching over the store could be an unpleasant task at Christmas, especially if he caught someone shoplifting, but it was one of those jobs that had to be done, and he was paid well for it. Not as well as when he'd been on the force, naturally. But since his hours were regular, and no one had even thought about coming at him with a knife yet, neither he nor his wife and three children had minded the drop in income one bit.

He caught sight of the bum out of the corner of his eye, and turned to observe him more closely, with a jaded ex-cop's detachment. Like all urban downtown areas, Denver's had a few transients—or homeless, to use the more current and politically correct euphemism. Most were only a danger to themselves, on a fast track to self-destruction.

This old guy looked to be one of those, except for the box he was carrying. He made his way unsteadily across the employee parking lot with it, heading for the Lyon's building. Paul stayed where he was, just doing his job. He was pretty sure he knew what the fellow was up to.

It was very cold out. Snow was falling lightly, and there was already a skift of it covering the cars in the lot. From all accounts, the mountains were getting hit hard and the storm was expected to drift east into Denver later tonight.

Paul figured that the old guy was probably just looking for a warm place to sleep, and the mission wouldn't let him bring a bottle in, so he thought he'd curl up on Lyon's steam vent. The cardboard from the box would serve as a blanket and keep the snow off him.

Paul moved into the light so that the other man could see his uniform. "Hey, guy," he said. "At least wait until I go off duty, okay?"

The man stopped in the shadows at the edge of the loading dock. "I have to speak to Pop," he said.

Paul blinked. This wasn't the sort of thing he expected to hear from a homeless ragamuffin. "Sorry. I don't think he's taking visitors this late."

"Listen, sonny boy, I didn't come here to take your guff." He moved so that his face was in the pinkish glow of the sodium vapor lamps overhead. There was a cut over his left eye, and it was swelling shut. "I got this shiner trying to protect his property. Don't ask me why," he grumbled. "It was just plain stupid. But there's a lot of that going around this time of year, I suppose."

"What property?" Paul asked, frowning.

"The Arnies, of course." The old man peered at him with his good eye. "For a hired gun, you sure don't know much."

At the mention of that name, Paul motioned for him to come up on the dock. "I know all about the Arnies. Question is, what do you know?" He eyed the box the old man held cradled in his arms. "Is that them?"

"None of your business! And I'm not in the mood for any more of your fool questions, either. I have to talk to Pop and right now! I told you I was trying to protect those ings. Didn't say I succeeded." He touched his eye ginerly. "Not quite the man I used to be, you understand."

Paul had no idea what the guy was going on about, but it concerned the Arnies, Pop would want to hear it. "I uess I can take you up," he said. "We can stop at the cafeteria and get some ice for that eye, too."

The old man pushed away Paul's helping hand. "I been alking on my own since before you were a glimmer in your apa's eyes, sonny boy. I figure to keep doing it a while onger. Lead on."

OEY WAS GETTING worried. It was like watching a time omb tick away the seconds to a horrendous explosion. Any moment, something terrible was going to happen, and here wasn't the slightest thing he could think of to prevent.

Leo and Irv were bored. After arriving at the Lyon ouse, they had played video games for a while, but Leo's ight nanny had decided he'd had enough of those and sent ll three of them down to the playroom. This close to Christmas, however, there was nothing quite so boring to child as his old toys, even with new friends to share them.

Besides, it wasn't the lack of things to do, necessarily. It as the sudden removal of the things they had been doing or the last two days. The Lyon house was very pleasant, nd no doubt a much better learning environment for a rowing boy, but it wasn't the Jeffrieses' place. Leo wanted o play in that unusual pool. Irv wanted to watch thirty econds of each of a hundred and fifty satellite stations one fter the other.

They were, in a word, inconsolable. And something had o give. Joey sat in one of the playroom's comfortable eanbag chairs, watching Leo watch Irv watch him. They ere having a staring match, and Leo was winning.

"You blinked!" Leo exclaimed.

"Did not," Irv objected.

"Did so!"

Joey closed his eyes. "Oh, man," he muttered. "Here it comes. The mother of all spit-wad fights."

But they were saved by the bell. Literally. Leo's cellular phone rang, and Joey grabbed it off the card table at his side. "Pop, that you?"

It was. As Joey listened to what the older man had to say, his eyes widened and his mouth dropped open.

"You're kidding!" Joey exclaimed.

Irv and Leo were practically on top of him, trying to find out what was going on. "What?" Leo asked.

"Shh. I'm on the phone, kid." Joey held up his hand for silence. "Okay, Pop. Don't worry, we'll go get 'em."

"Who?" Leo demanded. "Get who? Is it the Arnies?"

"Shh! Hey, Pop, I can take Leo, can't I?" Joey asked. When he nodded, Leo went into paroxysms of pleasure. "Good, because if I left him here, you might not have a house left when you got home. And don't worry, we'll be careful. Bye."

Joey hung up the phone and looked at the pair of children in his charge, one eight, the other twenty-eight. He grinned, feeling a bit childlike himself at the moment.

"Boys, grab your coats. We've got a rescue mission."

Among much hooting, hollering and dour looks by Leo's nanny, the trio left the house and piled into the fancy four-wheel-drive vehicle parked in Pop Lyon's driveway.

"Are we going to save the Arnies, Agent Joey?" Leo asked.

"Yeah, kid." He grinned. "I mean, Agent X. But first we're going into the mountains to rescue Shannon and Rick."

"Do the spies have them?"

Joey shook his head. "No, I think they're just stuck in the snow." That sounded boring, even to him. "But you never know, I guess. So we'll have to be careful."

"Yeah!" Leo exclaimed. "Put the snowplow blade up and dodge the bullets."

Irv hooted loudly. Then he frowned and leaned close to Joey and whispered in his ear. "But I though we were supposed to be hiding from those two, Joey."

"Not anymore. They're on our side now."

"Who says?"

"Pop. And since he's paying the bills, he calls the shots."

Irv nodded. "Right. Oh, and Joey?"

"Yes, Irv?"

"There aren't really going to be any bullets, are there?"

Joey grinned at him. "You never know, Agent Irv."

AFTER A DELIGHTFUL SOAK in the hot tub, Shannon and Nick had gone back upstairs, where they sated the appetite their cheese and fruit tray had whetted on a more substantial meal. They had then adjourned to the entertainment room.

It took a small cleaning frenzy, but they at last deemed it fit for adult habitation again and relaxed on the couch, sipping eggnog and watching a black-and-white version of *A Christmas Carol* on one of the satellite channels.

But finally their busy day caught up with them, and neither one made it through to Scrooge's reclamation. They fell asleep in each other's arms, oblivious to the ghosts of past, present and future. Except for the low voices of the movie on television, all was quiet, especially the snow-blanketed landscape outside.

Around ten, however, a sound that didn't fit into the peaceful scene reached their groggy brains, and they came slowly awake. It was a growling, scraping sort of noise.

Then, as quickly as it had started, it stopped. Rick reached over and muted the television. In the near-total silence that followed, he and Shannon heard something moving on the front porch.

"Rick?" she asked sleepily. "What's going on?"

"I don't know. But keep your head down. I'll—"

Suddenly, three commandos dressed in identical parkas and ski masks came bursting through the door, two big ones and a little one.

"Agent X fires a burst to soften up any resistance!" the little one cried.

A snowball came flying over the couch and hit the remains of Rick's and Shannon's eggnog, spilling it all over everything.

"Direct hit!" Irv cried. "Now me, kid."

Leo moved farther into the room, continuing his blow-by-blow commentary. "Agent Irv, a cagey veteran of the Arnie wars, sneaks slowly into the room. Agent X covers him. But wait! Agent Joey is making a full frontal assault! What bravery! He's a goner for sure!"

A pudgy, nearly bald man wearing a fleece-trimmed parka appeared at the edge of the couch and looked down at Shannon and Rick. "Hi, guys. We didn't catch you flagrante delicto, did we?" He saw that they were fully clothed and nodded. "Ah. Good. My men are kind of sensitive souls," he said with a wink.

Shannon was fully awake now. She sat up on the couch. When she saw Leo, tears welled up in her eyes and she jumped up, running to him. He accepted her hugs and kisses with as much decorum as possible.

"Oh, Leo! I missed you so much!"

He permitted himself one small return hug, then squirmed to be set free. "Gee, Shannon. Not in front of the guys."

"Oops. Sorry." She ruffled his fine blond hair and let him go. He promptly smoothed it. "Are you okay?"

"Sure," he exclaimed. "We came to rescue you, didn't we, guys?" He strutted proudly over to where Irv and Joey were standing near the couch. "And now, we can go save the Arnies."

Rick was eyeing the two men warily. "How about a little briefing first? We're not up to speed on this situation."

Joey looked at him appreciatively. "Hey. That's good. I like this guy, Irv," he told him.

Irv nodded. "Me, too. Who is he?"

"This is Rick, you goof," Joey replied, punching Irv on the arm. "You remember. Angela's ex-husband. We saw him a couple of days ago at Lyon's."

"Right." But Irv seemed puzzled. "I thought we didn't like him then."

"I didn't say I didn't like him. I said I didn't like it that he was there. But now, Pop says..." Joey trailed off with a sigh of exasperation. "Skip it. Just take my word for it. He's cool, okay?"

"Okay."

Rick was shaking his head. "Do I know you two?"

"We've never met," Joey replied. "But we, uh, sort of kept an eye on you for Nathan a few times. Back when you were still in Phoenix. No offense." He held out his hand. "I'm Joey, and this is my brother, Irv."

"Pleased to meet you," Rick said, shaking both their hands. "At least I think I am. Do you still work for Nathan?"

Joey laughed. "No, that arrangement has officially been terminated, I believe. I guess you could say we work for Pop now. In a way, we have for quite some time." He shrugged. "It's a long story, and we're supposed to get you back to Denver to see Pop pronto. He'll explain it all."

Shannon was still smiling, for Leo's sake, but there was no mistaking the anger in her voice. "Somebody better! Because if I don't get an explanation soon, I will personally pluck out all of your eyebrows hair by hair until I do!"

Irv winced. "Ouch. I guess it's true."

"What's that, Irv?" Joey asked patiently.

"Redheads really do have bad tempers."

NATHAN CONFRONTED his wayward wife the moment she came through the door. "Stop right there, Angela. I want the Lyon boy, a truckful of Arnies and that cheating little weasel of a driver. If you don't have at least one of those, you might as well just march your cute rear end back out into the cold and get them for me."

Angela scowled at him. "What on earth are you talking about, Nathan?" She sniffed the air. "You've been drinking. So help me, if Todd and Chelsea see you like this—"

"Shut up! They're with the nanny."

There was such vehemence in his voice that Angela took a step backward. "Nathan! What's gotten into you?"

"Some sense," he replied. "At last."

"If you say so." She edged past him toward the living room, looking for a suitable weapon to use in case this got out of hand. The fireplace poker would do. When she was close to it, she continued. "But to me it sounds as if you've taken leave of your senses. I don't have the boy."

"Then who does?"

She shrugged delicately. "I'm sure I don't know. But I think that by now it's a foregone conclusion that your longtime henchmen, Joey and Irv, have sold you out."

Nathan muttered several choice epithets under his breath. "And how about you, Angela?" he asked in a sullen, threatening tone. "Did you sell me out, too?"

"Now, what possible reason would I have to do that, dear?"

"Emilio."

Her eyes widened. "What do you mean?"

"You're having an affair with him, aren't you?"

"Me? With Emilio?" Angela managed a convincing laugh. "You must be joking, my love. He's gay."

"It certainly sounded as if he liked women well enough when I called you this afternoon at the lodge."

Angela's eyes narrowed, and she stepped closer to him, thoughts of bashing him on the head temporarily forgotten. "Now you've really lost me. I haven't spoken with you since last night, Nathan. In fact, I believe I left the phone off the hook up there. Your constant whining was driving me quite insane and I needed a break."

Nathan seemed confused. "Then who did all the moaning?"

"I have no idea. But it wasn't me. Obviously, someone is toying with us." She went to their wet bar and poured herself a stiff drink. "What Emilio and I were doing this afternoon was taking care of business. He had hired one of those sleazy sources of his to keep an eye on Rick. It paid off, eventually, and we found the Arnies in a warehouse near downtown."

"You took them?" Nathan asked, suddenly alert.

"Yes. For all the good it did us," she replied with disgust. "They were fakes. Of course, we didn't find that out until we tried to sell them to another of Emilio's contacts, this one a pipeline to the black market. He was not pleased."

"What?" Nathan cried. "Who authorized—"

"I did," Angela interrupted. "Did you honestly think I would allow you to jeopardize our position by selling this particular load of stolen merchandise at Bayer's? I'm sure that's just what Rick had in mind for us all along.''

Nathan shook his head as if to clear it. Obviously, she had been more on top of this operation than he'd thought. But that wasn't what troubled him. ''What's all this about Rick? What's his connection?''

''I don't know. But it's a solid one.'' She sipped her drink and smiled. It was a particularly evil smile. ''And that, jealous husband, is our ace in the hole. He has real Arnies around, I'm sure, or can get them. And when he does, we'll take them for ourselves—or better yet, his profits.''

''How?''

''The same way we got everything else he ever owned, my darling,'' she told him sweetly. ''Blackmail.''

Nathan came closer to her, breathing in her perfume. ''I'm sorry for flying off the handle like that. But the thought of you and that little...I mean, you're enough woman to make any man change his affiliation, you know.''

She patted his cheek. ''Honestly, Nathan, you're such a Neanderthal sometimes. It just doesn't work that way,'' she told him. ''Besides, if I were having an affair with the man, would I have left him stranded with a truckful of stolen merchandise, at the mercy of a very irritated hood?''

Chapter Twenty-One

Whatever else Joey was, he could certainly drive well. Of course, having a fancy vehicle with a snowplow blade didn't hurt. The two combined to get what Leo was now calling the spider brigade to downtown Denver in record time, in spite of several inches of snow left behind by the dwindling storm.

Still, by then, it was after eleven, and Leo himself was down for the count. Paul unlocked the doors to let them into the store and they put him on the couch in Pop's outer office without so much as a peep out of him. Then they all trouped in to see Pop, with a very determined Shannon in the lead.

"You owe me an explanation," she told him without any preamble. "And it had better be good."

He shrugged his thin shoulders. "Not much to explain, really, Shannon. It was actually more of a sequence of events that took on a life of their own."

"Then perhaps you'd better start at the beginning."

She sat down on the old leather sofa. Rick sat beside her, while Joey and Irv settled for chairs near Pop's desk. Irv looked decidedly worried.

"She's going to pull out all our eyebrows if you don't, Pop," he told him. "And she'll do it, too."

Pop smiled at him. "Yes, Irv, I believe she would. But I think we can forestall that unhappy probability by simply being honest with her." He then gazed directly at Rick. "All of us. Don't you agree . . . Mr. Bonner?"

Rick paled slightly. He didn't have to look at Shannon to know that her eyes were focused on him now, too. So he nodded his head in agreement. "I think that's wise."

"Good." Pop wheeled himself to a position where he could see the four of them comfortably. "First, it would be helpful for you to know that Joey's given name is Joseph, after his father, the late Joe Bayer."

"I didn't know Nathan had a brother!" Shannon exclaimed.

"Neither does Nathan," Joey replied. "Daddy dearest was quite a ladies' man, you see. I'm Nathan's half brother, the result of an affair Joe had with my mother. He saw to it that she was taken care of, and later hired me to do odd jobs, but never acknowledged my link to the Bayer family. Or the Bayer family fortune, naturally."

"Irv, by the way, is the product of another union," Pop interjected. "And that's about as much honesty as is needed in his case."

Joey shrugged. "What can I say? Mom got around, too."

"Joey brought me up," Irv said. "Didn't you, Joey?"

"Yeah, Irv." He grinned and punched him playfully on the arm. "But don't hold it against me, huh?"

"Nah."

"I think I'm getting the picture here," Shannon said. "I assume there is no love lost between you and Nathan, Joey?"

"Correct. He's done okay with the business, I'll say that for him. But only because he is, in most other ways, a slime.

I am ashamed to say that I have done some things in his employ of which I am not proud."

Rick was nodding. "Like follow me during the divorce?"

"Exactly," Joey agreed. "I have to tell you, though. I was pulling for you. That Angela is a real…" He trailed off with a glance at Shannon. "Well, I guess we all know what she is, don't we? If you ask me, you were justified in popping her one."

"But I didn't hit her," Rick vowed.

"Then who did?" Joey asked.

"If I knew that, I wouldn't be sitting here now." He frowned at the thought, and put his hand on Shannon's knee. "Which makes it all worth it, I suppose."

Shannon took his hand in hers, lifted it and dropped it in his own lap. "Speak for yourself, Mr. Bonner."

"That's just an alias," Rick assured her. "One I took on to hide my business dealings from the Bayers." He glared at Pop. "And mentioning it now is just a ploy designed to divert your attention from the real culprit here."

Pop held up his hands in a placating gesture. "I'm only interested in bringing out the truth, Rick."

"Then get on with it."

"Yes," Shannon agreed. "Please do."

"Very well," Pop said. "As you may or may not know, at one time, that old coot Joe Bayer took a run at my wife, as the current phrasing goes. She repelled his advances, thank heaven, because he repelled her. From that day forward, I made it my business to know who he was seeing, with the intention of blackmailing him at some point."

Shannon was flabbergasted. "Pop!"

"Sorry, but this is the honesty hour, after all," he told her. "And anyway, my sordid plans came to naught. He was a cagey man. I didn't learn he had sired a son out of wedlock until it was too late. He died before I could put the information to good use." Pop rapped his cane sharply on the floor. "Damn his eyes!"

Shannon didn't know why she should be so surprised. The rivalry between the two men was legendary. "But you did get in touch with Joey, I assume."

"Actually, I got in touch with Pop," Joey said. "For all his faults, at least my father admitted that I was his son and treated me as fairly as he could. After he died and Nathan took over, I just became the trashman, cleaning up after his messes. He also pays lousy. Knowing that I was in the position to help Lyon's from time to time, I offered my services to Pop." He grinned. "For a fee, natch."

Pop nodded. "It has been an equitable arrangement over the years. Since I was privy to Nathan's dirty deals, I was able to steer Lyon's on a safe path. Of course, that allowed him to become a very wealthy man, while I simply got by—"

"Pop," Shannon interrupted. "Honesty, remember?"

He cleared his throat. "All right. I became a wealthy man, too. But you know what I mean."

"Yes. You've done very well by all of us at Lyon's, and we appreciate it."

"You're my family," he explained simply.

"Was this kidnapping and plan to take over the Arnies one of those things Joey told you about?" Rick asked.

"It was. And I told you." Pop smiled. "Or rather, your company, Mr. Bonner. Anonymously, of course."

Rick chuckled and shook his head. The old man had been arranging this for a long time. "So you're the one. We had other hints that something was going on. Odd little inquiries, that sort of stuff. But it was the anonymous tip that made it clear who was doing the asking, and I came running."

"As I knew you would. Or rather, I knew someone would come. I didn't know you from Adam when Shannon introduced you to me. And you did give me pause, with your bluster and bold assurances that you would find Leo. I realized then that you could ruin everything." His smile grew broader. "But I also saw your potential, and that made it worth the risk."

"Meaning?"

"Meaning that I had more than one intention when I took over the kidnapping, so to speak," Pop informed him. He turned his dancing eyes to Shannon. "First and foremost, I intended to make Nathan look like a fool. Second, I knew the publicity might garner Lyon's some sympathy points."

"*You* leaked the story to the paper!" Shannon cried.

"I did."

"All that complaining and those dramatics over the ruthless media." She shook her head in disbelief. "You missed your calling, Pop. You should have been an actor."

"Precisely what a good salesman is, my dear. I sold you on the veracity of the kidnapping, too. Because that was necessary to achieve my third objective."

"Which was?"

"I am not a young man, obviously. Leo is going to need a guardian, and the closest living family member is his great-aunt Alice, whom he despises. You were always a candidate, but I worried about your ability to handle a crisis."

She sighed. "Because of the way I completely collapsed when I lost my daughter?" she asked sadly.

"Yes. I'm sorry to be so blunt, but the truth of the matter is, terrible things can happen to any one of us at any given time. It is a fact of life we must learn to cope with, and I am happy to see that your unfortunate experience taught you well. You steeled your nerve and went after Leo with a vengeance. But that alone is not enough."

"I love him," Shannon said. "And I would do absolutely anything for him. What else is there?"

"Leo needs a family, Shannon," Pop replied.

She looked away from his intense gaze. "Oh."

"I think that's why he got along so famously with Joey and Irv. They were like the brothers he never had." He looked at Rick. "And that, young man, is what I meant when I said you had potential."

Rick arched his eyebrows. "As a... You mean to say that you thought... You were playing Cupid!" he managed to exclaim at last. "Why, you tricky old goat!"

"It worked, too, I think. You pulled together. Together you made a unit stronger than the sum of your parts. And that, my children, is the essence of a good marriage."

"Whoa, there!" Shannon interjected, rejoining the discussion. "Nothing has been said about marriage. And at any rate, I am not marrying a man with two names."

Pop looked at him. "It's your turn, I believe. But be brief." He glanced at the clock on his wall. "I had intended to let all this reach a natural conclusion up there in the snow, but circumstances have changed. I have it on good, if somewhat liquor-soaked authority, that the Arnies you had hidden in the warehouse have been stolen by Angela Bayer and her chauffeur."

"But they're not Arnies, Pop," Shannon said. "Rick told me. They're fakes."

"Well, actually, that's not quite true," Rick said.

Shannon turned and glowered at him. "No, of course not!" She folded her arms and slumped on the sofa in total disgust. "Tell me, Rick. Is there anything you've ever said to me that *is* true?"

"Plenty," he told her. He touched her arm and his tone turned serious. "And I never really out-and-out lied to you. I could usually manage to just agree with what you wanted to believe at the moment. You said it, not me."

Pop chuckled. "*You said it*. Interesting phrase, isn't it? One can use it to avoid all sorts of things."

"That's right," he admitted sheepishly. "Both you and Shannon said I was an employee of the Arnie company, not me."

Shannon was now totally befuddled. "Meaning you're not?"

"I *am* the company," Rick said. "I invented Arnie the Arachnid and orchestrated this entire campaign. My lawyer friend, Charlie Prine, set up a blind corporation for me under the name Bonner. That way, if Angela got wind of anything before I had some kind of leverage against her and Nathan, she couldn't use her black-eye story to smear my name—or extort the profits out of me. A toy maker with an abuse charge in his background wouldn't stand a chance with today's media. That's why I was so secretive. I had no choice."

"I thought it was something like that," Pop said.

That surprised Rick. "How?"

"Your tale about the head of the Arnie company having one of my lions," Pop said. He clucked his tongue. "There are only three of those in this country, son. And while one does belong to the head of a toy company back East, he happens to be a friend of mine. So I called Ivan to see if he had some Arnies up his sleeve. Turns out he didn't even have any plain old spiders. Seems some bright young inventor came along and took them off his hands, millions of 'em. And even at a few pennies apiece, Ivan figured he'd ripped the boy off."

"Good old Ivan," Rick said. "In a way, he really is responsible for the birth of Arnie. If it hadn't been for the job he gave me on his loading dock, I wouldn't have had all those toy spiders to fool around with." He chuckled, albeit without much humor. "I owe some to Angela, too. I was dreaming of horrible ways to get back at her one day. I knew she was afraid of spiders. So I came up with a way to make one that couldn't be brushed off."

"So are the spiders they stole real Arnies?" Shannon demanded in exasperation.

"Not yet, but they can be, with a splash of the right formula." Rick grinned.

Shannon's mouth had dropped open. She was only beginning to comprehend the real meaning of everything that had just been said. Something this huge was going to take a while to soak in.

There was one thing she did realize, however. "You still don't have the leverage you need against the Bayers, do you?"

Rick sighed. "No. I had hoped to somehow orchestrate it so they could be caught taking the fakes. Obviously, that's out. And calling the police won't do much good—if they're smart, they've already transferred those bugs to the black market. Besides, involving the law in this would be tricky indeed, for the same reason it won't do any good to try to pin the kidnapping on them now."

"No," Joey agreed. He and Irv were looking uneasily at each other. "That wouldn't be such a hot idea."

"I'll just have to think of something else," Rick said. "But first, there are going to be an awful lot of disappointed Denver-area residents in the morning if I don't get busy."

"Then you can save the day?" Pop asked hopefully.

Rick nodded. "All I need is a little time, some help and the contents of that box." He pointed to the box that had been in the warehouse and was now sitting beside Pop's desk. "Dare I ask how you came to be in possession of that?"

"The same old man who brought the information about the spiders being stolen gave it to me," Pop replied. "He said you were kind to him and he was just repaying the favor."

"Where is he now?" Rick asked. "We owe him, big time. It would take a few precious hours to get more supplies."

Chapter Twenty-Two

Last night's storm had left another inch of snow on the ground, but no one minded standing in its slushy remnants. The sun was shining, it was a beautiful Friday morning and tomorrow night was Christmas Eve. Best of all, the Arnies had arrived, and even though the line to get one was over a block long, no one seemed to mind standing in that, either.

Pop had hired some musicians to rove the streets outside Lyon's and lead the crowd in carols. He had also set up a stand where people could get a free cup of coffee or hot cocoa while they waited.

Not that the wait was terribly long, in any case. Inside, Shannon had several clerks manning registers that were handling nothing but Arnie sales. There were, after all, a few people who had other shopping to do, and didn't want to battle the Arnie-buying crowds. They had crowds of their own to contend with. Simply put, Lyon's was a madhouse.

A similar condition existed in the storeroom, where an assembly line had been going since early that morning, with the goal of making sure as many people got as many Arnies as was humanly possible. Rick had ordered extras. And for labor, he hadn't had to look any farther than the nearest shelter. The work was boring and repetitive, but it was a happy group, nevertheless. In addition to their wage, each employee would receive an Arnie, as well as one for each of their children.

The process was extremely simple. Each six-inch-long rubber spider was dipped legs first into a small tray of what Rick called activator. It was then placed into a plastic bag, sealed tightly and sent along the line to be labeled as an official Arnie the Arachnid. Only Rick was allowed to touch the gallon jugs of Arnie activator, and he jealously guarded each drop. He also kept a sharp eye on the process, to make sure nothing but activated Arnies left in those bags.

Shannon had gone home to soothe and feed her cats, and to grab a shower and change of clothes. But Rick had insisted on staying to set everything up.

"You look amazingly chipper," she told him.

"I went down to the warehouse to check on things, and took the opportunity to shower and change. Did you miss me?"

"A little bit," she admitted, permitting herself a small, reluctant smile. "But that doesn't mean I've forgiven you. You could have made these things at any time. You should have trusted me."

"You're right. I've said I was sorry about a hundred times."

"Then try a hundred more."

Rick suddenly decided he couldn't take it any longer. He swept her into his arms and kissed her soundly on the lips, much to the appreciation of his workers.

"So?" he asked her.

Shannon sighed. "A hundred more of those might help."

Pop came careening into the storeroom. With Leo sitting on his lap as navigator and Irv providing the thrust, what he needed was a horn to warn of his arrival. Instead,

Joey just strolled along behind them, picking up anything or anyone they might knock over.

"Your public is clamoring for you, Rick," Pop said, giving him a knowing wink. "And the television crew is all set up for your so-called interview."

"So soon?" He nervously squeezed Shannon's hand. "I know we have this planned out, but suddenly, I'm not so sure."

Shannon hugged him. "Go on. It'll work. She'll fall for the bait like a hungry carp. Not a bad analogy, at that."

"She'd better," Rick said.

With a fatalistic shrug, he headed for the exit and the awaiting TV cameras, with his entourage following close on his heels. His expression was somber. Shannon reached out and poked him in the back.

"Smile," she ordered. "It's Christmas."

Rick did manage to smile, even though temporarily blinded by the television crew's lights. A woman with a microphone and a large, hungry-looking smile pounced on him immediately.

"Okay," the newswoman said quietly. "Everything is set. We even planted some of our people in the audience to give them the right idea when the time comes." She led him to some marks that had been put on the floor with blue tape near the giant dollhouse. "This is going to make great television."

"Right," Rick said, still a bit rattled.

One of the crew members pointed at the woman and she started asking him questions. His mind desperately shifted gears.

"Excuse me?" he asked.

She laughed, and her audience laughed with her. "I guess that is a pretty wild question, isn't it? But really, how does it feel to be a millionaire?"

"Well, I'm not really a millionaire," Rick told her. "At least, not yet. The store receipts for each location have to be tabulated, and then the percentage calculated for each one. There are also a few loans to be paid off and development costs to be considered. Eventually—"

"Eventually, you'll be a very rich man," the newswoman interrupted. She wasn't interested in the details. What she wanted was drama. "Tell us a little about why you chose our own fair city of Denver as the spot from which to direct this brilliant campaign. Is this the center of Arnie's web?"

"Well, it really wasn't planned this way."

Off camera, Shannon winked at him as he spun a web of his own, keeping the onlookers interested while not telling them very much at all. Meanwhile, Leo, Irv and Joey had taken up a position near the television crew's monitor bank.

Joey's interest was fixed upon the monitor hooked up to the outside camera. It showed the activities of the crowd waiting in line for Arnies.

"There," Joey said, pointing at the screen.

"What?" Leo wanted to know. The adults had planned something while he slept last night and so far he hadn't been able to figure out what they were up to. "What's there?"

Irv was nodding. "That's her, all right."

"Who?" Leo demanded. "Is she a spy?"

"That's right, kid," Joey replied. "Of the worst kind."

He waved at Pop, who nodded and whispered to Shannon. She, in turn, alerted Rick and the newswoman. Rick smiled, and kept answering her inane questions.

Outside, Angela was making her way alongside the line of people, muttering under her breath. Nathan was right behind her, hurrying to catch up. Until a moment ago, they had been standing in Nathan's office, looking out the window. When she had heard Rick's voice on television, however, something inside her had evidently snapped.

"Angela!" Nathan called out. "Where are you going?" She paused until he was by her side. "Where else?"

"Lyon's?" He looked around at the milling crowd and kept his voice low. "I thought we agreed it would be easier to let him be for now, and then go after his profits later, when all the attention has died down."

"I just want him to see my face, Nathan," she told him.

"But why?"

"Because he's enjoying himself too much, that's why!"

She strode onward, with Nathan right behind her. Now he was the one muttering under his breath. "You're an evil woman, Angela."

It took her a while to work her way close to the dollhouse, where the interview was still going on. But finally she managed, and positioned herself right in Rick's line of sight. She smiled at him and waved. Rick frowned.

The newswoman, quick to pick up on the arrival of her guest of honor, noticed this exchange and immediately worked it into her dialogue.

"And who is this in the crowd, Rick?" she asked, pointing to the beautiful woman in the low-cut sweater. "A special admirer, perhaps?"

"In a way, Sue, you could call her Arnie's mother," Rick told her, taking the opportunity to go on a first-name basis with the newswoman. He was also suddenly all smiles. The audience was laughing. "Seriously, this is my ex-wife."

"Isn't that interesting!" newswoman Sue exclaimed.

The camera operator took the cue and immediately focused on Angela. For a brief second, she looked alarmed, but quickly recovered. The camera loved her. The camera operator, a young male, loved her even more. He moved in for a close-up.

"Hi!" Angela said breathlessly.

"Wait a minute!" Sue cried, in a flawless pretense of surprise. "Ladies and gentlemen, will you please put your hands together for none other than Angela Bayer. Are you here on behalf of Bayer's Department Store?"

Angela nodded, her blond hair catching the lights and shimmering. "Yes, Sue. We're just delighted with the way things turned out." She looked directly at Rick. "And I hope my ex-husband understands that the future of our relationship with Lyon's rests in his hands."

Rick leaned closer to Sue's microphone. "That sounds like a threat, Angela."

"Take it however you like, Rick," Angela told him.

She suddenly sensed that something was wrong and turned to go. The huge crowd, however, had other ideas. They closed in around her like a wall.

The television people recognized an unfolding drama when they saw it. One camera followed Angela, while another stayed on Rick and the newswoman. An engineer who used to work on a soap switched deftly between the two.

"Is there trouble in Arnie-land, Rick?" Sue asked.

"There was. But it's about over," he replied.

Angela laughed. "That's what you think!"

"You see, Angela Bayer had me arrested the other day," Rick continued. "For the serious offense of talking to my own daughter, Chelsea."

"You can't mean Chelsea Bayer?" Sue asked.

"No, Chelsea *Hastings,*" he corrected. "My lawyer recently informed me that Angela had my daughter's name legally changed, using falsified documents."

Sue was so excited, she was practically jumping up and down. "My! What a tangled web we have here! Is this true, Mrs. Bayer?"

"You want truth? I'll give you truth!" Angela returned. She faced the camera again, going on the attack. "Do yo want me to tell them the real story, Rick? I will, yo know!"

Nathan, who had been standing off to one side, sud denly reached out and tried to restrain his wife. She jerke away, but the camera caught every move. A few key mem bers of the crowd shifted, as well, and he found himsel thrust into the spotlight beside her.

"Nathan Bayer!" Sue crowed. "What an unexpecte surprise."

He smiled uncomfortably. "Hello, Sue. I'd just like t say that my wife has been under a lot of strain latel and—"

"Shut up, Nathan!" Angela interrupted.

The crowd roared with laughter. Sue was loving ever minute of it. This was working out even better than it ha sounded when Hastings and his unusual little group ha pitched it to her. She was certain there was a talk-sho contract in her future.

"Just what is the real story, Mrs. Bayer?" she asked.

"I did have him arrested the other day. For violating restraining order I got to protect my child and myself fron his vicious wrath! This man, this so-called toy maker you'r all fawning over, is a wife beater! When I told him I wa divorcing him to marry Nathan Bayer, he became so en raged that he beat me up and blackened my eye!"

The crowd gasped. All eyes turned to Rick for a rebut tal. To their amazement, he was smiling. "Is that a fact?" he asked.

"I testified to it in a court of law, didn't I?"

He nodded. "Yes, you did. And that makes you guilt of forgery *and* perjury, Angela. Because it was a lie."

"That's absurd!" Nathan exclaimed.

"Is it?" Rick asked. With the camera following every ove, he reached behind him and knocked on the wall of e dollhouse. "Come on out, Emilio."

A silence fell over the crowd as they watched a raven- ired man emerge from the dollhouse, where he had been ling for the past few minutes. He looked at Rick, nod- d and then turned to face Nathan and Angela, who were th visibly shaken. They tried to move away from the mera, but the crowd wouldn't let them. Publicity, his emy for so long, was now working to Rick's advantage.

"Who are you?" Sue asked, again with flawlessly gned innocence. Why stop at a talk show? Maybe an ting career!

"My name is Emilio. Up until last night, when I was ruptly terminated," he said, his dark eyes shooting dag- rs at Angela, "I was the Bayers' chauffeur. I also per- rmed ... other duties for them on occasion."

Nathan pushed his way toward the dollhouse. "This man a deviant and not to be believed!" he exclaimed.

"Shut up, Nathan!" Angela said. She tried another tack. Emilio, please. We don't have to air this in public. Come me with me and we'll work something out. I'm sorry for e way I behaved last night."

Sue was thinking major network now. "What do you nk, ladies and gentlemen?" she asked, winking at the mera. "Did this man drive her car, or what?"

They laughed. But Emilio kept his somber demeanor and e crowd quieted down quickly. "I am not your puppet, gela," he told her. "And before you threaten me again, r. Bayer, let me assure you that I am prepared to take at comes my way for my part in this. Unlike you, I am a n of honor."

The veins in Nathan's neck bulged. "Why you—"

"I hit Angela Bayer," Emilio announced. "Because s
paid me to do it."

With her razor-sharp nails, Angela was more successf
in moving people out of her way. But she no longer car
about Emilio. As she approached Rick, however, she g
the surprise of her life.

"Lionman to the rescue!" Leo cried. He was standing <
top of the dollhouse, a big tub in his hands. With some <
fort, he managed to dump the contents right onto Angela
head. "Take that, you evil spy!"

It took a moment for anyone to realize what had ha
pened, including Angela. But then she felt the first Ar
wiggle its way onto the bare skin displayed by her low-c
sweater. She pulled on it, but it wouldn't budge. The h
lights had raised her skin to just the right temperature.

As Angela began screaming, Sue's eyes went as wide
the camera lenses that were now focused on her. "Oops!
think we'd better go to a commercial break now, folks."

Epilogue

aditionally, Lyon's closed at noon the day before Christ-
as and had a party for all the employees, at which Pop
ve out their Christmas bonuses. Although the sales for
e day had yet to be figured, Friday's Arnie receipts had
eady ensured that those bonuses would be the largest in
e store's history. Between that, profit sharing and the
credible publicity garnered by Angela Bayer's nervous
eakdown on live television, they were a very merry
unch.

As Shannon was closing down her department, she sud-
nly noticed that she was not alone. She looked curiously
the young girl standing in front of her register.

"Why, hello, Chelsea."

"Hello, Ms. O'Shaughnessy," she said.

"Please, call me Shannon. But I'm afraid you just
issed your father. He had some errands to run before all
e stores close. Would you like to wait for him?" Shan-
n asked.

Chelsea frowned. "I don't know. I mean, I actually came
see you." She looked around uncertainly. "Could we
ve that hot chocolate now?"

It took a moment for Shannon to remember what the girl
as referring to. But then she smiled and held out her hand.

"Certainly. Let's go up to the cafeteria. They'll be closin
but I'm sure we can manage to scare up some cocoa for t
two of us. Does your mother know you're here?"

"Nathan does. I'm not sure about Momma. She's st
freaked out." Chelsea blushed slightly. "I mean, she is
feeling well."

Shannon laughed. "Freaked out is a perfectly accep
able term. And it's understandable, after what happene
You know that Leo is very, very sorry for what he did, do
you?"

Chelsea nodded. "Nathan said he apologized."

"He's also up in the mountains right now, helping
clean a certain white Berber carpet," Shannon told her. "
Nathan mad?"

"It's always hard for me to tell what Nathan is," the g
told her. "He's...I don't know. Cold. Not like Daddy us
to be."

They arrived at the cafeteria and Shannon made the
some hot chocolate, waving off the help of the staff so th
could go about their business.

Shannon watched as Chelsea just stirred her cocoa wit
out tasting it. "Is that why you're here, Chelsea? Do y
need someone to talk to about your father?" she ask
softly.

Chelsea nodded. "I don't know what to do."

"What do you mean?"

"I do love him."

She looked up at Shannon, her brown eyes so much li
Rick's that Shannon felt her heart skip a beat. Shann
could tell there was more the child wanted to say.

"Go on," she prompted.

"But I love my momma, too. I know she's told some li
about him. She...she isn't always so nice to me, either

don't want to be just like her and she keeps trying to make me that way. I get mad at her. It doesn't feel right.''

Shannon reached over and stroked the girl's silken blond hair, reassuring her. ''It's okay to be mad at your parents, Chelsea. Just because people make us mad, that doesn't mean we don't love them.'' She had recently learned that firsthand.

Chelsea fixed her with an appraising gaze. ''You love my daddy too, don't you?''

The question took Shannon by surprise. But the answer wasn't hard to come by. ''Yes, Chelsea. I do.''

''Are you going to marry him?''

That one was a bit harder. ''Well, for one thing, he hasn't asked me yet. And for another, there are some things we have to resolve first.''

''Oh.''

''Why do you ask?''

Chelsea sighed deeply. ''Sometimes I wonder what it would be like if I didn't live with Momma and Nathan anymore. If she just visited me when she wanted to. It's not as if she's around all the time, anyway.''

Shannon took her hand and squeezed it. ''I know how that feels, Chelsea. My mother was that way.''

''Shannon?''

''Yes, Chelsea?''

The girl looked down at her hot chocolate, and her voice was very soft when she spoke. ''You'd make a good mother.''

Shannon could feel the tears well up in her eyes. She knew exactly what the child was hinting at, and didn't have the slightest idea how to respond.

''Why, thank you, Chelsea. Someday, maybe, I...I think I might like to try again.''

''Again?'' Chelsea asked, looking up at her.

"I had a little girl once. She passed away when she was very small."

"I'm sorry. That must have hurt."

Shannon nodded. "It did. But I'm better now."

"Good," Chelsea said. She took a sip of her cocoa. "Would you mind if I ask my daddy?"

"Ask him what, sweetheart?"

"If I could come live with him and you someday."

"No, honey. I wouldn't mind at all." She stood up abruptly. "Would you excuse me just a second?"

Shannon managed to get to the hallway before her tears started flowing in earnest. She sobbed quietly in the silence, everyone on this floor having long since gone to the party.

Or so she thought. A man cleared his throat, and she turned around, an excuse forming on her lips.

But Rick kissed it away. She clung to him until her tears began to subside. "I'm sorry," she told him with a sigh. "What a way to behave on Christmas Eve."

"Oh, I don't know. I've spent a few that way," he told her. "What on earth caused this?"

Shannon put a finger to her lips, then motioned for him to look through one of the round windows in the cafeteria doors. His eyes went wide.

"Chelsea!"

"She came to see me, but now, I think she'd like to talk to you, as well," Shannon told him.

Rick suddenly looked as nervous as a cat. "What about?"

"Lots of things, I imagine," she replied. She took his hand and held it against her cheek. "But she has a couple of tough questions I think I'd better prepare you for. And answer in advance. It's yes, both times."

"I don't understand."

"I'm ready to get married again, Rick. And I'm ready to have more children. If it's just Leo and Chelsea, then I'll consider myself the luckiest woman alive. But it would be nice to have some of our own." She tugged on his hand and opened the swinging cafeteria doors. "Now come say hello to your daughter."

Chelsea saw him and got up from her chair. She moved hesitantly toward him. Rick released Shannon's hand and got down on one knee, his arms spread wide. "Chelsea, honey! I'm so happy to see you!"

"Daddy!"

Chelsea ran into his arms and they hugged, while Shannon watched. She had changed her mind. Crying was just fine on Christmas Eve, as long they were tears of joy, and you shared them with the ones you loved.

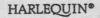

Fifty red-blooded, white-hot, true-blue hunks
from every State in the Union!

Look for MEN MADE IN AMERICA! Written by some
of our most popular authors, these stories feature fifty
of the strongest, sexiest men, each from a different state
in the union!

Two titles available every month at your favorite
retail outlet.

In December, look for:

NATURAL ATTRACTION by Marisa Carroll
(New Hampshire)
MOMENTS HARSH, MOMENTS GENTLE by Joan Hohl
(New Jersey)

In January 1995, look for:

WITHIN REACH by Marilyn Pappano (New Mexico)
IN GOOD FAITH by Judith McWilliams (New York)

You won't be able to resist MEN MADE IN AMERICA!

◈HARLEQUIN®

The proprietors of Weddings, Inc. hope you
have enjoyed visiting Eternity, Massachusetts.
And if you missed any of the exciting Weddings,
Inc. titles, here is your opportunity to complete
your collection:

Harlequin Superromance	#598	*Wedding Invitation* by Marisa Carroll	$3.50 U.S. $3.99 CAN.	☐ ☐
Harlequin Romance	#3319	*Expectations* by Shannon Waverly	$2.99 U.S. $3.50 CAN.	☐ ☐
Harlequin Temptation	#502	*Wedding Song* by Vicki Lewis Thompson	$2.99 U.S. $3.50 CAN.	☐ ☐
Harlequin American Romance	#549	*The Wedding Gamble* by Muriel Jensen	$3.50 U.S. $3.99 CAN.	☐ ☐
Harlequin Presents	#1692	*The Vengeful Groom* by Sara Wood	$2.99 U.S. $3.50 CAN.	☐ ☐
Harlequin Intrigue	#298	*Edge of Eternity* by Jasmine Cresswell	$2.99 U.S. $3.50 CAN.	☐ ☐
Harlequin Historical	#248	*Vows* by Margaret Moore	$3.99 U.S. $4.50 CAN.	☐ ☐

HARLEQUIN BOOKS...
NOT THE SAME OLD STORY

TOTAL AMOUNT	$
POSTAGE & HANDLING	$
($1.00 for one book, 50¢ for each additional)	
APPLICABLE TAXES*	$ _____
TOTAL PAYABLE	$ _____
(check or money order—please do not send cash)	

To order, complete this form and send it, along with a check or money order for the
total above, payable to Harlequin Books, to: **In the U.S.:** 3010 Walden Avenue,
P.O. Box 9047, Buffalo, NY 14269-9047; **In Canada:** P.O. Box 613, Fort Erie, Ontario,
L2A 5X3.

Name: _____

Address: _____ City: _____

State/Prov.: _____ Zip/Postal Code: _____

*New York residents remit applicable sales taxes.
Canadian residents remit applicable GST and provincial taxes.

WED-F

This holiday, join four hunky heroes under the mistletoe for

Christmas Kisses

Cuddle under a fluffy quilt, with a cup of hot chocolate and these romances sure to warm you up:

#561 HE'S A REBEL (also a Studs title)
Linda Randall Wisdom

#562 THE BABY AND THE BODYGUARD
Jule McBride

#563 THE GIFT-WRAPPED GROOM
M.J. Rodgers

#564 A TIMELESS CHRISTMAS
Pat Chandler

Celebrate the season with all four holiday books sealed with a Christmas kiss—coming to you in December, only from Harlequin American Romance!

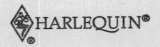